Prologue

CW01507943

Bournemouth
October 1987

The sky was gun-metal grey, but the menacing clouds were yet to release the forecast downpour. A deceptive calm hung over Seamoor Road as people went quietly about their daily business. No one noticed Charlie in his grubby mechanic's overalls, sitting nervously in a rusty Ford Cortina parked near the entrance to the Westbourne Arcade.

Suddenly the heavy air was pierced by the crack of gunshots: one, two, a pause and then a third. Reactions were mixed. Screams from inside the post office. Horrified expletives from those outside. One man dived for cover. Charlie fumbled with the ignition key, his fingers trembling as his mind tried to compute what he'd just heard. They'd gone in with replica pistols, as agreed. So, who the hell was shooting? And why? His gut told him something had gone terribly wrong.

Three men, dressed head to toe in black with balaclavas over their faces, ran frantically from the post office. They flung themselves into the car, three doors slammed shut, then Charlie swerved out into the road, cutting across the front of a grubby white van and skidding slightly as he took an almost immediate left turn into Robert Louis Stevenson Avenue. There was a flurry of activity as the men pulled off their balaclavas and shoved them into their pockets. Pete pulled on a multicoloured bobble hat and tugged it down over his tousled blond hair. Winston wriggled out of his black donkey jacket to reveal a red and black checked work shirt and donned a black and red beanie with the AFC Bournemouth badge. Teddy slipped a dirty royal blue hoodie over his black jumper and pulled the hood up to conceal his ponytail. Charlie's focus was on the road as he slowed down to the speed limit and anxiously scanned the road ahead for anything that might impede their escape.

By the time the car reached the junction with Alum Chine Road, the occupants bore little resemblance to the robbers fleeing the scene only seconds before. Charlie cautiously turned right and left and then left again as he negotiated the quiet residential streets, before pulling into a small car park behind a family-run guest house. There was little chance of them being seen as the owners were currently in Ibiza on their own holiday. He switched off the engine and swivelled to face Pete.

'Is one of you gonna tell me what the bloody 'ell 'appened?' he asked, looking anxiously from Pete's face to the two in the back.

'I'll tell you what bleedin' 'appened,' growled Teddy. '*He* only bloody decided to pull a *real* shooter, didn't he?' He poked his finger aggressively towards Pete.

'Keep yer 'air on!' chuckled Pete sarcastically. 'If I 'adn't, we'd 'ave been stymied by that bloody 'ave-a-go old battleaxe.'

'What the 'ell?' exploded Charlie. 'We agreed: replicas only! No one needed to get hurt!'

'Well, it's a bit late for that,' retorted Winston, glaring angrily at Pete. 'Bloody Buffalo Bill 'ere put two down in there.'

'Shit! What the 'ell did yer go an' do that for?' Charlie demanded, but Pete was already out of the car. He ducked his head back inside briefly.

'Are we gonna get going before the filth catch on, or what?' He grinned, jangling a set of car keys and nodding to the almost-new dark blue Montego neatly parked facing the road in a nearby space. With much grumbling and cursing, the gang switched cars and, with Pete driving this time, the robbers quickly disappeared into the deluge that finally fell like a waterfall from the leaden sky.

The Mystery of the Missing Wallet

by

WENDY BOYNTON

THE CHOIR PRESS

First published in the United Kingdom in 2025 by
The Choir Press

ISBN 978-1-78963-527-0

This book is a fictional story set in the beautiful and very real city of Salisbury in Wiltshire. I lived in the Salisbury area for many years and still return regularly to visit family and friends there.

Whilst I have tried to stay faithful to the real locations, I have altered or invented certain aspects for the sake of the story. For instance, there is no care home called Birtford Lodge, nor does the footpath across the water meadows from Tesco on Southampton Road to Britford Farm exist as described. All the characters in this book are entirely the products of my imagination, and any similarity to real people, living or deceased, is coincidental.

Acknowledgements

A huge thank you to everyone who read my debut novel, *The Mystery of the Missing Brooch*, especially those who took the time to leave a review. It was your kind words and encouragement that motivated me to bring forward the publication of Book Two in my Salisbury Murders series; I really hope that you enjoy it.

My grateful thanks again to all the lovely people at The Choir Press for guiding me through the publication process, and for their patience and understanding when I kept making additional changes in the page proofs. In particular, I want to thank my copy editor, Ann-Marie, who took on my second manuscript just before Christmas despite already being busy.

A quick shout-out to some special friends: Dawn, for all her encouragement; Andrew, for proofreading my work; and Heather, for her amazing artwork. And to my wonderful husband, who has supported me all the way through my writing journey. Becoming an author is most definitely not a solo adventure.

Finally, I want to say thank you to Robert, the owner of Britford Farm, who kindly allowed me to use his shop and café in this book.

I dedicate this book to you all!

Other Titles by Wendy Boynton

The Mystery of the Missing Brooch

Several months later, Charlie carefully cut out the final newspaper article on the subject:

Gang in Westbourne Heist Sentenced

Three armed robbers, who participated in last October's Westbourne Heist, were finally sentenced by the trial judge at The Old Bailey yesterday. Peter Blackett, 29, of Parkstone in Poole was given a life sentence with a judge's recommendation that he serve a minimum of thirty-five years for his part in the armed heist that saw Westbourne postmistress, Annie Taylor, 67, shot dead and post office customer Nigel Waring, 54, injured. Blackett, who was carrying a deadly Walther PPK pistol, is said to have masterminded the daring heist whilst gang members Napier and Crouch, who strenuously denied any intention to cause harm, were armed only with replica pistols. Winston Napier, 30, and Teddy Crouch, 31, both from Poole, were also sentenced to mandatory life sentences but with a lesser recommendation that they serve a minimum fifteen years each. Whilst both replicas were recovered, along with some of the money stolen during the heist, police have not been able to locate either the murder weapon or around £15,000 in used banknotes. The getaway driver, dubbed 'the fourth man', remains unnamed and is yet to be apprehended.

He added the cutting to several others in a large brown envelope, tucked it in his suitcase before closing it, put on his coat and left his miserable flat for the final time.

Chapter One

Salisbury
Monday 9th January 2023

Lauren Peachy hopped onto the bus in her home village of Downton, strode down the aisle and flopped into the corner of the back seat next to the window. She pulled her hands inside the sleeves of her overlarge hoodie and shivered. Her mum was right; she should've put a coat on this morning. She was cold and tired and fed up. Today was supposed to have been a day off. But Sharon had phoned late the previous evening and begged her to work today. She'd argued, this being her seventh day working in a row, but Sharon had been desperate and persuasive.

That was the problem with working for an agency. All the care homes were desperate for staff, yet the one she wanted to work at still hadn't advertised a job vacancy. She scowled. Perhaps she shouldn't be so fussy. But after her brief job at The Cedars, which had been closed after the dramatic events back in September, she didn't want to work for just any old care home. She wanted to work at the care home that Meg was in. And she was prepared to wait; after all, the pay for agency work was actually pretty good, and she needed every penny she could get whilst she was learning to drive.

Lauren Peachy was a petite nineteen-year-old with short pixie-cut blonde hair and aquamarine eyes. Mature for her years, she hadn't had the easiest of lives. An only child, her father had been killed in a road accident when she was sixteen. That had been followed by the cancer scare her mother had last year and then the dreadful events at The Cedars Residential Care Home, where Lauren had started her first job, which had lasted less than five weeks. Relieved to have been taken on by an agency supplying carers to the many care and nursing homes around the Salisbury area, Lauren was glad to have employment. It had meant she could contribute to the rent and bills that her mother had struggled to pay whilst off sick following a hysterectomy. Her mother had finally been given the all-clear before Christmas, giving them a double reason to celebrate the festive season. Now back fulltime at her job as a medical secretary at Salisbury District Hospital, Bekka had insisted that Lauren keep more of the money she earned and spend it on herself. Without hesitation, Lauren had started driving lessons.

As the bus rumbled through the small village of Britford on its way into Salisbury, Lauren peered through the misted-up windows and could just make out the outline of Britford Lodge. That was where Meg Thornton had moved to, after her brief stay in Salisbury Hospital. At eighty-one years of age, Meg, former resident of The Cedars, had been abducted by a murderer but had, thankfully, been unharmed. The one good thing to come out of it was that the surgeons had relented and finally operated on Meg's hip, and she was now well recovered. Whilst it might seem strange to an outsider that a nineteen-year-old carer should have formed such a close bond with an elderly resident, the fact was the two had hit it off immediately and had worked together to help solve a murder. Well, several murders, to be accurate. And Lauren had been visiting Meg regularly since her discharge to her new home. As the bus trundled its way through increasingly heavy traffic towards the city centre, Lauren wondered what Meg was doing at that moment.

✿

Retired schoolteacher Meg Thornton and her new friend Jeannie Lewis were sitting either side of an old gate-leg table that had been positioned near one of the day-room windows so that they could work on their jigsaw puzzle in natural light. Their silence was warm and companionable as two grey heads bobbed in search of elusive pieces. Meg, with a head of thick glossy grey curls, worked methodically on the sunset sky, whilst Jeannie, her white hair thin and wispy, struggled with the reflections in the lake.

'Tea or coffee, Meg?' broke in Kayla Higginbotham, one of the younger carers at the Britford Lodge Care Home. Dressed in a crumpled white uniform tunic, bleach-blonde hair escaping from clasps that struggled to hold it off her face, the carer looked about as bored as she sounded.

Meg sighed before responding, 'Tea, please. Milk, no sugar.' She'd lived here more than three months now and was still unaccustomed to the attitude of some of the carers. Kayla in particular seemed to make no effort to remember any of the residents' preferences, repeating the same questions day in and day out.

'Jeannie?' droned Kayla.

'Milky coffee, please, with one sugar,' replied Meg's petite ninety-two-year-old companion. Jeannie's wizened face lit up with an almost beatific smile that went entirely unnoticed by the twenty-two-year-old carer. Kayla poured the drinks into identical white mugs and plonked them gracelessly side by side on the edge of the table before moving to the next cluster of residents.

'Which is which?' asked Jeannie, peering curiously at the two drinks.

Meg lifted the nearest mug and sniffed. 'This is your coffee,' she pronounced, disgust wrinkling her face.

Jeannie took the proffered mug. 'You'd think Kayla would know by now that you can't stand coffee,' she remarked dryly.

'Exactly,' agreed Meg. 'That's one of the things I still miss about The Cedars; I felt part of a family there.'

'A very dysfunctional family,' teased Jeannie, who was one of the few people to whom Meg had disclosed the events of September. She waited for Meg to make some acerbic or witty response. But Meg was staring intently through the window, completely distracted by something that had caught her eye. Jeannie twisted so that she could see. A black BMW had parked near the main entrance to Britford Lodge and was discharging its occupants. She noted a well-dressed couple in maybe their mid-fifties before spotting an elderly gentleman who looked every inch a sea captain, complete with beard and moustache. He stood straight as a ramrod, looking around with some curiosity.

'I don't believe it!' gasped Meg, standing up quite suddenly.

'What?' Jeannie demanded in concern.

'Just as I was thinking about The Cedars too! It's Albert! Albert Grimshaw!'

Once Albert had been shown to his new room by Maureen Wilkinson, the care manager, his son and daughter-in-law helped him to start unpacking before hastily making their excuses and leaving.

Albert heaved a sigh of relief. Fifteen weeks and three days since he'd had no choice but to stay temporarily with his son after The Cedars had abruptly closed. That was about fifteen weeks too long, in his opinion.

'Now then, do you prefer Albert or Bert?' Maureen, quite matronly-looking in a dark blue dress, enquired politely.

'My name is Albert,' he retorted, 'Albert, *never* Bert!'

Maureen recognised a curmudgeonly old sailor when she saw one. Royal Navy, retired, she would've guessed. 'Well, come along, Albert.' She jumped in expertly before he could say anything more on that score. 'Would you like a tour of your new home?'

He glanced at her, with her steel-grey bob framing a stern-looking face, and thought better of pursuing his favourite lecture. 'Ah, thank you. But I would very much rather find one of my fellow residents, if you could assist?'

Maureen frowned. 'I thought, from reading your file, that you hadn't visited Britford Lodge in person?'

'That's correct! My son, Peter, had no intention of driving me fifty-odd miles each way just to see if I liked this home or not. He couldn't wait to get rid of me, and I was only too happy to come here, seeing as how I have a friend here already.'

'Really?' Maureen raised an eyebrow in surprise.

'Yes, Meg Thornton.'

'Of course, you were both at The Cedars previously, weren't you?'

'That's right.'

'Have you stayed in touch?'

'She was kind enough to send a couple of letters and a Christmas card, y'know!'

'Very good! She'll most likely be in the day room. I'll show you where it is.'

Chapter Two

Meg cast frequent glances towards the day-room door as she and Jeannie carried on with their jigsaw puzzle. She couldn't believe that Albert was actually here! She had written to him a few times in the intervening months but, in his replies, he had never once mentioned coming to Britford Lodge. And judging by the amount of luggage disgorged from the BMW's boot, Albert appeared to be moving in!

Of course, dear old Frances had passed away last week, and Meg had known the room wouldn't remain empty for long. But she hadn't expected to know its new occupant! She noted the departure of the couple who'd brought Albert and noticed also the smiles of relief on their faces as they relaxed into their luxurious heated seats before driving off into the thin January sunshine.

Meg looked up to see Albert and Maureen standing in the doorway. She rose and crossed the room to greet him, her stride so much more confident than when he had last seen her, thanks to her hip replacement. She had even dispensed with the stick she used to rely on. She was a little taken aback when Albert greeted her with a hug and a surprisingly enthusiastic kiss but was nonetheless pleased to see him too. The forty-two-year-old care manager smiled at the reunited octogenarians and excused herself.

Meg looped an arm through Albert's and led him around the day room, introducing him as 'an old friend who's just moved in', although in truth she'd only met Albert last April on her arrival at The Cedars. Five years her senior, Albert had at first appeared reserved and somewhat aloof and, indeed, she'd even called him an old-fashioned bigot on one occasion, but they had eventually become good friends, and she was aware that Albert had a great deal of respect for her clear thinking and deductive powers.

Alan, Frank and Donald, three of the home's six male

residents, were dozing in front of *Homes Under the Sun*, which played on the TV regardless of their inattention. Alan Watts, a lean man with sparse hair, smiled lopsidedly and waved his left hand at Albert. Frank Mitchell, a small wiry man with heavy-rimmed glasses, continued to snore unabated, and Meg hadn't the heart to wake him. Donald Macpherson, a Scot with a remarkably dry sense of humour and a shock of almost pure white hair, nodded to Albert and proffered a greeting. 'Ye'll be welcome tae join us.' Albert nodded his thanks.

Ruth Griffiths and Pauline Morgan, known as the terrible twins because they had been friends since nursery school and were nearly inseparable, looked up from their knitting and eagerly welcomed Albert before resuming their labours. Several others muttered greetings from behind newspapers, but Meg could see that Albert's attention was wavering. Bypassing the remaining residents, she steered him towards Jeannie and ordered him to sit down.

'Jeannie, I'd like you to meet Albert Grimshaw.'

Albert immediately stood up again to shake hands with Meg's friend. 'Nice to meet you,' he beamed. 'I see you're another jigsaw fanatic, like Meg, what?'

'Yes, do you like them too?' smiled Jeannie enthusiastically.

'Umm, well . . .' he spluttered.

'That means no,' put in Meg as they all sat down again.

'It doesn't matter,' Jeannie reassured him. 'It's just lovely to put a face to the name, Albert. I've heard all about you from Meg!'

'Only the good bits, I hope?'

They all laughed. 'Now, why didn't you mention you were moving to Britford Lodge in your last letter?' demanded Meg.

'Sorry, old gal, didn't know then! The care manager only phoned a few days ago to offer me the vacancy.'

'But you must've been on a waiting list, or something?' she insisted.

'Well, er, yes indeed.'

'And you never said a word?'

'Didn't want to jinx things in case they didn't work out, y'know.'

'Ooh, how exciting,' said Jeannie. 'Were you deliberately trying to get into Britford Lodge to be with Meg?' She looked mischievously from one to the other, noting Albert's flushed face and Meg's instant embarrassment.

'Of course he wasn't!' Meg snapped.

'Steady on, there! You certainly know how to make a fellow feel unwelcome!' grumbled Albert. Meg felt the heat rising to her face as she tried to bite back her hasty words but, fortunately, Albert seemed to take it all in good humour and the awkward moment passed. When further pleasantries had been exchanged, Jeannie excused herself and trundled nimbly away on her walking frame.

For a while, they reminisced, but eventually the conversation turned to their current situation. 'So, tell me about Britford Lodge,' demanded Albert.

'Well, I'm sure you've read the brochure ...' Meg began.

'Haven't seen it, old gal.'

'Oh,' gasped Meg, surprised. 'Weren't you at all concerned about whether it would suit you or not?'

'Not really, m'dear. You said in your letter that it was a pleasant enough place, if not quite as homely as The Cedars. That was good enough for me.'

'You weren't at all curious?'

'No. To tell the truth, I was about ready to take any place offered, just to get out from under Wanda's feet. Couldn't have been happier when this place came up!'

'You weren't happy staying with your family, then?' she probed gently.

'Put it this way: my son Peter was sufficiently well-brought-up to do his duty by his old dad and not make a fuss. But that witch, Wanda, she's another kettle of fish.'

'Your daughter-in-law?' Meg clarified.

'Yes, the dreaded "in-law". Always sniping at me and complaining to Peter behind my back, as though I was as deaf as the proverbial post.'

'How do you mean?'

'My newspaper cluttered her coffee table. I was an

embarrassment when her friends came round. She had to stop working to get me something to eat – as if she wasn't going to have a lunch break herself. She had so much more washing and ironing to do. And so on, and so on.'

'Were your grandchildren there too?'

'Not all the time, fortunately. Patrick lives and works in London, doing very well for himself apparently. And Jenny was away at university except over Christmas. Of course, Patrick and his girlfriend came down for the so-called festive season too, which meant I was in the way. Taking up one of the guest rooms when the family were coming to stay. As if I wasn't family as well!'

'I'm so sorry.'

'Not your fault, old gal!'

'I guess you'd have taken a place at any care home, then?'

'Well, ah, it hadn't quite come to that.' Albert shuffled a little uncomfortably.

'What on earth do you mean?' Meg asked, puzzled.

'I only put my name on one waiting list, you see. Although I told Pete and Wanda I was on the list for all the Salisbury care homes.'

'You mean, you only applied to Britford Lodge!'

'Yes. I wanted to go somewhere where I knew I'd have a friend.'

There was a momentary pause and then Meg chuckled. 'It's a good job Jeannie didn't hear you say that!'

'Well, come on then, old gal.' Albert swiftly changed the subject. 'Tell me all about Britford Lodge. It's a lot bigger than The Cedars, isn't it?'

'Yes, thirty residents and about the same number of staff, I should think.'

'And the building's quite modern, I'd say?'

'Yes, Britford Lodge was purpose-built about eight years ago. Caused an awful furore, getting the planning permission to build here, but money won the day.'

'Someone was bribed?' asked Albert.

'There were quite a few backhanders, from what I've heard.'

'What's so special about this site, then?' demanded Albert.

'The home is built on land formerly belonging to Britford Farm, which is further down Lower Road. Like many farmers this century, they've moved from traditional farming to more innovative ways of making money. There's quite a large farm shop and café there now, selling homemade stuff like jams and biscuits. Open seven days a week, so you'll see cars going up and down the lane quite often, particularly at the weekend.'

'Can you walk there?' interrupted Albert.

'Yes, indeed, there's a lovely wide footpath between here and the farm. Jeannie and I have got into the habit of going there once a week for afternoon tea and cake. I think a number of the residents do, those that are sufficiently mobile anyway.'

'My treat next time, if I may come along with you?'

'Of course you can.' Meg smiled warmly.

'So, the planning objection was that this was built on arable land, then?'

'Not really,' replied Meg. 'Not all of the farmland was arable. Beyond the farm, you can still walk across traditional water meadows. And that was the main objection: risk of flooding, spoiling an area of outstanding natural beauty, and so on.'

'I see. Don't tell me we have to paddle whenever it rains?'

'Of course not, the builders put in all sorts of drainage schemes. And in any case, we're quite a long way up from the river here. As a matter of fact, the building won some kind of architectural design award the year after it was finished. Something about blending in with the environment and maximising green energy.'

'Load of eco-whatsit-cobblers, you mean.'

'Albert! I see you haven't changed at all since September!' rebuked Meg firmly.

'Neither have you, old gal,' replied Albert with a twinkle in his eye as he studied her stern face, framed by lush curls, and admired the brightness of her brown eyes as she took him to task, not for the first time, for being politically incorrect. He really quite liked it when Meg was telling him off.

Fortunately, Meg didn't have time to dwell on that as Kayla came into the day room to announce that lunch was nearly ready. Meg escorted Albert to the dining room, comfortably matching him pace for pace. They seated themselves at a table for four, with Jeannie and another good friend, Betty. The three women made an incongruous trio, Meg had always thought. Betty Henderson was short, plump and motherly, with a slightly untidy appearance and long streaky grey hair escaping from an attempted bun, whilst Jeannie looked almost pitifully thin beside her. Meg, verging on the statuesque, towered over the two of them despite her arthritis. But Albert was half a head taller than her, she noted with pleasure.

Chapter Three

Meg enjoyed dining with Albert, who'd been charming to Jeannie and Betty, but she had a visitor coming this afternoon and didn't want him sticking to her like superglue. She determinedly led him to the trio of men in front of the TV when they returned to the day room.

'Albert, I think you would get along very well with Frank here,' she began.

'Oh?' Albert frowned at her. She hoped he wasn't going to be awkward.

'Yes,' she said firmly. 'Frank is about the same age as you, I believe, *and* he also served in the Navy.'

'Royal Navy, eh? How splendid!' beamed Albert.

Frank stood up, recognising a senior officer when he saw one, and carefully saluted. 'Petty Officer Mitchell, retired, Marine Engineering Mechanical, Electrical branch, at your service, sir!'

Albert returned the salute. 'Captain Grimshaw, retired. Delighted to meet you, Petty Officer.'

'I prefer Frank, these days, if you don't mind, sir.'

'Oh, er, yes, of course.' Albert tried hard not to sound disappointed as he lowered himself into the armchair beside Frank's. 'MEM electrical, eh? I take my hat off to your branch, all that complicated ship's wiring, what?'

'Thank you, sir.'

'No, no. If I'm to call you Frank, I suppose you'd better call me Albert.'

'Thank you, Albert,' corrected Frank with a wry smile. 'I came out after twelve years and was an electrician in Civvy Street for thirty-seven. I'm long out of the habit of using my rank.'

'I served the Navy for forty years!' boasted Albert proudly. 'Worked my way up through the ranks. When did you enlist, eh, Frank?'

'In 1951, straight after my sixteenth birthday.'

'Ah, I must be a year younger than you, then; I enlisted in 1952.'

'If you two gentlemen would excuse me,' interrupted Meg, happy that her plan had worked, 'I have a few things to do.'

They barely noticed her leaving them.

She visited the bathroom, patted her curls into place and checked in the mirror that she didn't have any food stuck between her teeth, before returning to the entrance foyer with perfect timing.

'Well, that's a bit of good luck, bumping into you here!' exclaimed Detective Inspector Daniel Bywater as he came through the front doors. They exchanged pecks on the cheek. 'Saves me having to hunt you down!'

'You *could* call it good luck,' mused Meg with a twinkle. 'But then again, you always know where I'll be when you come to visit!'

She linked an arm through his as he gallantly escorted her across the day room and out into the slightly more private conservatory, where they settled into well-padded cane armchairs.

The thirty-eight-year-old clean-shaven detective was deceptively unremarkable to look at, but it was his quick thinking that had rescued her when she'd been taken hostage by a murderer not so long ago. Although Dan himself might have argued that it was Meg's perspicacity that had helped him to solve the case.

In any event, a warm friendship had developed between the two, and Dan was happy for Meg to call him her honorary grandson. It also helped that Dan's father had been a fairly junior DC under Meg's late husband, who had been a DCI with Bournemouth CID.

'How are you?' enquired Dan, pleased to see that she was continuing to walk more easily each time he visited.

'I'm very well ... and I have some news for you,' replied Meg. 'But first, do tell me: how are you, Dan?'

'Oh, you know, okay.'

'Only okay?' She looked concerned for a moment before

seeing the big grin on his face. 'Come on, then, what is it? You look like the cat that's got the cream!'

'How would you feel about having an honorary *great*-grandchild?'

'Oh, my dear, that's wonderful news!' Meg reached over and squeezed his hand. 'Do tell me all about it.'

Dan told her that his wife, Katie, was now three months pregnant. He said he'd been bursting to tell her the news on each of his last few visits, but they'd agreed to keep it to themselves until she reached the end of her first trimester. Meg had met Katie at Christmas when they'd visited together to bring her a card and a box of very indulgent truffles. She liked the slightly plump thirty-three-year-old primary school teacher with a blonde bob framing a round face that always seemed to be smiling. She was genuinely happy for the couple, knowing that Katie had previously had a miscarriage and then spent two years trying to conceive again.

'And how's that nice young sergeant of yours?' she asked, when he'd finished talking about plans for converting their box room into a nursery.

'Viv? He's moping around a bit at the moment because he's just broken up with his girlfriend, Sacha.'

'Oh dear, that's such a shame.'

'Don't feel too sorry for him. He'll have another one by next week, just you wait and see.'

Meg chuckled. She could well imagine that the twenty-six-year-old smartly dressed, handsome Jamaican would have no difficulty in attracting women.

'What was your news?' Dan enquired, remembering that she had something to tell him too.

'You'll never guess who just moved into Britford Lodge today.' Meg paused before answering her own question. 'Albert Grimshaw!'

'What, Albert from The Cedars?' asked Dan, amazed.

Meg told him about Albert's unexpected arrival, before changing the subject. 'Now then, I need your help with something,' she declared.

'Of course! What can I do?'

'I've been thinking about buying a mobile phone.'

'You have?' Dan sounded surprised.

'Yes,' she nodded firmly. 'I realise now how much easier things would have been at The Cedars if I'd had one, so it's about time I put that right.'

'But didn't you say you have a phone in your room, here?'

'Oh yes, this place has all mod cons. But what if I needed to contact someone in an emergency, when I wasn't in my room?'

'Is that very likely?'

'Well, you never know, do you? I didn't expect to be sedated, locked in my room and then driven off to goodness only knows where, but it happened.'

'That's true,' he conceded, 'but surely you aren't expecting anything quite so dramatic to happen again, are you?' he asked, with amusement in his eyes.

'Of course not! But it's a good idea to be prepared, just in case.'

'Fair enough. Well, what do you want to know?'

Meg spent a bewildering half hour trying to assimilate Dan's patient explanations before conceding that she had little hope of walking into a phone shop and coming out with something she could use.

'I just want to make phone calls,' she interrupted, as Dan launched into the comparative benefits of Android versus Apple. 'Never mind taking photos or downloading whatever. I just need a nice simple phone, please. Like the one I had shortly before I retired.'

'Would you like me to come shopping with you?' smiled Dan.

'Yes, please. That would be very kind of you.'

'How about I pick you up at ten o'clock on Saturday morning then?'

'You're not working this weekend?'

'Not unless something major happens between now and then,' he chuckled. 'It's remarkably quiet at the moment; a few burglaries, but I'm mostly catching up on a backlog of paperwork.'

'I thought you weren't supposed to use the word "quiet". Isn't it supposed to be a jinx, or something?'

'You watch too much television,' he laughed, and she joined in.

'What-ho! Nice to see a familiar face!' boomed Albert, coming up behind Meg and making her jump.

Dan stood up and shook his hand. 'Good to see you, Albert,' he said politely.

'I say, well remembered, Detective Inspector.'

Dan smiled wryly, not sure he would have remembered the name if Meg hadn't already told him. He remembered the face well enough, though.

'You can imagine my surprise,' continued Albert, 'when Frank pointed out Meg walking past us with her *grandson* a few moments ago, and I looked up and saw that it was you!'

'I consider Dan to be my honorary grandson,' Meg explained.

'Oh, jolly good show!' beamed Albert.

To her dismay, Dan seized on the interruption as a sign that he should go, but she insisted on walking him to the door. 'Don't forget our shopping trip on Saturday,' she reminded him. 'Unless there's been a grisly murder or some terrible terrorist incident that requires your presence.'

'I'll see you on Saturday,' he said firmly, not imagining that any such thing was likely to happen in the next five days.

Chapter Four

When Meg returned to Albert, he was sitting where Dan had been, waiting for her.

'I do hope I didn't put my big foot in it?' he asked, studying her face anxiously.

She didn't have the heart to be annoyed with him. 'No, Albert, of course not. In any case, I shall see Dan again soon enough.'

'Does he visit very often, then?' Albert sounded surprised.

'It depends if he's busy with work or not. Hopefully, he's taking me out shopping on Saturday.' Albert looked as though he'd like to question her further, but she was saved by the appearance of one of the carers.

Ana-Maria Matei, tall and slender with long brown hair tied back in a neat ponytail, was the very antithesis of Kayla. Her tunic was crisply ironed, she was caring and took a great interest in every resident, and she knew just how Meg liked her tea.

'I sorry I interrupt you and your visitor, Meg,' she apologised, in her broken English.

'Oh, this isn't a visitor, Ana! This is our new resident, Albert,' corrected Meg.

Ana scrambled in her pocket for a piece of paper and referred to it for a moment.

'Oh, I sorry, Mr Grimshaw. Very nice to meet you.' She offered her hand to Albert.

Rising to his feet, he shook hands briefly. 'It's Captain Grimshaw,' he began. Then, noticing Meg's thunderous brow, he hastily added, 'But you can call me Albert.'

'Albert, I like this name. Is the name of husband of Queen Victoria . . . I think?'

'Yes indeed!' Albert seemed a bit surprised, but then,

Meg thought, he probably didn't expect a Romanian to know much British history.

'I hope you will be content to live here,' Ana said politely.

'Er, yes, I'm sure I will be.' He sat back down, slightly bemused.

'Don't mind him, Ana,' interjected Meg, 'did you want me for something?'

'Sorry, no, Meg. I only come to ask if you need paracetamol. I see on your chart you did not take any today.'

'That's very kind of you, Ana, but I'm fine today.

'No pain?'

'No pain, thank you.'

'Okay, thank you, Meg. I leave you to meet Albert.' Ana walked away, checking her list for her next patient.

'Another bloomin' foreigner,' grumbled Albert.

'And what's that supposed to mean?' Meg's voice was dangerously quiet; Albert should have known better.

'Well, there was Sonia and Milana at The Cedars and now this Ana. All these foreigners coming over here and taking jobs that nice British girls should be doing.'

'If it wasn't for carers like Sonia, Milana and Ana, our care homes would be struggling to find staff, because there aren't enough "nice British girls" willing to do this kind of work!' Meg frowned at him. 'And, I'll have you know, Ana is very nice. As are Stefania and Florin, who are also Romanian. And Taska, who is Latvian.'

Albert had the grace to look slightly abashed. 'But—' he began, but Meg cut him off.

'And every single one of those carers is a lot more caring than one of the British carers I could mention.'

'I stand corrected,' he managed to squeeze in when Meg paused for breath.

'Well, so long as you remember that,' she finished.

'I can't help being what I am, but I promise to try harder to be more tolerant.'

'Good.'

'Anyway, I didn't come across to break up your conversation with the detective inspector, I'm sorry about that. It's just, when I was telling Frank who your so-called grandson was, Alan got very agitated and kept repeating your name over and over.'

'Did he? He doesn't usually say much.'

'Well, I must admit it was very difficult to make out what he was saying.'

'That's because he has dysphasia, from a stroke two years ago,' explained Meg.

'Dys . . . what?' spluttered Albert.

'Dysphasia. Problems with speech. If the stroke is on the left side of the brain, it can affect your speech as well as causing weakness on the right side of the body. Alan's right arm is pretty much useless, and his leg is quite weak and jerky when he tries to walk. And he has problems forming his words, so he tends not to speak much.'

'I just thought he was a bit gaga!'

'Albert!' Meg rebuked.

'I know, I know, I'm sorry! I didn't mean it to be derogatory.'

Meg smiled despite herself; Albert was definitely mellowing.

'How come you know so much about this sort of thing?' Albert demanded with curiosity. 'I thought you taught English, literature and grammar and all that kind of stuff, not medicine.'

'Oh, Albert,' chuckled Meg, 'don't be so narrow-minded. I read a lot, I'm curious about the world around me. Aren't you?'

'I read my newspaper every day,' Albert retorted stiffly. 'I know what's what with current affairs and the financial markets, that sort of thing. And I keep up to date with the cricket scores, of course, whenever it's being played. Wrong season, now, of course.'

'Each to his own,' she chuckled. 'Personally, I can't think of anything more boring than cricket.'

About to take umbrage, Albert fortunately caught sight of Meg's face and realised that she was ribbing him. 'Steady on, old gal,' he warned her playfully.

'Well,' she said, as she eased herself out of the chair, 'I'd better go and see what Alan wants.'

'Shall I come with you, m'dear?'

'No, I think it might be better if I go on my own.'

Meg spoke briefly to Frank and Donald before settling herself in the armchair next to Alan's.

'Hello, Alan, did you want to see me?' she asked quietly, angling her body so that the others wouldn't hear. He nodded and she waited patiently whilst he tried to form a word.

'Po-lees,' he managed eventually.

'Police?' repeated Meg, to be sure that's what he'd meant. Alan nodded again.

'Yes. Dan, who visited me this afternoon, is a detective inspector with Salisbury Police. But he's also a friend, who I regard as my honorary grandson.'

'Con-fesh-an.'

'You want to make a confession?' asked Meg, surprised. Alan nodded vigorously.

'Con-fesh-an,' he repeated firmly.

'Do you want to tell me, and I'll pass it on, if that's really necessary?'

'No. Po-lees.'

'Do you want me to ask Dan to see you, next time he comes?'

'Yes pliz!'

'He's coming on Saturday morning. I'll ask him then, if that's okay?'

Alan nodded, his head drooping. Meg realised that the effort of trying to communicate had worn him out.

'Don't worry.' She patted his hand gently. 'I'm sure it can't be anything too bad.'

A solitary tear rolled down Alan's face as Meg walked away, but no one noticed.

✦

Trapped inside a body that didn't work properly and unable to communicate with the outside world, many people ignored Alan. Meg was one of the few who were aware that he could understand what was being said to him even if he couldn't reply. People like that were all too rare, he thought. Even a few of the carers treated him like he was an imbecile. Sometimes, he wanted to shout and scream at them but, of course, he couldn't. There were a few good ones too, here at Britford Lodge. Maureen Wilkinson, the care manager, was one of them, and that nice Romanian girl, Ana.

Of the residents, he had little time for most of them. Some of them really were imbeciles. Or totally senile. But Frank treated him okay, and Donald put up with him. And Meg, she seemed like a genuine sort of person. Although she hadn't been here that long, so he didn't really know her. But he trusted her enough to pass his message on without gossiping about it to everyone else. He'd noticed that about her. She wasn't the sort to go blabbing his business to all and sundry. Which was good, because he really didn't want everyone knowing what was weighing so heavily on his mind.

He lifted his left hand and clumsily wiped away the tear that had escaped. He just needed to get this off his chest before it was too late. And he had a feeling that time was running out.

Chapter Five

When their early shift finished, Kayla, Ana-Maria and another carer, Mandy, left Britford Lodge together to walk up to the bus stop at the nearby Britford Park and Ride. They were silent until they reached the brightly painted bus shelter, the air too cold for conversation and walking. Once there, they huddled together against the chilly January weather as tendrils of freezing fog drifted in, blotting out what little warmth the sun had offered.

Like Kayla, Mandy Cartwright was Salisbury born and bred, but she was closer in age to Ana, and the two older carers chatted sociably as they waited for the bus into town, whilst Kayla moodily said nothing. Once on the bus, Ana and Mandy sat together, the tall willowy Romanian waiting for the plump mother of three to sit first before perching on the aisle seat beside her. Kayla sat as far away from them as she could and was quickly absorbed by a game on her phone.

'You on diet?' asked Ana pleasantly. 'You have lost weight, no?'

'Sort of,' admitted Mandy, 'but there's still plenty to lose,' she added morosely.

'No, is good you lose weight slowly. You lose too quickly, you not look well.'

Privately, Ana considered that Mandy already looked too pale. Her wispy dark brown hair framed a face etched with worry lines that made her appear older than her thirty-five years. She could easily have been mistaken as five or even ten years older than Ana, despite there being less than a year between them. But then, Ana hadn't had children, although she hoped there might still be time for that one day.

'How old your children, now?' she asked.

'Olly's nearly eight,' Mandy replied, with a touch of

warmth to her voice. 'Amelia has just turned six, and Jack's three.'

'Olly?' queried Ana, not understanding.

'Short for Oliver,' explained Mandy.

'Ah, like Mandy is short for Amanda, I think?'

'Yes,' she confirmed.

Ana wondered what it would be like to have a husband and three children to go home to after work. It must be nice to cook for a family and to all sit around a table together, chatting about your day. It reminded her of better days at home in Romania, when they would all sit at the worn-out table and share stories. Today, she would return to her cold flat, all alone as usual. It made her feel homesick.

Ana was the first to get off the bus. She hopped off in Exeter Street, cutting through Carmelite Way to a housing estate known as The Friary. A few minutes' walk and she was inserting a key into the shabbily painted door to her flat. The corridor smelt vaguely of urine and curry, but at least inside her flat it was clean even if she couldn't afford to turn the night storage heaters on. She stumbled over an envelope on the hall mat, picked it up and dropped it onto a ring-marked coffee table in the lounge with barely a glance. She quickly changed into jeans and a roll-neck jumper, throwing her uniform into a plastic laundry basket in her tiny bedroom. She pulled a blanket around her shoulders for added warmth and made a cup of cheap instant coffee in the miniscule kitchenette. Only once she'd flicked the TV on to a music channel and slumped onto the lumpy sofa did she examine her mail.

As she'd feared, it was a letter from the letting agent. She knew she was behind on the rent, but it couldn't be helped. Papa had needed the operation or he would have died, and so she had sent the money to her parents. She was working hard to find more money and was sure she would be able to pay last month's rent soon. Hopefully, that would be enough to avoid eviction.

Mandy and Kayla both got off the bus opposite the Red Lion in the town centre. Mandy waved to Kayla before walking briskly round the corner into Queen Street. She crossed into Endless Street and, with a slight spurt of speed, she was able to board the number two bus waiting at the stop there. She was lucky she didn't have to wait for the next one. She sank gratefully into a seat halfway down the bus and struggled for a moment to get her breath back. She looked at her watch. Her mum would've collected the two older children from school by now, but she'd be home in plenty of time to give them their tea. Amelia would moan because she wasn't keen on spaghetti hoops, but they'd had the baked beans last night. It wasn't like there was a lot of choice; it was a tin of whatever she could afford between the three of them, with toast. At least they had a proper meal at school and her mum fed Jack at lunchtime, knowing her daughter wouldn't be able to cook in the evening.

Tears pricked at the back of Mandy's eyes. She hated not being able to afford to buy them nicer food, things like cakes and fruit and yoghurts. There had been a time when she'd loved cooking, but now she had to juggle what little money was left after the mortgage and bills had been paid. It had seemed like a good idea to buy their own house four years ago, and money hadn't been a problem whilst Darryl was working. But he'd been made redundant six months back and she hadn't seen or heard from him since he walked out in November. If things got much worse, she might have to go to the food bank, much though she hated the idea. And she couldn't remember the last time she'd been for an evening out. Much though she adored her children and wouldn't be without them, she sometimes wished she could be young, free and single again, like Kayla, with money to go out whenever she felt like it.

With a start, she realised that the bus was already at St Mark's roundabout. Ten minutes and she'd be home. She would smile brightly for her mum and pretend everything was okay. And maybe, just maybe, she'd be able to find enough money to treat them to a large fish and chips to share on Saturday. Her stomach rumbled at the thought.

❖

Kayla saw Mandy wave as she hurried away from the bus but chose to ignore her. Mandy and Ana both acted like they were so much better than her, so why should she bother with them? She took her time getting off the bus and then sauntered along the road to the Odeon in New Canal. She scanned the list of films showing, but there wasn't really anything she wanted to see. Not that Mack would want to go to the cinema anyway. A number one bus groaned to a halt and she got on board and opened her phone to continue her game, keeping her head down and ignoring the hustle and bustle as a load of grammar school boys boarded around her.

She got off the bus at The Valley and made her way reluctantly to the tiny terrace she shared with her boyfriend. She entered as quietly as she could and tried to sneak straight upstairs, knowing that there was every likelihood that Mack would be off his face on weed by now. But Mack burst out of the living-room door.

'Where do yer think you're goin'?' he demanded.

'Upstairs to change out of my uniform,' she replied, as calmly as she could. He grabbed her right arm tightly, just above the elbow.

'Not so fast!' he hissed. 'You got any cash on yer?'

'And where would I get cash from?' she protested petulantly.

'Don't be so snippy,' he snapped, grabbing at her handbag.

'Hey, keep your hands off!' she warned, but he shoved her suddenly, catching her unawares and sending her thudding into the banisters. 'Ouch!' she wailed as she sat down on the stairs nursing her knee. He took no notice, rifling feverishly through her bag, finding the twenty-pound note she'd hidden in a side pocket.

'What d'yer call this, then?' he sneered, with an unpleasant grin.

'Mine,' she retorted sullenly.

'Is this all you got?'

'Yes.'

'It's not enough. I need more.'

'What for?'

'What d'yer think? Billy's got some skunk in. I was going to nip round for a couple of baggies.'

'Mack, I thought you'd promised to quit that stuff?'

Mack backhanded her across the side of her face. 'Shut yer face,' he growled.

Kayla kept her head down until she heard the front door bang, then she hauled herself up the stairs. One day, she swore, she'd find the courage to leave him. If only she had a flat of her own, like Ana. As it was, she had the choice of here or the streets, and she wasn't sure which was more terrifying.

Chapter Six

Tuesday 10th January 2023

Ana and Kayla were on the same bus out of town the next afternoon, on their way into work for the late shift. They had greeted each other briefly at the bus stop but Kayla avoided Ana on the bus, and when they reached the Park and Ride, Ana walked ahead of Kayla, who limped along sullenly. When she arrived at the care home, Ana turned round to speak to Kayla and only then realised that she was lagging some way behind and appeared to have an injury.

'You are hurting?' she asked solicitously as Kayla caught up.

'Fell down the stairs last night,' Kayla mumbled.

'Is very bad?'

'I'll live.'

Ana was about to say something else, but Kayla edged around her, head down, refusing to look her in the eye. Ana glimpsed a slight redness across the side of Kayla's cheek and reached out a hand to stop the girl from moving away.

'You hurt your face also?' she enquired, with concern in her voice.

'It's nothing,' muttered Kayla.

Ana let her go and followed her through the door, but she couldn't let go of the idea that something was not right for Kayla. She would try to find out later.

There was an overlap between the late shift coming on duty and the earlies going off. This ensured there were sufficient staff to oversee the residents leaving the dining room after lunch, toileting those who needed help whilst the care manager handed over to the late staff.

After handover, Ana walked into the dining room in time

to see Mandy struggling to help Alan up from the table. She hurried to assist, knowing how awkward it was to get him up and into position with his walking frame, whilst the chair was effectively in the way. Given his tendency to lean heavily to one side, Mandy shouldn't really be moving him on her own.

'Thank you!' she gasped, looking very pale and tired after an exhausting early shift. The two of them walked either side of Alan, who seemed especially uncoordinated today.

'Now then, Alan, where would you like to sit?' asked Mandy, already halfway to Alan's normal seat in front of the TV. She wasn't really expecting a reply.

'Nothe,' struggled Alan. Mandy looked at him in surprise.

'Not there? Don't you feel like watching TV this afternoon?' she enquired.

'Vish-tor,' Alan tried to explain.

'Oh, is Tuesday today,' cried Ana. 'Alan's friend come every Tuesday afternoon!'

'Of course,' replied Mandy, 'I completely forgot what day of the week it was.'

They steered him across to a different group of faux-leather armchairs, where it was a little quieter, and helped him to sit down. Ana watched as Mandy wearily moved a small table to Alan's left side and positioned a plastic beaker of water there for him.

'You are unwell?' Ana asked, as they walked back towards the dining room together.

'No, what on earth gives you that idea?'

'You very pale today.'

'No, I'm fine,' laughed Mandy, just a shade too brightly.

'You ate some lunch?'

'Yes, of course,' Mandy lied. There hadn't been enough bread left after breakfast this morning to make herself a sandwich, so she'd skipped lunch again. A habit that was becoming all too regular, sadly. Now, she'd have to find enough money to buy a loaf for tomorrow on the way home. She sighed. 'I'm just a little tired,' she explained quickly to Ana.

Just then, a tall, thin gentleman with a bald head and gold-framed glasses pushed through the front doors, a supermarket bag for life over his left arm.

'Good afternoon,' Ana called out politely. 'Alan is waiting you in the day room!'

He nodded his thanks as he retrieved a large white handkerchief from his coat pocket, setting his bag on the floor carefully before taking off his glasses and removing the condensation that had formed the instant he'd entered the warm care home.

The two carers had disappeared by the time he'd finished, but it didn't matter. He came every week at exactly the same time, and Alan was always waiting for him in exactly the same chair.

'Good afternoon, Alan,' he said, as he approached his longtime friend. Despite being a good ten years younger than him, Ed had known Alan for most of their adult lives, on and off.

Alan looked up and smiled, albeit a little lopsidedly. He reached out his good arm and the two shook hands warmly. 'Ed!' he said, quite clearly.

Ed took off his coat and scarf and folded them neatly across the arm of his chair, before sitting down.

'It's very cold out, again,' he said, knowing that Alan could understand well enough, even if he struggled to say anything, 'but it's nice to get a glimpse of the sun, and at least it's not raining.' He paused. 'Or snowing, for that matter.'

'Boot?' asked Alan anxiously.

'Yes, I brought the book you asked me to get for you in Waterstones.' Ed pulled a hefty paperback from his bag and put it on Alan's lap so that he could see it. Alan nodded enthusiastically at the latest Lee Child novel. He wouldn't be able to read it sitting here in the day room, but he had a gadget in his bedroom that held the book for him so that he could read. He spent a lot of time reading in bed.

'I've brought some grapes for you too,' added Ed.

'They're the small green seedless ones that I know you like.'

'Than you,' Alan managed, as Ed showed him the plastic box of fruit.

'Shall I take them upstairs with your book for you?'

'Yes, pliz. Wal . . . let?' He struggled with the word.

'Is your wallet in your bedroom?' verified Ed. Alan nodded. 'No problem, shall I bring it down for you?'

Alan shook his head.

'Shall I just take out the money for the book?' asked Ed, knowing his friend so well. 'It was £9.99.'

Alan nodded.

'Won't be long.'

As Ed walked away, he passed by Meg and Albert, who were just coming into the day room. He wished Meg 'Good day' and smiled, recognising her. He wondered who the man with her was, for he'd not seen him before. Perhaps he was her brother.

Meg stopped as they drew level with Alan. 'Nice to see your friend here again, Alan. He's as regular as clockwork, isn't he?'

Alan nodded and lifted his left hand to beckon Meg closer. 'Po-lees,' he reminded her.

'Don't worry, Alan, I haven't forgotten.' She sat down briefly in the chair Ed had vacated, motioning Albert to carry on without her, and laid a hand gently on Alan's arm. 'Is there any particular reason why you suddenly feel the urge to confess something?' she enquired.

Alan didn't reply, but he had a sort of faraway glazed look in his watery blue eyes.

'You're not terminally ill, are you?'

Alan shook his head and eventually managed one word: 'Time.'

Before Meg could think what that meant, Ed returned in a hurry, slightly breathless and clearly worried.

'Oh dear, oh dear,' he sighed.

'Is there a problem?' Meg asked, as she vacated his chair and motioned for him to sit down.

'Alan,' Ed looked directly at his friend as he sank into the chair, 'did you leave your wallet in the top drawer of your bedside locker, where you normally put it?'

Alan nodded with a slight frown.

'In that case, I'm sorry to have to say that it appears to have gone missing. It's neither in the drawer nor on top of the locker. I checked the dressing table too. Are you *sure* you put it in the usual place?'

Alan nodded vigorously, looking anxious.

'Oh dear, what should I do now?' Ed looked up at Meg for advice.

Meg thought for a moment. 'Would you like Albert and me to go and search your room, Alan?' she asked. 'It's just possible your wallet's fallen down behind the furniture or under the bed, or something.'

Alan nodded.

'That's very kind of you,' said Ed gratefully, 'but I don't want to spoil your time with your visitor. Perhaps I should ask one of the carers?'

'Albert's not a visitor, he's a new resident,' she chuckled. She beckoned to Albert, who had been hovering a short distance away. Albert had already pricked up his ears on hearing his name and came quickly to Meg's side.

'Can you describe what exactly we're looking for, please?' she asked Ed.

'It's a black leather wallet, the sort that folds in half, and quite new. I gave it to Alan for Christmas because his last one was falling apart.'

'Come along, Albert,' she ordered her bemused friend, who hadn't a clue where they were going but faithfully followed her out of the day room.

Chapter Seven

Alan's bedroom was on the ground floor, whereas both Meg and Albert had rooms upstairs. They methodically searched in, under and behind every bit of furniture, but there was no sign of a wallet. Meg straightened up from having another look under the bed.

'Well, it's definitely not here,' she pronounced.

'I must say, he keeps his room nice and shipshape,' remarked Albert, looking around with curiosity. The ground-floor rooms were a bit bigger than those on the first floor, although they contained the same furniture, and they had a glass-panelled door leading to the paved terrace that ran along that side of the building.

'They mostly use the ground-floor rooms for the residents with wheelchairs or walking frames because they need the extra space,' she replied, reading his mind. 'Not that I'd like a door to the outside in *my* room,' she said firmly.

Albert walked over to the door. 'It's got a good solid lock on it. And the glass looks like toughened safety glass, if I'm not mistaken. You wouldn't break in here easily!'

'Still not my cup of tea,' she declared.

They returned to the day room and explained their lack of success. Alan was upset by the news and became very agitated; so much so that Meg insisted Ed go immediately to the office to report the theft to the care manager. Once she'd marched off with Ed in tow, Albert sank down into an armchair and closed his eyes. Where did the woman get all her energy from? he wondered. Ah well, she was a few years younger than him.

❀

Maureen Wilkinson was working at her desk when Meg arrived with Alan's visitor. She put her pen down, giving them her full attention as they explained the problem.

'Thank you for telling me,' she replied earnestly. 'We take any report like this very seriously, so you can be assured I will follow up on it, Mr . . . er?'

'Call me Ed, please,' he insisted with a wry smile.

'Ed, thank you. Perhaps you would be kind enough to help me fill out a form for missing property and, if we do manage to find Alan's wallet, I'll phone you to let you know it's been found.'

Meg waited until the paperwork was done and then escorted Ed back to where Alan was anxiously waiting. She was about to wake Albert, who was now snoring quite loudly, but Ed invited her to leave him be and to join Alan and him for a while. She was later pleasantly surprised to discover she'd spent over an hour conversing with the erudite visitor who, it transpired, had been a mechanic with a penchant for self-education. She was amazed at the breadth and depth of his knowledge and had thoroughly enjoyed their discussions on subjects as diverse as climate change and the Booker Prize. It wasn't every day that she found someone as well read as herself.

❖

Maureen frowned. Mrs Thornton had insisted they'd searched Alan's room very thoroughly, but she'd better get a couple of carers to double check. And, if the wallet didn't turn up by tomorrow, she'd have to phone the police. She hated the idea that any of her staff might have stolen it, so it was imperative to get to the bottom of this quickly. She called Sarah, who was in charge of the late shift, and Kayla into the office and briefed them on what had happened. Sarah Fielding, senior care assistant, pushed the unruly auburn curls off her freckled face as she went with Kayla to search Alan's room. But they had no more luck in finding the missing wallet than Meg and Albert had had. Maureen also checked with all of the other carers working that day, thankful that both shifts were still on duty. But no one had seen Alan's wallet.

Before she went off duty, Maureen went to talk to Alan. She reassured him that she was taking the theft of his wallet very seriously.

'Don't worry, we'll do everything we can to get it back for you. Can you tell me, when did you last see your wallet?'

'S'morn-ing,' he replied instantly.

'And you're sure of that?'

'Yes,' he insisted adamantly.

'And it was in the top drawer of your bedside locker, where your friend Ed told me it normally was?'

'Yes.'

'Do you have any idea who might have stolen it?'

'No,' Alan mumbled sadly.

'Was there very much money in it?' Maureen asked, sympathetically.

'Al-mos two … two hun-ded,' Alan managed with an effort.

'Two hundred pounds?' gasped Maureen, taken aback. 'Whatever did you have that much cash for?' It was a rhetorical question because she knew he couldn't explain. Perhaps his friend had withdrawn some of his pension for him? Still, it was a lot of money given the small amount Alan would likely have needed.

'Was there anything else in the wallet?' she asked.

'Pho-to.'

'You had a photo in there?' Alan nodded. 'Was it of someone special?' A tear appeared in Alan's eye but he didn't reply. Not that it mattered. She knew that many of her elderly residents kept treasured photos, often of long-lost loved ones. She understood that the pain of losing a precious memento was probably just as upsetting for Alan as losing the money. It made her all the more determined to get to the bottom of this.

✿

Why, oh why did someone have to go and steal Alan's wallet?

They already had Alan's murder carefully planned out. Think!

Perhaps if Alan was killed tonight, suspicion would fall on whoever stole the wallet? He was going to make it look like natural causes – but now that Maureen was planning to contact the police, how would that affect their plans?

In the end, she dashed off a text and left the decision to him.

✿

As she got ready for bed that evening, Meg's mind was uneasy. On the face of it, it was just a missing wallet. But her brush with murder at The Cedars had started with a missing brooch, and look where that had ended up! She told herself not to be so silly. But it didn't help; she just couldn't shake the ridiculous notion that this was the start of something more sinister. With this playing on her mind, sleep was impossible. Half an hour after turning her light out, she turned it back on again. *Margaret Thornton*, she scolded herself. *You are being a fanciful old woman.* She picked up her book and tried to distract herself. One of the carers poked his head around the door a little while later. Kai, a lad in his mid-thirties at a guess, was half Chinese, half British and had the typical eyes and jet-black hair of the Chinese.

'Are you all right, Meg?' he asked solicitously.

She told him that she was finding it difficult to sleep, without explaining why. He asked if she needed some paracetamol for pain. When she politely refused, he insisted on fetching some warm milk and a hot water bottle. 'It will help you to settle,' he said. Strangely enough, it must have worked, for not long after he'd gone, she finally drifted off to sleep.

Chapter Eight

Lauren had been for a night out with her boyfriend. Or her now ex-boyfriend, to be precise. Since they'd met at The Cedars in September, she'd been going out steadily with David, an agency carer who had been working there on that final day when all the craziness had happened. If it hadn't been for David and his car, they would never have been able to follow Brenda's car with Meg, being taken away to God only knows where. She shivered at the thought of what might have happened if they hadn't been able to guide the police as to the direction Brenda had taken.

After that was all over, a casual invite for a drink had turned into a few dates and some incredible sex. For a month it had been sooo good. Then it started going downhill. She wanted a steady relationship; he was happy to keep it casual. She'd text him and sometimes he'd reply, all sexy and wonderful, and other times he'd ghost her. Just before Christmas, he'd stood her up, leaving her waiting in Pizza Express feeling like a lemon. She'd been really mad at him, but on Christmas Day he'd turned up at her house with a beautiful pair of silver earrings shaped like little snow angels, full of apologies. And who could stay mad at that gorgeous smile of his? Now, she felt stupid for falling for it.

This evening, they'd been for a quick burger and then gone to the cinema. All had been great until they were leaving at the end of the film. A group of girls were messing about and giggling in the foyer. One had broken away from the others on seeing David and literally thrown herself at him. 'Hey, babes,' she'd muttered before planting a smacker on his lips. Then she'd realised that Lauren was there. 'Who's this?' she'd demanded, looking Lauren up and down like she was a piece of dirt.

'I could ask the same,' Lauren had retorted hotly, tears pricking the back of her eyes.

David had tried to laugh it off but, in a flash, Lauren had realised why her relationship had felt so on and off again. 'You two-timing piece of fucking shit!' she'd screamed at him before storming off. It spoke volumes that he hadn't attempted to follow her. Not that she'd wanted him to.

She was still seething when she got off the bus near The Bull and, for a second, she contemplated going in for a drink. But it was nearly closing time. She walked home briskly, still fighting back tears. She slammed the front door, ran into the lounge and threw herself down on the sofa beside her mum, and the dam burst. Her heaving sobs gradually calmed down, with her mum gently stroking her back and wisely not saying a word. When she'd let go of all the pent-up hurt and anger, tinged with a bit of embarrass-ment, Lauren told her mum what had happened.

'What a bastard!' her mum finally exclaimed, surprising Lauren as she rarely heard her mum use strong language. Her mum made her a lovely soothing hot chocolate, with marshmallows, as it was an occasion that demanded them, and she began to feel a bit better.

'What about work?' Lauren suddenly asked.

'What about it?' her mum replied, with a slight frown.

It was David who had helped her to get the job with the agency and, just occasionally, they had both been sent to the same care home.

At that precise moment, she felt like she never wanted to see David again, despite her mum's assurances that she was better than him and would be able to deal with the situ-ation should it arise. Perhaps the time had come to stop waiting for a job to miraculously appear at Britford Lodge and to start looking at current vacancies elsewhere?

Once in her bed, she opened her notebook and started looking at job adverts. She was busy filling in online forms well into the night.

✿

Early hours of Wednesday 11th January 2023

Petra Orlova, senior care assistant, was in charge of the night shift. Russian, tall and strongly built, she had once been cruelly likened to a shot put champion. But not by any of the residents, who all adored her for her compassion and willingness to help. It was four-thirty in the morning, the most difficult part of the shift for many nurses and carers, when tiredness stealthily overwhelms but it's too early to start on the morning workload. Petra's answer was to keep busy regardless. She and Taska, a petite Latvian who was the home's youngest member of staff at twenty-one, were carrying out a round of the residents. They trod quietly and deliberately from one door to the next, stopping and peering through each small porthole-like window to view their sleeping charges. Taska had once asked what they were supposed to be able to see when it was so dark, to which Petra had patiently explained how to study a person's silhouette to see if they were moving around restlessly, which might mean they were possibly in pain or unable to sleep. These things are important to note, she'd explained.

Taska peered through Alan's window and reported that he was sleeping. As Taska moved towards the next room, some sixth sense made Petra take a second look. That was odd. In the faint light of the moon shining through the curtains, she could just make out an arm hanging over the edge of the bed. She watched to see if she could detect the rise and fall of his breathing but he was eerily still.

'Taska,' she whispered softly.

The young Latvian returned. 'What is it?' she asked impatiently.

'I think we should check Alan.'

Petra eased the door open and flicked on a small pencil torch, pointing it down at the floor as they crossed the short space to the side of Alan's bed. Taska started lifting Alan's wrist with the intention of taking his pulse, but she withdrew her hand abruptly with a gasp. 'Is very cold!' she whispered in alarm.

Petra felt the arm and then gently felt Alan's forehead. He was extremely cold. She felt for a carotid pulse but, unsurprisingly, there wasn't one. Alan had apparently died in his sleep.

Petra put the lights on and conducted all the correct checks to confirm death. Whilst she was doing that, she didn't notice Taska absent-mindedly stoop to retrieve a piece of rubbish she'd seen on the floor near the door, dropping it into the bin in the room. Petra and Taska then quietly withdrew to the office, leaving Alan as they'd found him, in the dark with his door shut. Petra telephoned Dr Phil Baker, with an apology for waking him but procedure dictated that the doctor be called immediately. She calmly explained the situation and Dr Baker accepted her diagnosis without query, knowing Petra to be very experienced. Alan was only seventy-six, but he'd already had one major stroke and a couple of minor ones, so death was not entirely unexpected. Petra agreed with the doctor that there was no rush for him to attend.

Chapter Nine

Wednesday 11th January 2023

At half past six, Phil Baker, a forty-five-year-old GP with short silvery grey hair and glasses, arrived at Britford Lodge muffled in a heavy coat and scarf. He discarded these in the office and looked through Alan's notes briefly whilst blowing on his hands in an effort to warm them. He wanted to get this death certificate handled before he went into the surgery as he had a busy day ahead.

'Right, remind me which room Alan's in,' he said, looking towards Petra, who was sitting at the desk updating the residents' notes.

'Jess will take you,' she replied, nodding to a carer who was waiting nearby.

Several minutes later, Phil and Jess returned to the office, just as Maureen Wilkinson arrived ahead of her early shift.

'It's Alan,' Petra explained to Maureen, 'he died in his sleep.'

Maureen glanced at Phil's face, which was unusually grim. 'Is there a problem, Doctor?' she enquired.

'To be honest, I'm not sure. But I would like to call the pathologist for a second opinion.'

'His death is suspicious?' gasped Petra in alarm. 'What did I miss?'

'Don't worry, Petra, I'm sure you were very thorough. But there's a couple of anomalies suggesting that it wasn't a fatal stroke that killed him, which is what I would've expected. I suspect he died of asphyxia, which is odd when there is nothing obvious obstructing his airway.'

'There will have to be an investigation?' asked Maureen.

'I'm sorry, yes, I think it's necessary,' replied Phil. 'Maybe I'm being a little overcautious but ...' He took a deep breath, memories of a previous death that he'd signed off as natural causes and had later turned out to be murder echoing in his mind.

'It is what it is,' said Maureen, ever the pragmatist.

By seven, the early staff had all arrived and Petra took them into the deserted day room for handover, the office being occupied by Dr Baker, who was briefing the two DCs who were first on the scene about the situation. Recently promoted Detective Constable Moira Gordon made detailed notes before taking up position on the front door, having established that this was the only entrance to the home that was unlocked. She would keep a log of anyone entering or leaving the building. DC Aaron Johnson settled himself into position outside Alan's door, knowing better than to enter and risk contaminating a possible crime scene. Phil Baker waited impatiently in the office, worrying whether he had perhaps overreacted and hoping he hadn't made a fool of himself.

Next to arrive was Dr Graham Hamnet, the pathologist, followed closely by Detective Sergeant Vivian Williams, who yawned and stretched as he climbed out of his Vauxhall Astra. After signing in with DC Gordon, the two men went straight to the office, where Phil explained his concerns. Dr Hamnet then went to Alan's room, where he donned a forensic suit before entering to conduct his preliminary examination. Viv decided he may as well take Phil's statement whilst they were waiting for the pathologist's verdict, to save a little time later if this turned out to be a suspicious death.

He was learning to dot all his i's and cross all his t's, as the DI would often say.

❖

Meg had woken up early that morning and had read several chapters of her book by the time Taska brought in her early-morning cup of tea, shortly before seven.

'Good morning, Taska,' she smiled, then noticed the tension in the Latvian's face.

41

'Is everything all right?'

'I do not know! Mr Alan Watts is dead and police come,' she blurted out anxiously. Then she put her hands to her mouth. 'Oh! Perhaps I should not say that?'

Meg felt a sudden lurch in her stomach, and an intense feeling of *déja vu* washed over her. Somehow, she just knew that Alan had been murdered!

'Don't worry, Taska,' she said, trying to reassure the distraught carer. 'It won't hurt for you to have told me, but perhaps it might be better if you don't tell any of the other residents.'

'No, I not say anyone. I say only you, Meg.'

'Good girl. Do you know when Alan died?'

'Sometime in night.' Taska shrugged her shoulders as though that detail was unimportant.

'He was in his bed?' checked Meg. Taska nodded.

'What time did Alan settle down to sleep, do you know?'

'I know this. Alan ring his bell a quarter before eleven and I take his book stand so he can lie down.' She mimed the actions as she spoke. 'I pour him some water, make him comfortable, then I turn out his light.'

'And when did you find out he was dead?'

'Petra and me, we find him at four and a half.'

'Half past four.' Meg couldn't stop herself correcting the girl.

'I sorry, my English no good. I go to college but is difficult language.'

'That's okay.' Meg smiled warmly. 'You're doing very well.'

Taska beamed back at her. 'Thank you.'

'Now, describe to me how Alan looked when you saw him.' Taska did her best, with Meg asking further questions until she was satisfied there were no more details to be had. 'I think you'd better go and finish the teas, now, don't you?' suggested Meg. 'And not a word to the other residents!'

Taska hurried out of the room, eager to oblige.

Meg got out of bed, put on her warm dressing gown and slippers and rummaged through a drawer to find a notepad and a biro. She settled herself down in the armchair with her cup of tea and carefully wrote down everything she could remember of her recent conversations with Alan, as well as what few facts she knew about his murder. If indeed it was murder and she wasn't putting two and two together and making five. She wondered if Dan and Viv would investigate.

✿

Dr Hamnet popped his head round the office door, still suited up so that only his bushy grey eyebrows and steely blue eyes were showing.

'I agree, Phil,' he stated bluntly. 'Definitely a suspicious death. You did the right thing by calling me in.'

Dr Baker let out a long sigh of relief, glad that he had followed his hunch.

'DS Williams, would you come with me so I can talk you through a couple of things before the CSIs arrive and take over the scene?'

Viv stood up and went with the pathologist. He pulled on a pair of shoe covers and followed Dr Hamnet into Alan's room, standing just inside the door and being careful not to touch anything.

'What do you see?' asked the pathologist, in the tone of a consultant testing a junior doctor. Viv looked. If it hadn't been for the wide-open eyes and limp arm dangling over the side of the bed, Alan might just have been asleep as there were no apparent injuries that he could see.

'It looks like he died peacefully in his sleep,' he said, baffled.

Dr Hamnet pointed out pinprick bruises in the eyes, some very faint bruising across the nose and a small amount of dried blood just inside the victim's nostrils. Then he showed Viv the pillow discarded across the red armchair in the room, which had one or two very faint traces of blood on it.

'He was smothered with a pillow?' exclaimed Viv.

'Yes, and I've never known a person do that to themselves, so you're definitely looking for a third party,' Dr Hamnet replied dryly.

'I wonder if that door is locked,' Viv mused to himself, moving towards the patio door.

'Yes, it is. I already thought to check it,' interrupted the pathologist tersely.

'Then it has to be an inside job?' Viv perked up, thinking this made things easier.

'Unless there's another way someone could have entered the building.'

Viv's face fell. 'I don't suppose you've got anything useful on our killer?'

'Possibly. I reckon we've a chance of getting skin or blood from under the victim's fingernails on that left hand.' Dr Hamnet pointed. 'Can you see how one of his nails is torn?'

'Why only the left?' puzzled Viv.

'Because the victim was paralysed on the right side from a stroke.'

'Oh, I didn't know that.'

'That's why I had Dr Baker tell me the victim's medical history before examining him.'

'Hmm. If the murderer knew that, they'd have known that Alan wouldn't be able to fight back as strongly. Does that mean a woman could have done this?' asked Viv. 'Or perhaps even one of the residents?'

'Oh aye, quite easily. Although I'd say the murderer used far more force than was actually necessary, which implies either a strong person who doesn't know their own strength, or someone who was very angry.'

The two men left the room and returned to the office.

Chapter Ten

Meg finished her notes and her tea and got herself washed and dressed with as much speed as she could manage. There was no one on the first-floor landing, it still being quite early for many of the residents to be up and about. She was able to take the lift to the ground floor without being questioned by anyone, emerging into the entrance foyer just as Detective Inspector Daniel Bywater walked in through the front doors.

'Meg!' He seemed taken aback.

'Dan, I'm so pleased to see you! Are you in charge of the case?'

'I barely even know if there *is* a case,' he said, amazed that Meg was once again one step ahead of him. 'I only just got the message that Viv was looking into a suspicious death.'

'Oh, it was almost certainly murder,' said Meg, in a matter-of-fact tone. 'I think you'll find that Alan was killed sometime between eleven last night and four-thirty this morning.'

'How on earth do you know that?' Dan asked incredulously. Fortunately, Meg was saved from having to answer by Viv's arrival.

'Morning, guv, nice to see you finally made it,' the Jamaican teased sarcastically.

'I didn't want to waste my valuable time attending a death that turns out to be natural causes,' returned Dan, in the same bantering tone. 'That's what sergeants are for!'

'Well, it's definitely murder ...' began Viv, breaking off when he saw Meg hovering behind Dan. 'Mrs Thornton!'

'Don't beat yourself up, Viv. Meg's already informed me it was murder,' Dan replied.

'But how? I only just found out myself!' Viv exclaimed.

'I have my reasons,' Meg said airily, reluctant to get

Taska into trouble. 'Which I will happily explain to you whenever you're ready to take my statement,' she added, when she saw the look on Dan's face.

Before he could reply, Maureen came out of the day room and approached.

'Good morning, I assume you're with the detective sergeant?' she asked, before doing a double take, recognising him as one of Meg's regular visitors. Dan nodded and introduced himself in his official capacity, showing his police ID to the care manager. As Maureen leant forward to check it out, she was surprised to see that Meg was also there.

'Ah, Meg, perhaps you wouldn't mind excusing us?'

Meg moved towards the lift but neglected to press the call button so that she could listen discreetly whilst appearing to wait for the lift. Introductions were exchanged and Maureen demanded to know what was happening. Viv outlined Dr Hamnet's findings to them.

'I'm afraid that means we'll have to conduct a full investigation,' explained Dan, 'which will involve, among other things, us needing to talk to everyone who was in the building between eleven last night and four-thirty this morning.'

Meg risked a glance and was amused to see the astonishment on Viv's face. She felt absurdly pleased that Dan had accepted her time frame without question.

'I'm afraid there will be a number of police and crime scene personnel doing what needs to be done. Alan's room is, of course, out of bounds, but we will also need to examine the rest of the building, especially the corridor outside his room and any exits and entrances. I don't suppose we can minimise movement around the home until we've had a chance to do that?' Dan smiled hopefully.

'Most of the residents are currently in their rooms, Inspector, but they would normally be getting up and dressed and coming to the dining room for breakfast over the next hour or so. In the circumstances, I suppose we could serve breakfast on trays to their rooms. But to do that, the carers would need to be able to move freely round the corridors.' Maureen paused. 'I suppose you'll want to

46

question the night staff before they leave? Only, they're just about to go off duty.'

'Yes, I'm afraid we do. And we'll need a private space to conduct our interviews, please. Perhaps the office?' Dan suggested.

'I'd rather you used the dining room for your police activities this morning, please. The staff and I need to have constant access to my office.'

Dan nodded his consent.

'Very well, I'll brief the carers immediately and make an announcement over the PA system for residents to stay in their rooms.'

Meg kept her head down as Maureen spun round and headed for the day room. Then she jumped as Dan spoke from close behind her.

'I'm sure you heard all of that because I noticed that you forgot to call the lift.' He pressed the call button for her. 'And can I urge you to leave the investigating to the police this time, please?' he added as the lift doors opened.

Meg was about to argue but she saw the look on Dan's face and thought better of it. Not that she intended to pay any attention to his warning. After all, she knew all the staff and residents far better than he did, and she had a feeling they would talk to her more readily.

❖

Dan was keen to talk to Meg to find out what she knew, but he resisted the urge to question her immediately. Not only was there a lot to be done but he didn't want her thinking that she was an integral part of the investigation. He spoke briefly with the pathologist and Dr Baker before they left, issued instructions to his two constables and informed them that he and Viv would be found in the dining room, if needed.

Over the next hour, CSIs moved in to process Alan's room, and several police constables arrived and started a search of the corridors and communal rooms, having been instructed not to get in the way of the carers or to disturb the residents.

Dan and Viv, meanwhile, questioned each of the night staff before allowing them to go home to sleep. Taska reluctantly revealed that she had settled Alan down to sleep shortly before 11pm, and Petra and Taska both stated that they'd found him dead at about 4.30am. That confirmed Meg's time frame, Dan noted, guessing that Taska might well have been her source. Petra insisted that she had locked the main entrance overnight, unlocking it at 6am as usual. All in all, none of the night staff had seen or heard anything suspicious or had anything useful to add.

Dan's next move was to interview the care manager, Maureen Wilkinson, so that he could get a list of the residents and a rota to ascertain which staff were on duty when. To his surprise, she had already prepared photocopies of both. She also supplied him with floor plans for the two-storey building, with the names of the residents added in very neat blue ink. He was impressed by her calm efficiency but thought he wouldn't like to get on the wrong side of her!

'What about doors with access to the outside? How many rooms have an external door, like Alan's?' he asked, looking at the plans.

'There are ten residents' rooms on the ground floor, and they all have a door to the patio on the south side of the building,' she indicated on the plan with a well-manicured finger, 'but they can only be opened from the inside.'

'Could someone have left one of these doors unlocked?' he enquired.

'Impossible!' she replied firmly. 'Besides the lock, they're on a self-closing latch; the doors close automatically unless they're opened fully and fastened in that position. Once closed, they cannot be opened from the outside.'

'What about fire escapes?'

'There are four fire escape doors on the ground floor: at the end of this corridor and in the dining room, day room and staffroom.' Dan watched as her finger pointed to each as she mentioned them. 'There are also two on the first floor, one at each end of the corridor, where the emergency stairs are situated. But they are all linked to the fire alarm,

48

so the staff would know immediately if one of those was tampered with.'

'Are there any other doors?'

'There are sliding doors from the conservatory out into the garden on the east side and an entrance to the kitchens, here. But they are attached to an alarm system that activates automatically between 10pm and 6am.'

'And the main entrance?' he persisted.

'The night staff are responsible for locking and unlocking that.' She sat back and folded her arms, almost daring him to criticise the home's security. Even if he could, he wouldn't have had the courage.

'What about CCTV?' he asked hopefully.

'There are cameras both inside and outside the main entrance, which upload to a cloud storage site where the images are stored for thirty days. I can arrange for your team to access the site.'

'Thank you, that will be very helpful,' he said. 'I'm sorry to take up so much of your valuable time, but can you talk me through the daily routine here?'

She succinctly described a typical day and responded to Dan's questions until he could think of nothing else to ask. He thanked her and wandered out of the office, deep in thought. He then issued instructions for a couple of the PCs to walk around the exterior to check for possible signs of a break-in, regardless of the care manager's confidence.

Finally, he consulted the floor plan and was about to make his way to Meg's room when one of the CSIs approached him.

'You've got something?' Dan asked hopefully.

'Just wanted to let you know that we've found a spot of blood on the bedcover in addition to the few smears on the pillow, Inspector,' a young woman almost completely concealed in a protective suit reported.

'Good work!' exclaimed Dan.

'The blood on the pillow is almost certainly the victim's; likely the result of a broken nose. We'll get it all analysed, of course, but it seems possible that the blood on the bedcover might not be from the victim; it's a clean drop, not a smear, and from its position it's very unlikely to have come from the victim's nose.'

'That could be our murderer's then!' exclaimed Dan.

'We should be able to establish that, if we can get a DNA match to the scrapings taken from under the victim's finger-nails.'

'Excellent! Now, what about fingerprints?'

'Lots of them, sir, but they're not a lot of use until we have prints from all the staff for comparison, plus those of recent visitors and any of the residents who've been inside that room. It's going to take a long time to sort them all out, I'm afraid.'

'Doesn't it always?' sighed Dan. 'I don't suppose there was any sign of that patio door being tampered with?'

'Sorry, sir, no.'

'Well, thanks anyway.' He headed for the staircase.

Chapter Eleven

Dan knocked and waited for Meg's invitation before entering her room and looking round it with interest. Meg, who had been reading a book, was sitting in a yellow armchair of the type typically found in hospitals, next to a generic light oak-coloured dressing table. A matching chest of drawers and a single wardrobe occupied another wall. There was a bedside locker next to the bed and on the near side of that, a door to the bathroom. He noted that the furniture was identical to that in Alan's room, although the room itself was slightly smaller. Even the flooring was the same nondescript grey vinyl. The only difference appeared to be the subtly patterned bed cover, which was multiple shades of rose pink in Meg's room, whilst Alan's had been blue.

'Are all the rooms furnished identically?' he asked.

'So far as I know, yes,' replied Meg.

'It's rather sterile,' he remarked.

'Yes, it's not as homely or individual as my room at The Cedars was, but it is comfortable and well equipped.' She indicated for him to sit on her bed.

'I wondered when you would get around to visiting me,' she said dryly.

'I'd have come sooner but there was a lot to be done,' he smiled. 'Now, perhaps you'd explain how you knew Alan had been murdered?'

Meg explained her reasoning to him without mentioning Taska's name. And Dan saw no reason to press her for it, given that he'd already deduced who her source was. However, he was very interested to hear her account of the recent conversations she'd had with Alan.

'He didn't give you any indication of what it was he wanted to confess?' he asked.

'I'm afraid not.'

'Or any reason as to why now?'

'Just that one word: "time".'

'Surely you asked him about it?'

'Are you saying I'm nosy?' Meg challenged playfully.

'If the cap fits . . .'

'Well, I didn't question him further because he found it hard enough to speak following his stroke, without me putting any more pressure on him. In any case, it was none of my business.'

'Fair point. What do you think he meant by the word "time"?' he enquired.

'I've been thinking about it quite a lot this morning. I presume it means that it was the right time for him to tell someone. But he wasn't terminally ill, and I doubt he would have known that he was about to be murdered. I did wonder whether whatever it was he needed to confess had a statute of limitations and he knew he could no longer be prosecuted for it. Or maybe some external event had come to his attention, and he wanted to get whatever it was off his chest?'

'Interesting ideas,' he said, 'but without knowing what it was, I doubt we'll ever find the answer to that.'

'Now then, what progress have you made?' she demanded.

He stared at her in mock horror. 'You really don't expect me to answer that, do you?'

'Well, it was worth asking,' she replied, with a merry twinkle in her eye. 'But will you at least confirm that he was smothered with a pillow?'

'Very well, although how you worked that out, I'll never know. Yes, he was smothered with a pillow. It looks as though he was either already awake or he woke up and tried to struggle with his murderer, so we have high hopes for some useful forensic evidence.'

'I see, from under his fingernails, I presume?'

'Yes,' he marvelled, shaking his head at her perspicacity.

'Have you started interviewing the staff?'

'Just the staff that were on duty last night, so far. And the care manager, who has provided a lot of general information.'

'Did Maureen tell you about Alan's missing wallet?'

'No, she didn't! What missing wallet?'

Meg filled in the details for him. 'I did wonder if one of the staff could have stolen it.'

'When was it stolen?' he asked.

'Sometime yesterday, I believe. Alan told Maureen it was still in his bedside drawer first thing in the morning, but it was gone by about quarter past two.'

'And Maureen was going to report it to the police?' he confirmed.

'That's what she told Ed.'

'Who's Ed?'

'He's Alan's friend. He comes to visit every Tuesday. He didn't tell me his surname, but I expect Maureen will have it on the missing property form.'

'Thank you, I'll add him to the list of people to interview. Does that give us a possible motive, if whoever stole the wallet also killed Alan?'

'Oh, I very much doubt it,' replied Meg carefully. 'I wouldn't have thought there was much point in killing Alan when so many of the staff already knew about it.'

'Hmm.'

'Do tell me, please. How did the killer get in?'

Dan frowned; he really didn't want to tell her that it was looking increasingly like an inside job. 'You know I can't tell you that.'

'I just wondered, because Albert said that the lock on Alan's patio door was very sturdy, so it seems unlikely that someone came in that way.'

'And how on earth would you know that?' he exclaimed.

She told him how she and Albert had searched Alan's room for the missing wallet.

'Oh, great,' he replied, tongue-in-cheek. 'Seeing as how your fingerprints will be all over his room, I suppose I'll have no choice but to arrest you.'

'I think you might need some more evidence first,' Meg chuckled.

'Oh, I never let a little thing like evidence get in the way of making an arrest,' Dan teased. 'Although it's likely the room is going to have so many fingerprints it will take a month of Sundays to work out if any of them are relevant to the case.' He sighed.

'Listen, I'd better get on with some work,' he said, rising from the bed. 'But I'll see you on Saturday at ten o'clock, if not before.'

'You're still okay to take me shopping?' Meg asked in surprise.

'Well, I've got this murder case now, but I think I should be able to get away for an hour.' He winked as he stooped to kiss her cheek and then quickly left.

The residents were asked to stay in their rooms for the entire morning whilst the police searched for and gathered forensic evidence. For those who were either more physically disabled or afflicted with some form of dementia, this had little impact. Some, like Meg, were patient and understanding of the reason for the inconvenience. Others, like Albert, had bristled with indignation at being deprived of their freedom, even though they would have done little more than sit around in the day room. So, when the residents were finally released from captivity in time for a late lunch, Maureen having insisted that their routine return to normal as quickly as possible, there was a buzz of excited chatter in the corridors as residents greeted each other. Downstairs, the volume in the dining room steadily increased as everyone gathered, and rumours spread like wildfire.

Meg remained stubbornly silent throughout lunch, much to Albert's annoyance. He wanted to get her thoughts about the murder. It wasn't that he was particularly ghoulish, but he hadn't known Alan and he had fond memories of the last case he'd helped Meg to solve. After his third attempt at getting a response, she hissed somewhat dramatically, 'Shh! I'm trying to listen!' He tried listening too, but there were so many conversations going on around the room that he found he couldn't focus on any one in particular.

Chapter Twelve

After lunch, when Meg had taken Albert through to the conservatory, she explained that she'd been trying to pick up clues.

'Don't know how you could pick up anything in all that babble,' he grumbled crossly.

'You'd be surprised,' she replied. 'It's a skill I developed as a teacher when trying to keep ahead of a more unruly group of students. It sometimes pays to know what they're planning.'

Albert couldn't imagine that any student of Meg's had ever dared be unruly. 'Well, what did you find out?' he challenged belligerently.

'Consider Jeannie and Betty's conversation, to begin with. They assumed that an outsider had broken into Alan's room and killed him, and now they're scared witless that Jeannie could be next, what with her bedroom being next to his on the ground floor.'

'I heard that myself. We were all at the same table, after all. What about it?'

'Well, you remarked just yesterday how sturdy that patio door was,' she explained. 'And even if someone could have broken in, why choose that particular door when there are ten to choose from? It's not like Alan's room was at the end of the row.'

'Aha, so you don't think it was a random attack?' Albert's eyes glinted.

'Exactly! And when I asked Dan earlier how the murderer got in, he refused to answer me.'

'I see. If no one broke in, the murderer must have already been *in* the building!'

'Possibly, or perhaps they had an accomplice who let them in,' Meg said thoughtfully.

'Good show! What other clues have you collected?' Albert asked.

'I picked up three interesting comments amid a lot of wild speculation. The first was from Donald, although I already knew what he had to say. I just didn't expect *him* to know it! He said he thought Alan was murdered because he had something to confess to the police.'

'Did he, by Jove?' spluttered Albert. Meg told Albert about the conversations she'd had with Alan. He was quite disappointed to find that she had no idea what Alan had wanted to confess but was intrigued by the idea that Alan had a criminal past.

'It might not have been anything he did himself,' she warned, 'but I wish he'd been able to tell me what was on his mind.'

'I knew he was a criminal,' continued Albert to himself. 'He had that kind of shifty look about him.'

'Albert!' Meg snapped crossly. 'Only two days ago, you thought he was gaga! And you were wrong about that, weren't you?' Albert had the sense to look abashed.

'Sorry, old gal, must stop leaping to conclusions, what?'

'Exactly!' Meg paused and took a deep breath to calm herself. 'Anyway, I'm more concerned that Donald was obviously listening to what Alan said. I wonder why.'

'Just being nosy, I expect. After all, he's Scottish, isn't he?'

'And what's that got to do with it?' Meg threw him a warning look.

Albert coughed apologetically. 'Carry on, m'dear. What was the second comment you heard?'

'Well, that was the senior care assistant, Sarah, talking to Maureen over by the door.'

'But you couldn't possibly have overheard what they were saying, they were too far away,' Albert exclaimed incredulously.

'Don't you believe it, I've got remarkably good hearing,' Meg chuckled.

'Hmm. Very well then, what did you hear?'

'To be fair, not every word. But I caught enough to gather

that Sarah was quizzing Maureen as to which member of staff might have stolen Alan's wallet. And whether that might in any way be connected to Alan's murder.'

'Ah, a likely motive. Good thinking.'

'It's possible, yes, but why kill Alan? Too many people already knew that his wallet had been stolen. If the thief had killed Maureen to stop her calling the police in, that might have made more sense. But, even then, another staff member would likely have reported the theft sooner or later.'

'Oh,' said Albert, somewhat deflated.

'Anyway, I caught the names of three possible suspects for the wallet thief: Kayla, Ana-Maria and Mandy.'

'Why only three suspects?' demanded Albert. 'Surely it could've been any of the staff? And why those three?'

'Good questions, Albert. I don't know. It's possible they mentioned another name or two and I didn't hear it because of the noise in the dining room. As to why those three, well, I'm pretty certain they were all on duty yesterday.'

'But they weren't the *only* ones on duty,' Albert persisted.

'No, you're right. Perhaps the senior staff have some reason to suspect those three? I think it's time to do some digging into them, see if we can work out who the thief is.'

'And that will give us our murderer!' exclaimed Albert.

'Not necessarily,' warned Meg, shaking her head.

'Harrumph!' Albert snorted, unconvinced. Why did Meg always have to make things so complicated?

'There was a third thing I overheard in the dining room,' Meg reminded him.

'Ah, yes, what was that?'

'It was the terrible twins.'

'Who?'

'Ruth and Pauline.' Albert looked blank. 'The two ladies knitting? I introduced you to them on Monday,' Meg reminded him.

'Ah, of course!' Albert looked like he didn't have a clue, but Meg continued anyway.

'They were discussing how Alan had upset quite a few

57

people around the home, back in the days before his stroke. Apparently, he could be quite an obnoxious man.'

'Really? Do you think that means one of the residents could've killed him?'

'I somehow doubt it, given that any upset Alan caused would've been some time ago. I mean, why wait this long to kill him?'

'They do say that revenge is a dish best served cold,' Albert suggested.

'That's true, and revenge can be a powerful motive. We need to dig deeper into Alan's history. And we can't rule anyone out just yet.'

'What do you propose we do?'

'We watch and we listen,' Meg instructed, not wanting Albert to go around tactlessly questioning people on his own. 'And we need some outside help, I think. Leave it with me.'

※

Later that afternoon, Meg returned to the privacy of her own room and made a phone call. She was delighted to find Lauren at home but a little concerned at the flatness of her tone. 'Is something wrong?' she asked.

'There's no hiding anything from you, is there, Meg?' Lauren told her what had happened with David, and Meg empathised, having found out after ten years of marriage that her first husband had done something very similar.

'Don't let it jade your opinion of all men,' advised Meg. 'There are some good ones out there. You just haven't found the right one yet.'

'Yeah, I know. But it sucks. I feel angry and upset, and I don't know what to do with myself at the moment.'

'I might have just the antidote to that.' Meg succinctly explained what had happened and what she wanted. Lauren, thrilled at the thought of being involved in another murder investigation, was only too eager to help.

'I'll get straight on the internet and do some research,' she assured Meg, already sounding much more like her usual cheerful self. 'But we need to get together as soon as possible to discuss the case in more detail. I've finally got a day off tomorrow. How about I come and visit you?'

'No, don't come here. I'd rather people didn't see or, more importantly, overhear us talking together. Why don't Albert and I walk down to the farm shop café, and you meet us there?'

'Albert?' exploded Lauren. 'You don't mean Albert, never Bert, from The Cedars?'

'The very same,' Meg chuckled, and filled Lauren in on recent events. 'Tomorrow morning then, I'll see you at about half past ten in the café.'

Chapter Thirteen

Thursday 12th January 2023

The next day dawned bright and frosty, but the white hoar had all but disappeared by the time breakfast was over. Meg and Albert wrapped up warmly and declared their intention of walking down to the farm shop. 'I just want to show Albert around the local area,' she explained to Maureen, who required residents to check out and back into the home. Maureen nodded her approval, noted it in the day log and thought no more of it.

There was still one police car parked outside, and a small forensics van pulled into the driveway as they walked in the opposite direction towards the footpath to the farm.

'I say, old gal,' began Albert, 'I rather thought we'd be questioning potential suspects this morning, not gallivanting off out.'

'We're not gallivanting,' Meg explained. 'We have a rendezvous.'

'What? What? That sounds intriguing.'

'I didn't want to tell you in front of anyone at the home.'

'Secret, eh?' Albert tapped his nose.

'My outside source. You remember Lauren from The Cedars, of course?'

'Lauren! Ah, the pretty little blonde-haired girl that started working there not long before poor Marianne . . .'

'Exactly.'

'Didn't know you stayed in touch.'

'I've tried to stay in touch with as many people as I can.'

Albert quizzed Meg on who was where and doing what, and she happily obliged insofar as she could. She knew where each of the former residents of The Cedars had gone, scattered across care homes in the region. She had been to visit Janet twice at her nursing home in Ringwood, but the hundred-and-one-year-old had sadly passed away from pneumonia shortly before Christmas.

'Sorry to hear that, m'dear,' Albert said sympathetically. 'I know you were good friends.'

'She'd had a good life,' Meg said sorrowfully.

'And have you seen any of the others?'

'Sadly, no. I had a Christmas card from Annie, but that was all.'

'And have you kept in touch with any of the staff?'

'Just Lauren. She's working for an agency now until she can find another permanent position.'

'I thought care homes were crying out for staff, from what you said the other day?'

'Some of them are, but apparently Lauren is fussy.'

Albert wasn't sure what to make of that.

They approached Britford Farm and drank in their surroundings. Beyond a visitors' car park lay the livery stables, and Meg could just see two horses being saddled in the courtyard and, just ahead to the left, some kind of farm machinery was being reversed out of a well-maintained barn. As they walked on, Meg checked her watch and, realising they were early, she steered Albert to the right of the café's welcoming door so that she could show him a couple of smartly painted holiday cottages that appeared to be occupied despite it being mid-winter. Behind them stood a big rambling farmhouse with its blue-painted door and wisteria-clad walls.

'Impressive,' he conceded, blowing on his gloved hands to warm them.

They returned to the café, which doubled as a shop, and felt a blanket of warm air wrap around them as they entered the cheery room. Albert admired the counters with their impressive displays of goodies and vowed to buy some rather tasty-looking ginger biscuits before they left.

Just then, Lauren entered through the latch door and strode confidently in.

'Well, I didn't expect to be seeing you again, m'dear,' announced Albert as she approached.

'Nor me you,' replied Lauren with a cheeky grin. 'Yet here we are.'

Meg suggested a table for three quite close to the door and they sat down. They exchanged pleasantries and ordered their drinks before getting down to business.

'Are you going to give us a résumé of what you know about the murder then, Meg, before I tell you what I've found?' asked Lauren, eager to get started.

'Ah, yes, of course.' Meg lowered her voice and the other two leant in. 'Alan Watts was settled down for the night at about eleven on Tuesday evening. At some point during the night, he was smothered with a pillow.'

'How do you know that?' interrupted Albert.

'I will explain,' Meg reassured him before continuing. 'He was found by two of the night staff, Petra and Taska, at four-thirty Wednesday morning. I was rather lucky to have been able to question Taska in some detail before the police did, else they might have warned her not to discuss what she had seen.'

'Jolly good show!'

'He was lying on his back, which is his normal sleeping position, but one arm was hanging over the edge of the bed, which is why Petra went to investigate. He was cold to the touch and Petra confirmed he was dead. I pushed Taska to tell me everything she could remember. She noticed that he had traces of blood around his nose, as though he'd had a slight nosebleed, and that his pillows had been disturbed. I asked her what she meant, and she told me that he usually sleeps with two pillows under his head, but one of these had been removed and discarded on the armchair. The bedclothes were disturbed; she thought maybe he'd tried to get out of bed, but I think it's more likely there was some kind of a struggle. And one more thing: she noticed that he had a badly torn fingernail on his left hand.'

'I'm guessing the bloody nose, the torn fingernail and the discarded pillow all suggest he was smothered?' Lauren interjected.

'Yes. And I confirmed that was the likely cause of death with Dan.'

'Oh, good, DI Dan's investigating! And what about his sexy sergeant?' asked Lauren.

'Yes, DS Williams is investigating with Dan,' smiled Meg, thinking that Lauren was evidently getting over David already.

'That means we have cause of death and a window for the time of death,' added Albert, wanting to put in his two pennies' worth.

'Exactly. Now: means, motive and opportunity.' Meg paused. 'Well, the means are easy. Anyone could have used the pillow to smother Alan, so that doesn't help identify or eliminate any suspects. And with Alan's debilitated condition, I don't think we can discount a woman or even a resident as having sufficient strength to do the deed.'

'In other words, anyone could have done it,' grumbled Albert.

'Precisely. Opportunity is a little trickier. Obviously, any of the residents and staff who were present in the home during that time frame could be suspects. The interesting question is whether an outsider could have gained entry to Alan's room or not.' Meg described the layout of the room for Lauren's benefit. Whilst it didn't sound likely that anyone could have broken in through Alan's patio door, they decided it needed further investigation in case there was a way for an accomplice to have left the door unlocked from the inside. 'Who was the last person to see Alan alive?' asked Lauren.

'That was Taska,' put in Albert. 'Makes her the prime suspect, what?'

'Not necessarily,' replied Meg, 'but it's worth bearing in mind that she *could* have been an accomplice.'

Albert suggested they might also look for footprints outside the door. Meg agreed that they may as well look, although she was sure the CSIs would have examined the area already.

'And we also need to find out if there was any other way of getting into the building,' added Lauren. Meg nodded approvingly.

'Now, motive is the trickiest of them all,' Meg announced.

'Oh?' said Albert with a frown. 'I thought we'd already determined the possible motives yesterday, old gal.'

'Those that we know about,' Meg cautioned. Then she explained to Lauren that Alan might have: A, been murdered by the person who stole his wallet, to prevent its loss being reported to the police; B, been murdered to prevent him from confessing something to the police or C, been murdered as revenge for something he'd done in his life, having apparently not been the nicest of people. 'Unless, of course, there's another motive we don't know about yet,' she added.

'Next, we need to start looking at possible suspects. We have three, so far, for the possible thief . . .'

'And that's where I come in,' jumped in Lauren. She pulled out a compact laptop computer and set it up on the table before reading from the notes she'd made. 'Right, those three names you gave me. Mandy was the easiest one to research. She was born Amanda Pincent on 5th November 1987, so she's thirty-five now. Lived all her life in Salisbury from the looks of it, went to St Edmunds' School, same as me though not at the same time, obviously. Married in 2012 and became Mandy Cartwright. Has three children: Oliver, Amelia and Jack. Lives just off Bishopdown Road. The most interesting thing on her Facebook page is that she changed her relationship status back to single only last month.'

'That suggests her husband has disappeared off the scene,' remarked Meg thoughtfully. 'Now I come to think of it, she has looked unusually tired and stressed recently. That might explain it.'

'Probably, although there's no record of divorce that I could find,' Lauren added. 'Next up was Kayla. Unusually, she doesn't have any social media presence! But from the Britford Lodge website staff page, I can tell you that she's Kayla Higginbotham and she's twenty-two and single. I managed to look her up on the electoral register and she's listed as living on Bemerton Heath at the same address as a

Matthew Dooley.' Lauren rolled her eyes at the mention of the heath. Unfortunately, it had a reputation as one of the rougher areas to live in Salisbury, although that wasn't necessarily fair to all the residents there. 'I also found court records for Matthew Dooley, aka Mack, on the *Salisbury Journal* website – he's been done for petty theft, drug possession and carrying a weapon with intent, namely a kitchen knife.'

'Doesn't sound like a very savoury character to me,' said Albert, shaking his head disapprovingly. 'Makes sense that Kayla is a wrong'un too.'

'Let's not jump to conclusions,' Meg warned.

'Well,' continued Lauren, 'I know even less about the third person you asked me to research. Ana-Maria Matei is a thirty-four-year-old Romanian who immigrated four years ago to work at Britford Lodge. That's it.'

'It's a very good start.' Meg praised her warmly to make up for Albert's lack of appreciation. 'Now, did you find anything about our victim?'

'There's evidence of an Alan Watts living and working in Salisbury since the early '90s, but nothing before that. I couldn't find a birth certificate or anything; we simply don't have enough information about him yet.'

'Not to worry. After I've paid a visit to the bathroom, we can plan where we go from here.' She stood up stiffly and stretched before heading towards the toilet.

'I'll grab another coffee,' said Lauren, springing up. 'Do you want another one, Albert?'

'Don't mind if I do, thank you. And you'd better get a fresh pot of tea for Meg while you're at it, please. Here, take this towards it.' He handed over a ten-pound note, which Lauren gratefully accepted.

Chapter Fourteen

In the end, Meg and Albert barely made it back to Britford Lodge before lunch. Maureen raised an eyebrow at them as they hurried into the office to report their safe return, wondering where on earth they could have been all this time on such a chilly morning. Whilst Albert enthused about their visit to the farm shop and café, Meg discreetly studied the staff rota on the board behind Maureen. She noted that, of their possible prime suspects, only Ana was on the early shift that day. Kayla would be in for the late shift, but Mandy was on a day off. Most annoyingly, Taska appeared to have finished her run of nights and wasn't due in again until Monday.

Then Maureen shooed them out of the office to go and get their lunch.

Jeannie and Betty were quite put out during lunch to discover that Meg and Albert had been to the café without them. Meg asked them to forgive her for wanting a little time to catch up with her old friend, at which Jeannie beamed and winked at Albert, who coughed and sputtered into his soup. Meg quickly changed the topic of conversation.

As soon as lunch was over, Meg dispatched Albert to join Frank and Donald, warning him not to give anything away if they should happen to discuss Alan's murder.

'Of course not, old gal. What do you take me for?'

Meg declined to reply, setting off instead to find Ana. She waited until the slender Romanian had finished settling a couple of other residents into the day room before approaching.

'Ana, are you very busy at the moment?' Meg asked her.

'No, I have time for you, Meg. What can I do?'

'Would you be able to come up to my bedroom and cut my fingernails for me, please? I seem to have broken one this morning and it keeps catching on my cardigan. I'd do it myself if it wasn't for this blasted arthritis making it so difficult to hold the scissors.' She held up the offending nail, which Lauren had carefully ripped.

'Of course. I just get some tablets for Clara, then I come.'

Meg took the lift upstairs, found her nail scissors and a file, and waited. Ana appeared about twenty minutes later, flustered and apologetic, having had to run several other errands before she could get away. She settled down to manicure Meg's nails.

'Now, tell me, Ana, you're from Romania, aren't you?' Meg began.

Ana happily talked about her childhood, how she'd grown up in a small village in a forested area of Romania. How she'd played with her brothers and sisters and the neighbouring children. How poor they had all been, compared to the English children she saw around Salisbury. 'But I think we were happier, you know?'

She told Meg all about her mama, who took in sewing for a living, and her papa, who worked in the local sawmill and whom she adored. Tears shone in her eyes as she spoke about her parents and siblings. It was clear to Meg just how close a family Ana had come from.

'You must miss your family very much?' Meg asked gently.

'Yes, I do,' Ana replied a little sadly.

'So why did you come to England to work?'

'I had job in factory that make food,' she explained. 'I was going to be married with man I work with, Andre. But he had another woman. I very sad when I find out. I not marry him. I not want to work in factory with him.'

'That's very understandable,' Meg sympathised, 'but surely there were other jobs in your village?'

'Not so much,' Ana explained, 'and in Romania the pay is very low. If I want more pay, is necessary I come to England. Here is good pay.'

Meg smiled wryly; not many British people would consider a carer's salary good.

'Do you like living in England?' she asked.

'Ye-es,' replied Ana doubtfully. 'Is nice town, Salisbury. But my flat is lonely. I miss my family.' She bit her lip, on the verge of tears. 'And it was hard being here when Papa was so ill.'

'Do you have friends here?' Meg asked, tactfully changing the subject.

'Some of the other carers are friendly, yes.'

'Can I ask you about Mandy? Is she one of your friends?'

'Yes, we often on same bus. Why you ask?'

'I'm worried about her. She's been looking very tired and stressed recently.'

'Yes, and she lose weight. I think she not eat enough.'

'Oh, why do you think that?'

'She is pale. And she not have . . . strength?'

'She's feeling weak, you mean?'

'Yes. That is word. Weak.'

'Ana, do you think Mandy needs some help?'

'Yes, I want to help, but she not say what is problem.'

'Of course, I quite understand. What about some of the other carers who live in Salisbury? Kayla, perhaps?'

'Hah!' scorned Ana. 'She is not good friend. She not sit with us. She not talk with us. But I think she have problem too.'

'Oh, why's that?'

'She is sometimes . . . hurting?'

'Do you mean upset?' queried Meg. 'Or is she injured?'

'Yes, injured. That is word,' Ana said with a nod. 'Yesterday, she have bruise on face here,' she indicated, 'and she not walk good.'

'She was limping?'

'Yes, limping. Is not first time I see her have bruise.'

'Does she play a lot of sports?' mused Meg thoughtfully.

'I not think so,' replied Ana dubiously, finishing the manicure and standing to tidy up.

'What about some of the other Romanians who work here? Surely you all get together from time to time?'

'Stefania and Florin?' Ana shrugged her shoulders. 'They are together always.'

They're good friends, you mean?'

'More . . . they are couple. They live in same flat.'

'I see.' Meg watched as Ana finished tidying up and washed her hands. 'And Taska?'

'Taska is not from Romania. She is from Latvia. And she is lot younger me.' Ana moved to the door. 'Shall I shut door or you come downstairs?' she asked kindly.

'Oh, just leave the door. I'll follow you down in a minute.'

Meg tidied herself and then followed the carer downstairs.

✿

Lauren had returned home on the bus after their morning meeting and was now curled up on her bed with her computer. At Meg's suggestion, she studied the staff page of the Britford Lodge website. Then she set up an Excel spreadsheet of the names, adding what little information the page gave. The senior manager of the care home, Kevin Percival, was based in an office somewhere, so he was unlikely to be a suspect. Maureen Wilkinson was the care manager on days, and Fiona Holland the care manager on nights. Then there were four senior care assistants who worked rotation days and nights and took charge whenever one of the care managers wasn't on duty: Petra Orlova, Sarah Fielding, Brandon Smith and Hazel Wright. She remembered that Petra had been in charge on the night Alan was murdered. Then there were sixteen care assistants, including Ana-Maria, Mandy, Kayla and Taska. Plus three cleaners and four kitchen staff. That was quite a long list of names to research!

She took a deep breath and got busy online, finding out whatever she could about each person. Gradually, she filled in a few details such as nationality, age, address and phone number. Not that she was able to track down details for all the staff.

When her mum called her down for her dinner, she

groaned in frustration. She'd been at it all afternoon and still had only patchy information. And she wasn't sure what use, if any, that would be.

It was evening before Meg managed to get Kayla alone. She was sitting on her own reading her book, Jeannie having already gone to bed, when Kayla arrived with the late-evening drinks round.

'Hot chocolate, Horlicks or decaf tea?' she asked, with little enthusiasm.

'I'll have hot chocolate, please.' Meg studied the young carer's face as she delivered the drink to a low side table. Sure enough, despite a layer of concealer, a bruise was just faintly discernible. 'Oh, I dropped my bookmark earlier and it slid under that chair,' Meg indicated. 'I don't suppose you could retrieve it for me?'

She watched intently as Kayla limped to the chair and, as she bent over to recover the bookmark carefully deposited by Meg, a bit of bandage was visible around one knee.

'Here you go.' Kayla passed her the bookmark.

'Do you play a lot of sports?' Meg asked casually, before her quarry could turn away.

'Sports?' Kayla scoffed. 'Yeah, right, when do I get time to play sports, eh? Why do you wanna know?'

'I couldn't help noticing the bandage around your knee.'

'Oh, that. I fell down the stairs at home, if you must know.'

'Oh, my dear, that's dreadful. I hope you weren't home alone at the time. It's my worst fear, you know, falling down-stairs and having no one there to help. But perhaps you live with your parents?'

'I live with my boyfriend. Fat lot of help he was!'

'Oh? Why's that?'

'It was . . .' She broke off. 'It's none of your business,' she finished dourly.

'Did he hurt you?' Meg asked gently, laying a hand on

the young girl's arm. Kayla ripped it away as though stung and stepped backwards with a confused look on her face.

'I never said that,' she snapped. 'I fell, that's all.'

Meg watched as the carer limped away with the trolley.

Chapter Fifteen

Friday 13th January 2023

On Friday, the freezing fog lingered all day, shrouding the care home and hiding it from the outside world. Over breakfast, Meg managed to share her findings of the previous day with Albert before Jeannie and Betty joined them, at which point the conversation turned to the weather and other desultory topics.

When she emerged from the dining room, having left Albert regaling her friends with naval stories, Meg could hear voices in the office and casually strolled that way to find out that it was Maureen speaking.

'... and it's still as important to find out who stole his wallet, so far as I am concerned, even if he is dead. I want to find a thief; you want to find a murderer. Has it not occurred to you that they might be one and the same person?'

'Of course,' Dan's voice soothed. 'It is one of *several* lines of inquiry that we are actively pursuing.'

'And have you got any suspects yet?' Maureen demanded.

'Not as such,' Dan admitted regretfully. 'As I explained, our crime scene technicians were still processing the crime scene all day yesterday.'

'Speaking of which, when can we have the room back?' Maureen asked. 'I don't want to seem callous, but every night a room is empty it costs us money. My senior manager is pressuring me to fill it again as soon as possible.'

'I understand that, and we'll release it as soon as we can. My officers have been busy gathering intelligence on the victim as well as cross-checking all the statements taken so far. And the post-mortem today will hopefully give us more information, as will the results of the forensic tests. But these things take time.'

'Well, I could've told you about the *victim*, if you had asked me. Alan was a car mechanic in Salisbury, working at the big Renault garage on Churchfields. He lived alone in a flat on Wilton Road until his first mini-stroke rendered him less capable of looking after himself. Having no close family, and consequently no one to look after him, he chose to move into this care home. He was ambulatory for about three years before his major stroke, two years ago. I can tell you that he only ever had one visitor, who came as regularly as clockwork every Tuesday.'

'Ah yes, his friend Ed. We need to interview him. I don't suppose you have his details, do you?'

A drawer opened and closed, and there was a rustle of paper followed by the sound of the photocopier.

'This is the Missing Property report I filed after Ed reported Alan's wallet stolen. As you can see, it has his details on it.'

'Thank you,' Dan replied. 'Ed Smith ... I do hope that's his real name!'

'Why wouldn't it be? He seemed like a perfectly respectable man. And plenty of people *are* called Smith, you know.'

'Hmm, we'll see. Tell me, what kind of a man was Alan, before his stroke?'

'Very reserved, kept himself to himself. He wasn't educated to a very high level, I'd say. He wasn't one for reading books or the papers. Preferred the TV. I noticed a couple of times that he needed help with written documents, but his friend Ed took care of all that for him.'

'What about friends here?'

'He never seemed especially close to anyone in particular, I'm afraid.'

'But he was well liked?'

'Not really. I don't like to speak ill of the dead, but he could be a bit of an argumentative character. He did upset one or two people in the past. Just petty things, you understand. Nothing to get himself murdered over.'

'Is there anyone in particular that he upset?'

'Not that I can remember.' Maureen sounded unwilling to say anything further.

'Very well. Now, about that space for myself and my two detective constables...'

'You can use the conservatory for your interviews today. I believe you know where it is?'

'Yes, I do. There is one more thing. A crime scene technician will be here to take fingerprints and DNA swabs—'

'Is that even legal?' snapped Maureen.

'We'll be asking people to provide them voluntarily, purely for elimination purposes. We can't force anyone to comply at this juncture.'

'So long as my residents are not harassed into giving samples against their will,' Maureen conceded. 'When your technician arrives, I'll ask one of my staff to accompany them at all times. To ensure the safety of my residents, you understand.'

'Of course.'

Hearing people moving towards the door, Meg beat a hasty retreat before turning round, just as Dan and his two DCs came out of the office, so that she appeared to be coming from the dining room.

'Dan,' she smiled, 'I was surprised not to see you here yesterday.'

'I can assure you, we were actively investigating the case all day,' he replied with a grin.

'I never doubted it. So, what's on today's agenda?'

'We need to interview the residents and any staff we haven't managed to take statements from yet. We're just heading to the conservatory now.'

'Do you want to start with me?'

'Sorry, Meg. I've already written up your statement from what you told me on Wednesday. We've got a lot of other people to get through today.'

'No Viv to help you?'

'He's attending the post-mortem and chasing up forensic results.' Meg grimaced at the thought.

'Right, we need to get on.' Dan nodded a curt goodbye and led DCs Gordon and Johnson away.

Meg and Albert spent the rest of the day engaging in several fruitless conversations, without being any better informed by the evening. They might have felt slightly less frustrated had they realised that Dan felt exactly the same way! Dan's only hope was that the fingerprints and DNA samples might throw up something interesting.

⚙

Lauren worked a busy early shift in a nursing home in the Milford area of Salisbury, wishing she could've been at Britford Lodge instead. As soon as she got home, she carried on with the task of filling in gaps in her spreadsheet, stopping only for dinner.

'Whatever have you been doing all this time up in your room?' her mum asked as they ate their sausage and mash.

'Oh, just a little project I've got on at the moment,' Lauren replied airily. She didn't want to worry her mother by telling her she was investigating another murder.

'I was listening to the radio while I was cooking dinner,' her mother said. 'The news was on and they said that police are investigating the suspicious death of a resident at Britford Lodge Care Home. That's where your friend Meg lives, isn't it?'

'Umm, yes, that's right.'

'I'm guessing you already knew about it? It might even have something to do with your "little project"?'

Lauren muttered something unintelligible, hoping her mother wouldn't push it.

'Please, darling, don't go getting involved again. Last time, it was your friend Meg in danger. What if this time it was you? I don't know what I'd do without you.'

'Oh, Mum,' Lauren rolled her eyes, 'I'm just helping Meg with a little research. How on earth would that put me in any kind of danger? It's not as if I work there, like I did at The Cedars.'

'Well, make sure you take care, love.'

'I will.'

Lauren continued her research through the evening whilst listening to Spotify. By the time she eventually closed her notepad and settled into bed for the night, both her mother and Meg had long been asleep.

Chapter Sixteen

Saturday 14th January 2023

Meg woke up early and spent some time getting herself dressed and ready to go out shopping later with Dan. She couldn't wait to talk to him about the case. But there was one more person she really wanted to talk to before seeing him. Her wish was answered almost immediately when Mandy popped her head around the door.

'Are you on your way down to breakfast, Meg? If so, I'll pop in and change your bed. If you're not, don't worry, I can come back later.'

'No, come on in, my dear. I'm nearly ready.'

Meg fiddled with her hair, watching in the mirror as Mandy wearily stripped the bed, sighing as she laid the bedspread across the chair.

'Are you okay, Mandy dear?' Meg asked solicitously, turning round.

'Just a bit tired.'

'It must be very difficult, being a mother and having to work full time. Remind me, how old are your children?' Mandy told her. 'And does the youngest sleep through the night?' Meg asked.

'Not very often, I'm afraid.'

'But I expect your husband takes turns getting up?'

Mandy didn't reply.

'Are you sure everything's all right?' Meg said gently. Mandy seemed about to answer but then had second thoughts. She focussed on making the bed with a grim determination.

'Forgive me, but I couldn't help wondering if perhaps you were having some problems in your marriage? I know it's none of my business, but I am a good listener, you know, if you want to talk to someone.'

Mandy's lip wobbled and she sank down onto the edge of the freshly made bed.

'I'm just so tired,' she whispered. Meg held out a hand and the younger woman took it, tears now trickling down her cheeks.

'He left me,' she said. 'A couple of months ago. Not that things were exactly great before that ...'

'Your husband?' Meg clarified.

Mandy nodded. 'Darryl. He lost his job back in May. After that, there was never enough money and all we did was bicker. Then one day he just upped and left.'

'But he pays you maintenance or child support or whatever it's called these days?'

Mandy shook her head.

'How are you managing?'

'Truth is, I'm not.' Mandy gulped. 'Oh, Mum's been brilliant helping me with the kids and with bits of food here and there. But she can't afford to pay the mortgage or the gas or the electric or anything.'

'So, you're behind with the bills, and not eating properly, either, by the look of it.' Meg kept her voice very calm and non-judgemental.

'Oh God, not you as well! Ana keeps nagging me about eating properly, not skipping meals. She says I need "strength". But she doesn't say what I'm supposed to use to buy food with, does she? It's all right, her being single. She's no idea what it's like to have children and to wish you could give them all the nice things you had as a child.' She took her hand back from Meg's and covered her face as the tears fell freely now. 'I'm such a failure,' she sobbed.

Meg comforted Mandy as best she could and suggested that perhaps the carer should plead a headache and go home for some rest.

'Oh, good grief, no! I can't do that! This job is all I have. God only knows what we'd do without my wages, even if they aren't enough.' She sat up and wiped her face with her hands. Then she went into Meg's bathroom and splashed water on her face, using paper towels to blow her nose and pat her face dry afterwards. She was a little more composed when she returned to the bedroom.

'I'm sorry, Meg, I shouldn't have told you all of this. Please, promise me you won't say a word to anyone else?'

'On one condition,' Meg said gravely. 'Please tell me it wasn't you who stole Alan's wallet.'

Mandy looked shocked. 'What the . . .! You can't think I would do such a despicable thing as steal from a resident? I would never—'

'It's okay, my dear, I believe you,' Meg hurriedly reassured her, convinced by the girl's reaction that she was telling the truth.

✦

Meg went downstairs and had her breakfast then returned to her room to brush her teeth and collect her warm outdoor clothes. She was just about ready to go out when her phone rang.

'Meg Thornton here,' she answered.

'I'm so sorry, Meg,' Dan began.

'That's okay,' she reassured him. 'I half expected you to phone.'

'I hate letting you down. And I'm sorry for the short notice; our morning briefing has only just finished. But, as there's no leave for anyone on my team this weekend, it's not fair of me to sneak off, even for an hour.'

'I quite understand.'

'LIsten, I promise we'll get you that mobile phone, just as soon as I can. Although I really hope you never need to use it in any kind of emergency.'

'I have no intention of needing to, honestly. It's just that I shall feel happier carrying it with me just in case.'

'Well, it's a good idea to have one,' Dan agreed.

'Can you tell me, did the post-mortem throw up anything interesting yesterday?'

'You know I shouldn't be sharing that kind of information. Nor should you be doing any investigating,' Dan warned sternly, 'but I'm not giving anything away if I say

79

that the cause of death is exactly what we suspected it to be.'

'He was smothered with a pillow?'

'Yes.'

'What about results from any of the samples the CSIs took?'

'It'll be sometime next week, at the earliest, before we get anything back. Thanks to financial cutbacks, we're not allowed to fast-track anything unless the superintendent signs off on it and, in this case, she won't.'

'I suppose the murder of an elderly man isn't important,' Meg muttered darkly.

'It's not that. The super has got it into her head that whoever stole Alan's wallet is our prime suspect. I've had her on my back, demanding to know why I haven't ident-ified the thief yet.'

'But you're not sure the two are linked?'

'If only it could be that easy.' Dan sighed. 'Anyway, I've been focussing all my enquiries on the night that Alan was murdered. Now I need to spend some of my precious time investigating how and when his wallet was stolen. And just hope that it throws up something useful.'

'Actually, I think I might be able to help you there.'

'Please tell me you've not been investigating again, Meg?' Dan sounded exasperated. 'Look at the trouble it got you into last time. Eh?'

'Dan, trust me, I've been really careful. But I do think you're going to want to hear what I've uncovered.'

'Go on, then.'

Meg filled him in on her conversations with Ana, Kayla and Mandy. Dan listened incredulously.

'Let me get this right,' he exploded when she'd finished. 'You've already identified three suspects, despite me telling you not to investigate. There's Kayla Higginbotham. I can confirm that her boyfriend, Matthew Dooley, aka Mack, is *very* well known to the police for drug possession and a whole string of petty thefts and burglaries. He also likes to threaten people with a knife, so I can quite easily see him threatening her to cough up money for his habit. There's

Mandy Cartwright, a single mother struggling to pay her bills and put food on the table. So it's no great leap of the imagination to think that a wallet full of cash would've been very tempting to her, despite her denial to you. And then you've got Ana-Maria Matei, who is a lonely Romanian with no apparent motive, so far as I can see. Unless you've suddenly become a xenophobe, which I very much doubt. Why these three?'

Meg explained how she'd overheard two of the senior staff discussing it. 'And although I can't identify Ana's motive yet, I definitely think that she's holding something back. But, I must admit, there could also be other suspects that I haven't identified yet.'

'Exactly. And you have no idea how dangerous the thief could be if they think you're investigating. Please, stop asking questions.'

'Just promise me you'll look into these three,' Meg asked.

'Of course I will. I've already asked Johnson to get background on all the staff on duty on Tuesday. And I've asked Viv to conduct some follow-up interviews this afternoon, so I'll tell him what you've told me and ask him to prioritise those three.'

'Thank you.'

Dan said goodbye and Meg put the phone down thoughtfully. It was true she had a gut feeling about Ana, but she had been rather remiss in not finding out if any of the other staff on duty that day also had a motive. She obviously had more work to do.

Chapter Seventeen

Going back downstairs, Meg went to the office and tapped firmly on the open door, hoping it would be empty. It was. She looked around and then slipped in, gently pushing the door nearly closed behind her. She went straight to the notice board and looked at the staff rota, jotting down names in a small notebook she'd brought with her. Petra, Taska, Kai and Jess had been on duty on Monday night, so it was just possible one of them could have stolen the wallet before going off shift. Maureen, Stef, Florin, Sue and Emma had all been on the early shift with Mandy. They had to be the prime suspects. And Sarah, Irene and Lyn had been on the late shift with Ana and Kayla. Fifteen suspects in all, and she'd only questioned three of them so far! She groaned. Not only did she have fifteen suspects for stealing Alan's wallet, but one of these, possibly even the same person, could have been an accomplice to the murder. If indeed there had been an accomplice.

That was her next mission, she decided, to find out whether or not an inside person could somehow have assisted the murderer in gaining access to Alan's room.

Meg made a beeline for Albert, who was once again deep in naval reminiscences with Frank in the day room.

'What ho, m'dear,' he barked when she approached.

'Excuse me interrupting, gentlemen.' She nodded at Frank and Donald. 'Albert, I wonder if you're free now, to go for that walk with me?' she asked, staring pointedly.

'What? What?' Albert looked puzzled but then the penny dropped. 'Of course, old gal. I'm ready if you are.' He followed her into the hall and immediately demanded to know what was happening. 'I thought you were off shopping with the DI this morning?'

'I was. But, rather as I feared, this investigation has put paid to that. I thought we could go for a walk instead.'

'In this freezing weather?' he asked incredulously. He pointed towards the window. 'The frost hasn't even gone off the grass yet!'

'Do stop arguing, Albert. It's just a short walk. Come on, let's go and get our shoes and coats.'

In the lift, Meg explained their mission and Albert begrudgingly fetched his coat, hat, scarf and gloves. He didn't like the cold.

Once outside, Meg and Albert walked around the perimeter of the building. A tarmac path made the going easy but also meant there was no hope of footprints. As they reached Alan's room, they scanned the surrounding ground for clues. But if there had been any, the CSIs must surely have been there before them, Meg thought. Then they tried every which way they could think of to open the patio door from the outside, but it was impenetrable.

'That settles it, then. It must have been an inside job, just as I thought all along,' Albert decreed. 'I bet it was one of those foreign night carers.'

'Albert!' Meg glared at him warningly.

'Oh, I know, I know. Don't go leaping to conclusions, what? But really, m'dear, I don't mean to be racist or anything. I'm just saying that the night carers *were* the ones with the best opportunity, and they *were* foreign.'

Meg refused to dignify that with a reply. Jess was certainly not foreign and neither was Kai, despite his Chinese ancestry.

As they were getting colder and colder standing around outside, she suggested they give up and go indoors. They stripped off their outdoor clothes just in time for morning coffee. Or tea, in Meg's case.

'Right, now for part two of our mission,' Meg announced, after they'd both warmed up. 'Come with me.'

They made their way through the hall, past the office and past Alan's room, which was still sealed off with tape but without a guard outside now. They made it into Jeannie's room without being seen.

83

'Why aren't we in Alan's room?' grumbled Albert.

'Because we daren't disturb the crime scene tape across the door,' Meg replied acerbically. 'However, all the downstairs rooms have identical patio doors, so Jeannie's door will do just as well as Alan's. We need to find out if it could be left unlocked somehow.'

'You're still persisting with this idea of an accomplice, aren't you, old gal?'

'At the very least,' Meg replied tartly, 'we need to investigate whether or not it's possible.'

The problem, they soon discovered, was that the door had a self-closing mechanism. As soon as it was opened, it inexorably swung closed and the latch clicked firmly into place. There seemed to be no way of locking the latch in an open position. Moreover, there was no keyhole on the outside, so if the key had been turned on the inside, the door would've been securely double locked. Even if an accomplice had left the key unturned, the latch would've held the door firm. The only way of keeping the door open was to take it all the way back against the outside wall and fasten the hook there into a small eyelet attached to the bottom of the outside of the door. And Meg was fairly certain that the night staff would've noticed the draught from a wide-open door in this weather!

'It's no good, old gal,' Albert proclaimed. 'I don't think anyone could've got in this way.'

Meg looked around Jeannie's room, deep in thought. There had to be a way. She spotted a folded envelope in Jeannie's bin and it gave her an idea. 'How about we wedge this between the latch and the doorframe?' she suggested. She sent Albert outside the door and tried repeatedly to get the envelope wedged, but it was too flimsy. Even if the latch didn't click immediately, every time Albert tried to prise open the door from outside, the slightest movement and it annoyingly clicked into place. 'We need something thicker,' she declared. She hunted around Jeannie's room and found a cardboard box from Amazon under her bed. She tore off a strip, hoping Jeannie wouldn't mind, and folded it. And, at last, the latch stayed wedged open!

'But, there's still the problem of how you pull the door from outside,' Albert pointed out. 'There's no handle!'

'What about that eyelet?' she suggested. 'Can you pull on that?'

'No good, old gal. I tried that and there's just not enough to get a hold of. And the door's quite heavy, y'know.'

Meg's brow wrinkled. Then she spotted Albert's laced-up shoes. 'Albert, can I borrow one of your shoelaces, please?'

With a bit of effort, he pulled the thick black lace from his right shoe. 'This better be worth it,' he grumbled, panting from the effort of bending down.

Meg took the lace and went outside the door, instructing Albert to wedge the latch. She then bent down and fed the lace through the eyelet, before tying it into a loop. She hooked her hand through the loop and pulled with all her might ... and the door opened just enough for her to grab the edge before it closed again.

'By Jove, you've done it!' Albert exclaimed.

'So, we know how the murderer *could* have got in from the patio,' Meg mused, as Albert struggled to replace his shoelace. 'Now we just need to find out who the murderer was. And who the accomplice was.'

'Isn't it also possible that the murderer could have got in some other way?' Albert asked. Meg tilted her head to one side and thought about that.

'You have a point,' she admitted. 'We'd better check all the other entrances to the building too, to be thorough.'

Once in the corridor outside Jeannie's room, Meg could see that the nearest entry point to Alan's room was the main front door. 'But that's too obvious,' she said under her breath. 'If the murderer was let in through the front door, or somehow broke in, there would have been a high risk of them being seen by anyone in the office as they passed.' Then she spotted the CCTV camera on the wall opposite the front door. 'And they'd have to be an idiot to risk getting caught on camera!'

'Talking to yourself?' chuckled Albert.

'Of course. I always talk to myself if I want a sensible conversation!'

'Thanks for that, old gal,' Albert replied indignantly.

'Sorry, I didn't mean you.' She squeezed his arm. 'Come on, let's have a look at the fire escape doors at the end of this corridor.' They wandered down the gently curving corridor. But when they got there, they discovered a notice warning that opening the fire escape doors would trigger the fire alarm.

'Don't think anyone could have got in that way,' sighed Albert.

'No, you're right. And I'm willing to bet that all the fire escape doors are the same. In any case—'

She never got to finish her sentence because Hazel, the senior care assistant in charge that morning, came out of the staffroom nearby. 'Whatever are you two doing all the way down here?' she asked suspiciously.

'Just taking a little stroll, what?' said Albert. 'Stretching our limbs and all.'

'But didn't I see you going out for a walk earlier?' she asked.

'You did,' he replied. 'We tried going outside before coffee and discovered just how cold it was, so we didn't go very far. But my legs were still somewhat fidgety, don't y'know, so Meg suggested an inside walk.'

'Fair enough.' Hazel accepted his explanation. 'That wind is so cold this morning, it goes straight through you. Now, come along, it's nearly lunchtime.'

She walked with them back to the hallway, leaving them to go into the dining room as she went into the office.

'Narrow escape there, old gal,' Albert remarked quietly into Meg's ear.

'Thank you for bluffing our way out of it. An inside walk, eh?' she chuckled, and Albert joined in. Jeannie and Betty wanted to know what was so funny when they joined them at their regular table.

Chapter Eighteen

Meg and Albert took the afternoon off sleuthing to recover from their exertions; Albert watched TV with his eyes closed whilst Meg indulged in a bit of jigsaw puzzling with her friend Jeannie. She didn't tell her that they'd been in her room, not wanting to involve her frail companion.

After a little while, Meg looked up to see Viv walking into the day room with DC Moira Gordon. After a brief 'hello', they moved into the conservatory to start their interviews. Meg watched as Mandy went in nervously and came out nearly twenty minutes later with red-rimmed eyes. Meg felt sorry for her, but she understood that the police couldn't just take her word that Mandy was not the thief. At least, she really hoped that the young mother hadn't lied to her.

Then they questioned Kayla, who went in wearing a truculent expression and came out with a face like thunder. That clearly hadn't gone well. Meg was slightly alarmed when Kayla marched directly up to their table. 'Can I have a word?' she demanded, glaring at Meg.

'I think it's time I went and had my afternoon nap,' Jeannie said diplomatically.

They watched until Jeannie was out of earshot, then Meg motioned to Kayla. 'Why don't you sit down?' she said calmly.

Kayla sat opposite Meg in Jeannie's seat, looked warily around the day room to make sure no one could overhear them, and then thrust her head towards Meg.

'What d'ya have to go and tell the police for, eh?' she hissed angrily.

'What exactly do you think I told the police?'

'They knew about my knee and they kept asking if my boyfriend was responsible. It's odd, isn't it? Just yesterday

87

you were asking the same kinda questions. I'll thank you not to go blabbing my business to the pigs.'

'Kayla, my dear, don't you think you might be overreacting? After all, you are limping, so it's quite easy to see that you've had an injury.'

Kayla was silent for a moment. 'Whatever!' She shrugged and made as though to stand up. 'It isn't fair,' she grumbled. 'Just 'cos he's been in trouble with the law, they think I'm the same.'

'I'm sure that's not true.' Meg crossed her fingers, knowing that it probably was a factor. 'You see, they are interviewing all the staff who were on duty last Tuesday when Alan's wallet was stolen. They're not singling you out.'

Kayla sank back down again with a sigh. 'Is that true?' she asked warily.

'Yes, my dear. They interviewed Mandy before you. And Florin's just gone into them now.'

'I saw Mandy coming out as I went in. She looked like she'd been crying.'

'I doubt very much if you're the only one with problems at home,' Meg said, as diplomatically as she could.

'Yeah? And what do you know about my problems, eh? And Mandy's, for that matter? Why do you keep sticking your nose in where it isn't wanted?'

'I'm sorry you think I'm being nosy. I'm just concerned, that's all.'

'Huh, you concerned about the likes of me? That'll be the day.'

'Kayla, what I see is a young woman who's chosen to work in a caring profession, which says a lot about your character, and who is obviously unhappy about something.'

There was a lengthy pause as Kayla seemed to be battling against herself.

'He does drugs, did you know that?' she threw out challengingly. 'And, before you ask, I don't!'

'I never thought you did,' Meg said sympathetically. 'I'm sure you couldn't hold down a job if you did. But doesn't your boyfriend's habit cause problems for you?'

'It certainly doesn't make life easy,' Kayla scoffed.

'No, I wouldn't think it did. Drugs cost a lot of money.'

'I suppose you think I stole Alan's wallet to fund Mack's habit, is that it? You're no better than those pigs in there.' She gestured furiously towards the conservatory.

'I haven't accused you of anything,' Meg reassured her, 'but, tell me, did you?'

'No, I bloody didn't! I'm no thief, even if Mack is!' Meg could see tears in the corners of Kayla's eyes and hear the indignation in her voice.

'That's okay, then. I believe you.'

'You do?' Kayla seemed surprised.

All of a sudden, the fire seemed to go out of her.

'You wanna know what happened to my knee?' she said quietly. 'I'll tell you. I got home from work on Monday and Mack wanted money to buy skunk. I didn't wanna give him my handbag, but he grabbed it off me and pushed me away. I fell against the post at the bottom of the stairs.'

'And does that sort of thing happen a lot?' Meg asked gently.

'Too bloody often. I never have any money to buy nice things with.' A tear trickled down Kayla's face.

'And did he hit you as well?'

'What?'

'I couldn't help noticing a bruise on your cheek the other day.'

'Yeah, he hit me. He does that too bloody often, n'all.'

'Why don't you leave him?'

'Oh yeah? And where would I go, eh?'

'Wouldn't your parents help you?'

'Huh! Dad buggered off years ago. And ever since Mum's had a new bloke hanging around her, I'm not welcome at home anymore.'

'I'm so sorry to hear that,' Meg said, wishing she could help.

Kayla pushed herself up from the table, wiped a hand across her face and took a deep breath. 'Look, I've said more than I should. Promise me you won't tell no one?'

'If you really don't want me to, I won't,' Meg promised, 'but I wish you'd tell the police what happened. Maybe you could press charges? Maybe they could help you?'

'Yeah, like hell.' Kayla was back to sounding truculent, and Meg wisely decided she'd pushed Kayla as far as she could. She watched as the carer limped away then returned to her jigsaw puzzle, turning things over in her mind.

Just as the daylight was fading to the point where she would soon have to abandon her puzzle anyway, Meg looked out of the window to see Lauren striding towards the front door. She went into the hall to meet her.

'Hi, Meg,' breezed Lauren cheerfully.

'What are you doing here?' Meg demanded. 'Not that I'm not happy to see you, of course.' She leant forward and whispered, 'But I don't want us to be seen together too much in case it raises suspicion.'

'I've brought that book you wanted to borrow.' Lauren winked and Meg understood that her friend had already thought of a cover story.

'Thank you so much,' she gushed. 'Shall we go up to my room?' They got into the lift and grinned at each other. 'Don't tell me you really brought a book with you?' Meg asked as the lift ascended.

'Kinda,' Lauren chuckled. 'I've got my notebook in my bag!'

They ensconced themselves in the privacy of Meg's room, Meg sitting on the chair and Lauren perched on the dressing-table stool. She deftly whipped her notebook out of her bag, put it on top of the dressing table and opened it up. Then she sat back and gestured with a flourish, 'Ta da!'

'When you said you'd brought your notebook, I was thinking of a paper one that you write in with a pen, like mine,' Meg commented dryly.

'Yeah, well, a notebook is also a kind of laptop computer,' Lauren explained.

'So I see.'

Meg shuffled to the edge of her chair and studied the notebook. 'What am I looking at?' she asked, confused by a screen filled with incredibly small typing that she couldn't even begin to read.

'It's a spreadsheet,' Lauren explained. She showed Meg how it worked. Meg quickly understood that it was essentially an enormous table, with the names of every person who worked at Britford Lodge down the first column and headings across the top row, such as date of birth, age, nationality, and so on. Lauren demonstrated how she could highlight a row to make it easier to follow it across the columns, and how to zoom in to read the information in each of the cells. 'That's amazing,' Meg breathed in wonder, marvelling at the hours of work Lauren had clearly put into this.

'Well, you said you wanted background information. I'm just not sure how useful all of this is going to be.'

'Oh, I'm sure it will be very useful,' Meg said, nodding to herself.

'That's good,' Lauren pulled a sheaf of papers from her bag, ''cos I printed it all out for you, so you can have a copy to keep.'

Meg took the printed papers gratefully. 'You wicked girl,' she scolded playfully. 'Why didn't you just give me this to begin with, save me trying to get my head around that computer of yours?'

''Cos I wanted to see the expression on your face. Oh, it was so worth it!'

Together, they studied the information Lauren had somehow garnered off the internet. 'I can use this to know what questions to ask each of our suspects,' Meg declared.

'Just glad I can be of service.' Lauren stood up and took a mock bow.

Meg motioned for her to sit down again. 'You're not the only one who's been busy.' She told her young companion everything that she and Albert had been up to.

'Then there's definitely an inside person who wedged the door so that the murderer could get in?' Lauren looked concerned.

'I'm sure of it, even if neither Albert nor the police are quite so convinced yet. And don't you look at me like that, young lady. I've already had a lecture from Dan about not putting myself in danger. I don't need a repeat from you.'

Lauren shrugged. 'Fair enough.'

'There is something else you might be able to help me with.'

'Anything I can do,' Lauren assured her.

Meg explained how Dan had been intending to take her shopping for a mobile phone but was now too busy with the case.

'You want a mobile phone?' Lauren exclaimed incredulously.

'Yes, why shouldn't I?'

'Do you even know how to use one?'

'I had one for a while before I retired, but it didn't look anything like that high-tech device you've got. But, surely, you could teach me?'

'I'm sure I can.' Lauren thought for a moment. 'Tell you what, rather than rushing out and buying a new phone, I'm sure I've got a couple of older ones lying around at home somewhere. I'll have a look and see what I've got. I can pick up a pay-as-you-go SIM card for you—'

'Explain it all to me whenever you can bring the phone,' Meg interrupted, wondering what on earth a SIM card was and why she needed one.

'How about tomorrow afternoon? I'm working seven to three again in Milford. I can walk to Tesco after work and get the SIM card, and then cut across the water meadows to Britford Lodge. See you about four o'clock, all being well?'

'That's excellent. Thank you, my dear.'

Lauren looked at her watch. 'I'm going to have to leave soon to get my bus, I'm afraid. The sooner I can get my driving licence, the better, then I won't be tied to a flippin' timetable.'

'That's okay.' Meg smiled at her. 'I'll see you tomorrow.'

'Bye then, see ya tomorrow!' Lauren scooped up her notepad, thrust it into her bag and hurried off.

Chapter Nineteen

Lauren ran lightly down the stairs and dashed across the hallway, literally bumping into DS Viv Williams, who was just coming from the day room.

'Oh God, I'm so sorry,' she gasped breathlessly.

'Not to worry,' he grinned cheekily. 'It's not every day you get a pretty girl throwing herself into your arms.'

'I'm not a girl, I'm a woman,' she said haughtily, pulling herself up to her full five foot two inches. Not that that was a lot beside his six feet one.

'Steady on, it wasn't meant to sound derogatory,' he apologised. 'It was meant to be a compliment.'

'Huh!'

'Anyway, where are you rushing off to in such a hurry?'

'Got a bus to catch.' She glanced at her watch and winced. 'If I hurry!' She turned away from him, making for the door.

'Wait a moment, are you going into town?' Viv asked.

'No, Downton,' Lauren called back over her shoulder.

'I'll give you a lift, if you like?' he offered.

Lauren stopped. Was she hearing this right? Did the sexy sergeant just offer her a lift? 'Are you sure that isn't going out of your way?' she asked breathlessly.

'Not at all, I live in Redlynch so I go right through Downton.'

DC Moira Gordon emerged from the day room at that moment, clutching a sheaf of papers.

'Don't you have to go back to the station first, or something?' Lauren muttered, glancing at the DC in embarrassment.

'Don't worry about me,' Moira chuckled. 'I'm planning to walk home. I only live in Ridings Mead.' She referred to a small housing development just down from the hospital, not far from Harnham junction.

'I can give you both a lift, if you like, Moira?' Viv offered.

'Thanks but no. It'll only take me twenty minutes and I need to get my steps in for today. You two are free to carry on hatching whatever plans you were hatching.' She winked at Lauren, who blushed. 'So long as I can dump these papers in Viv's car before you go.'

'Come on, then.' Viv led the way to his Vauxhall Astra outside.

After Moira had handed over the papers and set off on foot, Lauren looked critically at Viv's car. 'You still driving this piece of junk?' she teased, tongue in cheek.

'Hey, don't you go calling my car junk,' retorted Viv in a similar vein. 'It'll get you home far more comfortably than the bus you just missed.'

'*Touché*.' Lauren got into the passenger seat.

Viv slid into the driver's side and started the engine. 'I didn't know you lived in Downton,' he remarked, easing the clutch up.

'You've never asked before.'

'Fair comment. Whereabouts do you live, exactly?'

'You can drop me outside The Bull, thanks. That'll be fine.'

'No problem.'

'How did your interviews go this afternoon?' Lauren asked hopefully.

'Like I'd tell you!'

'And why not?'

'Because you're a civilian, that's why not. That, and Dan would have my guts for garters.'

'But he'd tell Meg, wouldn't he?'

'Probably. But there's a reason he trusts her: Dan once told me that his dad worked with Meg's late husband back in the day. Apparently, his dad told him that Meg had a reputation for helping the DCI to solve some of his cases. Personally, I just think the old man's a bit soft on her, to be honest.'

'Dan's not *that* old,' chuckled Lauren. 'He can't be more than ten years older than you?'

'Twelve,' corrected Viv. 'He's thirty-eight.'

'That makes you twenty-six.' Lauren nodded to herself. Only a little more than six years older than her. Not too much of an age gap.

'And you're what? Eighteen? Nineteen?' he probed.

'I'll be twenty next week, I'll have you know.'

'Ah, so you're leaving the terrible teens behind soon?'

'I was never a terrible teenager,' she retorted.

'So you say!'

'Don't judge me by your own standards.'

'Ooh, I think I've hit a nerve there somehow.'

'Yeah, well, the teens weren't exactly great to me. I can't wait to leave them behind.'

'Yeah, sorry. Dan mentioned you'd lost your dad. That can't have been easy.'

'It wasn't.'

'Mind me asking how he died?'

'It was a car crash. On the A303.'

'Nasty.'

'Yes, it was.' Lauren fell silent and for a while Viv concentrated on his driving. After a few minutes, he said softly, 'I hope I didn't upset you, mentioning your dad?'

'No, it is what it is,' she sighed. It didn't feel like talking about her dad would ever get any easier, but it wasn't something she wanted to avoid, either.

'Have you got anything nice planned for this evening?' Viv asked airily.

'Nope, just me and my mum and the TV.'

'Don't suppose you'd like to come out for a drink or two?'

'With you?' Lauren held her breath.

'Yes, with me. Unless you want to go on your own?'

'Duh, not likely.'

'Well, I'm not a fan of drinking on my own, either. How about it?'

'Yeah, okay. That'd be nice.'

'Great.' Even in the dark, the oncoming headlights lit up his smile and Lauren grinned to herself. A date with the sexy sergeant? Yes, please!

That evening, Meg managed to tick three more names off her list of suspects.

After dinner, she settled herself into an armchair in the day room to read her book and looked up a little while later to see Stef approaching. Stefania Popescu was one of the other Romanians working at Britford Lodge, and she had been on duty on Tuesday. 'Do you need any paracetamol, Mrs Thornton?' she asked.

'Please, call me Meg. Every time someone calls me Mrs Thornton, I feel like I'm back in my classroom again.'

'You were teacher?' asked the twenty-six-year-old with long black hair.

'Yes, I taught in a secondary school. English.'

'Perhaps I should ask you to teach me?'

'I don't think you need my help. Your English is very good.'

'Thank you, that is very kind. But I make mistakes.'

'English isn't an easy language for foreigners to learn,' admitted Meg. 'Far too many verb tenses, for a start.'

'Yes, I try to learn when to use past simple and when to use present perfect, but it is very confusing.'

'Yes, I'm sure it is,' Meg remarked, musing that a lot of English people her age would struggle to even identify those verb tenses. 'Where are you from?'

'Romania.'

'Oh, like Ana, then? Perhaps you are friends?'

'Ana is Romanian, yes, but she is not like Florin and me. We are from Bucharest, a big city. She is from mountains in the north of my country. Very different.'

'I'm afraid I don't know anything about Romania,' sighed Meg.

Stef spent several minutes telling Meg about the geography and history of Romania; her passion for her home country very obvious.

'What about Florin? Are you friends with him?'

'We live together. And soon, I hope he will ask me to marry him.' Stef's face lit up.

'How lovely! Did you know him from Romania?'

'No, we met when he came to work here. Three years ago.'

'And is it difficult, both working shifts? Do you get the same days off, or is that not always possible?'

'Mrs Wilkinson is very kind. She gives us days off together when it is possible.'

'Were you both working here the day Alan died?'

'Ah, that day, Florin had to work but I had a day off. We had Thursday off together, though.'

'Were you both working on Tuesday?'

'Yes, why you ask?' Stef's demeanour changed to one of suspicion.

'Oh, I just wondered if you might have seen anyone going into Alan's room on Tuesday. I suppose you know that someone stole his wallet from his room that day?'

'Yes, I know. Mrs Wilkinson asked everyone about it. It is not nice to have someone ask if you are thief. I am not thief!' Stef declared vigorously.

'Sorry, my dear, I didn't mean to imply that you were. No, it's just that I promised Alan's friend, Ed, that I would see if I could find anything out.'

'I understand. Yes, Ed is very nice man. Not like Alan. Before his stroke, he was often rude to me and other carers.'

'I'm sorry to hear that.'

'Some people not like foreigners,' said Stef with a shrug, 'but we are not bad. Florin and me, we would never steal a wallet. We are not like that.'

'Of course not,' soothed Meg.

'Is true we not have much money. But we are very happy in our little flat together.'

'I'm pleased to hear it. Now tell me something, did you go into Alan's room at any time during the day before he died?'

'I already told you, I am not thief.'

'I know, I just wondered if you might have noticed anything odd about Alan's room. Anything out of place or that shouldn't have been there?'

'No, I don't remember anything different,' she said, shrugging her shoulders. 'Now, I ask you about paracetamol. You need some before you go to bed?'

'No, thanks. I'm fine,' Meg answered.

She was reasonably confident that neither Stef nor Florin would've stolen Alan's wallet, although she'd still like to question him as well. But he had been on the early shift today and already gone home. She'd just have to catch him next time he was on duty. And she didn't think Stef had anything to do with the murder; she seemed genuinely perplexed by her questions.

A little later, she was pleased to catch Irene on her own in the hallway. She started a rambling conversation with the statuesque forty-one-year-old who was mainly interested in dogs and long-distance running. But she managed to ascertain that Irene apparently thought herself well-off, with her carer's salary and a room in a shared house. 'At least the landlord allows me to have my Jasper there,' she said, referring to her greyhound. Meg wondered what her housemates thought of sharing with a dog! By the time Meg had finished, she was certain that Irene was neither the thief nor the accomplice.

Chapter Twenty

On Sunday morning, Meg ticked another two names off her list, with Sue and Emma both working the early shift. Sue, a matronly woman in her fifties, strenuously denied stealing Alan's wallet and pointed out that her husband was an architect, they'd finished paying off their mortgage and their children had both left home, so why on earth would she need to steal anything? Her reasoning didn't necessarily follow but Meg believed her. She also insisted that she hadn't noticed anything unusual in Alan's room the day before he was murdered. 'If I had, I would have said something,' she declared. Meg thought it unlikely but didn't like to contradict the woman. Hindsight was a wonderful thing!

Emma was another older carer, perhaps in her early sixties. She looked permanently anxious, and her hair gave the impression of having been dragged through a hedge backwards. She was very suspicious of Meg asking questions, but Meg managed to tease out of her that she couldn't have stolen Alan's wallet even if she'd wanted to, as she'd been working upstairs with Florin all morning that Tuesday. The two of them had taken their lunch break together in the staffroom and then spent all afternoon cleaning out the treatment-room cupboards. She was clearly not happy about being lumbered with such a menial task, as she had a few choice words to say about Sarah, who had 'waltzed in at lunchtime' and given them the most boring job. Meg made a mental note to check her story with Florin when she got the chance. But, if her story was true, then she couldn't have been the accomplice either as she'd never had the opportunity to enter Alan's room alone.

It just so happened that Florin and Stef were also on the early shift. Meg managed to catch them just before lunch, when she passed the open office door and saw the two in a close embrace.

'Hello, Stef, Florin.' She stepped through the doorway and smiled at the couple as they sprang guiltily apart. They had clearly been catching a moment together, there being no other staff in the office at the time. 'Stef was telling me yesterday how you both come from Bucharest. It sounds like such a lovely city.'

'Yes, it is.' Florin glanced knowingly at Stef, and Meg guessed that his girlfriend had told him about their conversation.

'You want to know if I stole Alan's wallet?' he asked directly.

'I'm sorry if it seems intrusive, but I promised Alan's friend Ed—'

'Yes, yes. Stef told me that,' Florin reassured her. Then he described his movements on Tuesday, which confirmed what Emma had said. That meant he also couldn't have entered Alan's room unnoticed.

Meg reassured the couple that she didn't for one second believe that either of them had stolen Alan's wallet. Then she went and found Albert so that they could go into lunch together.

✿

Meg had seen no sign of a police or CSI presence at Britford Lodge that morning, and for a while the residents seemed to have settled back into their usual routines. Conversation over lunch had returned to mundane matters such as what was on TV and the weather. It was almost as if nothing had ever happened!

Of course, when the visitors started to trickle in after lunch, there was a buzz of gossip around the murder, but Meg and Albert refused to be drawn into speculation. By the time Lauren finally arrived, Meg was fed up with hearing ridiculous and fanciful theories.

'Come up to my room, dear,' she urged. Once there, Meg

could see that Lauren was bursting to tell her something. 'What is it?' she asked.

'You'll never guess who I went on a date with last night?'

'You went on a date?' Meg was surprised. 'I thought you'd only just split up with David?'

'Yeah, that was last week,' Lauren said dismissively.

'Well, you didn't let the grass grow under your feet!'

'You sound as though you disapprove,' Lauren said with a pout.

'Not at all, my dear, although I guess that all depends on the suitability of the lucky young man in question.'

'Viv took me for a drink.'

'Viv? As in Detective Sergeant Viv Williams?' exclaimed Meg.

'Yep, that Viv,' grinned Lauren, looking a bit like the Cheshire Cat.

'Well, well,' mused Meg. 'Did you manage to get the inside story from him about their interviews yesterday?'

'No, he refused point-blank to answer any questions about the murder.' Lauren sounded put out.

'Very commendable,' remarked Meg. 'I'm sure Dan would have approved.'

'It's not fair, though, is it? I mean, Dan shares things with you.'

'You've had one date with Viv! And I for one am very glad to hear that he didn't spend the entire evening talking shop. Hopefully, he was more interested in you.'

'Yeah, he was.' Lauren blushed slightly at the memory.

'Well, I'm pleased for you. He's a very presentable young man. A little older than you, though, isn't he?'

'What are you? My mum?' Lauren laughed.

'Perish the thought!' Meg laughed with her. 'Now then, did you bring me anything?'

'Oh yeah, I nearly forgot! Look, I dug out Mum's old Nokia 3310. It's probably the easiest to use, although it is absolutely ancient—'

'Will it make a phone call?' Meg interrupted.

'Duh, ye-es! But the camera is shi ... rubbish ... and it's not a smartphone.'

Meg smiled. 'Just show me how to make a phone call.'

Lauren took the back off the phone and inserted the SIM card, explaining what it was. 'I've put ten pounds credit on it for you ...'

'You must let me pay you back,' Meg insisted firmly, 'and for that tiny card thing.'

'You think that's tiny? You should see the micro-SIM cards a lot of the smartphones use nowadays.'

'No, thank you,' grimaced Meg. 'That one looks quite fiddly enough.'

'Yeah, but now I've put it in for you, you won't have to do anything with it. It just stays there now.' She fixed the back onto the phone and turned it over.

'Well, at least that looks more like a phone than your smartphone does,' Meg said approvingly as she saw the number buttons.

Meg listened patiently as Lauren explained how to make a phone call and how to send a text message. She wasn't quite sure about her ability to type a message, though. And she wasn't at all bothered with the camera, although she did watch as Lauren demonstrated. 'How do I phone *you*?' she asked.

Lauren showed her the phone book, which contained just the one number: Lauren's.

'Do you want me to add some more numbers to the phone book?' Lauren asked.

Meg found her address book and read off Dan's mobile phone number.

'Is that it?'

'Yes. I can't think of anyone else I would need to call on a mobile. I suppose I can still dial 999 on this thing in an emergency?'

'You can. Although 112 is a better number to use from a mobile,' Lauren said, repeating what she'd been told on a recent first aid course.

When Lauren finally left to get her bus home, Meg felt more confident than she'd expected to feel about using her new phone.

Why, oh why, had he broken Alan's nose?

It was so stupid: without that, Alan's death might have been passed off as natural causes. But now the police were all over it.

She was sitting at home and gnawing anxiously on her thumbnail. They had planned the two murders meticulously. The first should have gone unnoticed, and he'd set up a cast-iron alibi for the second, knowing the police would quickly connect the victim to him. Despite the debacle with Alan, he'd insisted on continuing with their plans.

The thing was, would he be able to get away with it? She really didn't want to see him banged up again. Not now that she finally had a chance to get to know him.

She understood his anger. He'd been unfairly singled out. Had wanted vengeance.

And she'd been only too happy to help.

Chapter Twenty-one

Monday 16th January 2023

Monday morning dawned wet and blustery, but Meg was pleased to see that the frost and ice had gone as she looked out of her bedroom window. She took her notebook from her drawer, a paper one that you write in, unlike Lauren's, and checked her list of staff on duty the day Alan's wallet was stolen. Of her original fifteen suspects, she'd crossed out seven names and put a question mark next to Ana's. She noticed that the remaining seven included Maureen Wilkinson, the care manager, who should surely be above suspicion? Very well, six more to question.

Sarah Fielding was the senior care assistant in charge that morning, and one of Meg's targets. Of medium height and average build, with her auburn hair scraped back into a ponytail today, she was just dispensing the morning medications outside the dining room when Meg came down for breakfast. Before Meg could decide whether or not this would be a good time to question her, Dan and Viv walked through the front door.

'You're here again?' Sarah asked, sounding quite put out. 'What do you want this time?'

'We still have a few more staff members to interview,' Dan explained patiently. 'We can use the conservatory again, if that's all right with you?'

'Yes, I suppose so,' Sarah replied with a shrug. 'Do you need to talk to me? Only, I'm busy right now, as you can see.'

'We'd like to start with Ana-Maria Matei, if that's possible?'

'She's in the dining room, I think. Meg, could you have a look, please?'

Meg obliged and spotted Ana helping a resident named Ray to cut up his breakfast. She made her way over to the carer and asked her to come and talk to the police.

'What, they want me?' asked Ana, looking concerned.

'They've been questioning all the staff over the last few days, my dear. It just happens to be your turn now.'

Meg watched as the Romanian smoothed her hands nervously down the sides of her trousers as she walked towards the waiting men. She had an uneasy feeling about Ana. She just hoped that if she was guilty of theft as she suspected, Dan wouldn't rush to charge her with murder as well. She was sure the two crimes were not linked.

❁

Half an hour later, Meg and Albert were just walking into the day room when Meg saw Ana leaving the conservatory with Dan and Viv. They all looked very solemn. Meg felt a sinking feeling in her stomach. As they drew level with her, Dan stopped and nodded to Viv to carry on with Ana.

'Have you arrested her?' Meg whispered anxiously.

'Not yet,' replied Dan in a low voice. 'We're just taking her down to the station to make a formal statement under caution. She's given us cause to think she might have been the thief, just as you suspected. I want to get our interview on tape so that it holds up in court, if necessary.'

As soon as Dan had gone, Albert demanded to know what was happening. After a quick glance around the room, Meg took him into the recently vacated conservatory and brought him up to speed.

'Blimey, old gal,' he said in admiration. 'You have been busy.'

Suddenly there seemed little point in chasing around after her other suspects, so Meg chatted with Albert until they could hear the clink of cups on the coffee trolley. They went through to the day room, where Albert went to join Frank and Donald, whilst Meg sat down with her friend Jeannie.

'Are you still investigating?' Jeannie asked.

'Well, I think the mystery of the missing wallet is just about solved. But there's still Alan's murder to investigate.'

'Did Ana steal the wallet? Only, I saw her going with those two detectives in their car.'

'I can't confirm that.' Meg shook her head. 'Not yet.'

'But you think she did?' Jeannie persisted.

'Yes. I suspect she was sending money home to her family in Romania. She said, "Papa *was* so ill." Not Papa *is* ill. Or Papa *has been* ill.'

'Oh, you and your verb tenses. I can't see what difference that makes. You'll have to explain it to a dunce like me.'

'You're no dunce,' Meg chided, 'but you see, if she had used "is" or "has been", it would have meant that he is ill *now*. By using the past simple, it implies that he is no longer ill. And I doubt very much that a poor family in rural Romania could have afforded healthcare. There's no NHS there. So it seems logical that Ana must have sent them money. In fact, I think that's why she came to England in the first place. She earns so much more here than she would in Romania; she said as much to me. I know many foreigners working in the UK send money back home to their families.'

'So she's the thief,' Jeannie said, nodding thoughtfully, 'but you don't think she murdered Alan?'

'Ana is one of the most caring professionals here,' Meg said. 'I really can't see her murdering anyone. And, in any case, it makes no sense. Why murder Alan because you've stolen his wallet? His friend Ed knew it was stolen. I knew. Albert knew. Maureen knew. In fact, I'm pretty sure that all the staff knew, because Maureen was asking everyone about it. Killing Alan wouldn't change anything.'

'I'm sure you're right, my dear. Where do you go from here?'

Meg was trying to think of a polite way of fobbing her friend off, not wanting to put her at risk by involving her. She was saved by the arrival of Dan's silver Nissan Juke in the car park outside.

'I wonder why Dan's back so soon?' she cried.

Jeannie looked out of the window. 'He looks very

106

serious, you'd better go and find out.' She flapped her hands at Meg, encouraging her to go immediately. 'I might have finished this puzzle by the time you come back, though,' she teasingly called after Meg.

✿

Dan had disappeared into the office but, to Meg's relief, the door was slightly ajar. After a quick look round to check that the hallway was empty, she tiptoed across to stand outside the office door. She kept looking first left and then right as she listened, praying that no one would come along.

'I'll need to notify senior management,' Sarah was saying.

'That will be Maureen Wilkinson, the care manager, I presume?' asked Dan.

'No, she's having a few days off, and I'm pretty certain she's gone away somewhere. I'll have to contact the senior manager, Mr Percival.'

'Right then. If anyone has any questions for me, you've got my card.' There was a pause before Dan continued. 'Very well, I'm just going to talk to one of the residents briefly and then I'll be off.'

Sarah said something in reply, but Meg was already hurrying away. She went to stand in front of the lift as though waiting for it to arrive.

Dan came out of the office and strode across, spying Meg immediately. 'I see you've forgotten to press the call button again,' he hissed into her ear. 'How about we go to the conservatory instead?'

Once they were settled into cane armchairs, Dan spoke quietly. 'We've interviewed Ana under caution and she's confessed to stealing Alan's wallet.'

'Was she sending money to her family in Romania?' Meg asked.

'How the hell did you know that?' Dan shook his head in amazement. 'Yes, she's been sending small amounts every month, apparently. But then she sent a much larger sum last month, for her father to have an operation. Poor girl, it seems he might well have died without the surgery, and her family were in no position to afford to pay for it. It really makes me appreciate just how lucky we are to have the NHS, for all its failings. She sent every penny she had to save her father's life. But then she couldn't pay her rent and was facing eviction. She only took the wallet because she was desperate.'

Meg grimaced. 'I suppose you've had to arrest her?'

'You understand, I had no choice. She's been charged with theft.' He paused, knowing that she wouldn't like what he had to say next. 'And we're also detaining her on suspicion of murder.'

'Oh, Dan, no! That dear girl is no murderer. I'd stake my life on it!'

'Unfortunately, she has a motive, of sorts, and no alibi for the night Alan was murdered. I'm not convinced myself, but by applying for an extension we can hold her until, fingers crossed, we get some DNA results back. If the blood droplet on the bed cover and the skin cells under Alan's fingernails match hers, then we've got her.'

'They won't match, I'm sure of it,' Meg insisted.

'If that's the case, we'll be able to release her. But I'm afraid that, as a foreign national with a conviction for theft, she'll probably lose her visa to work in this country.'

'She'll be sent back to Romania?' Meg was horrified.

'Quite likely.'

They both fell silent for a moment.

'There's one thing that's still baffling me, you know,' Dan said. 'If the murderer, whether Ana or someone else, got into Alan's room without being seen, how on earth did they do it?'

'Ah, well, Albert and I have solved that one, I think,' Meg announced triumphantly. She explained and he listened incredulously.

'Ha!' he laughed, shaking his head. 'That explains the piece of string the CSIs found on the grass not far from Alan's room. We couldn't work out if it was relevant or not.'

'I'll lay odds that it's what the murderer used to pull open the door,' Meg said, with a twinkle in her eye.

'But . . . if the door was wedged open from the inside . . .'

'. . . that means there was an inside accomplice.'

'Damn it! That could put you in danger again. You've got to promise me that you'll stop investigating.'

'I won't make a promise I can't keep,' said Meg, 'but I will promise to be very careful.'

Dan shook his head in frustration.

Chapter Twenty-two

After lunch, Meg tried using her mobile phone for the first time, to call Lauren. But it rang out and she got a rather abrupt answerphone message commanding her to *Leave a message if you want me to call you back*. Meg didn't. She hated talking to a machine.

An hour later, she and Jeannie were sorting out the edge pieces for a new jigsaw puzzle, when her phone rang. At first, she couldn't work out what it was but, with a start, she finally realised what was making that atrocious sound. She'd really have to ask if Lauren could change it to something more melodic! Fortunately, she managed to answer it before it stopped ringing.

'Meg Thornton here.'

'You don't need to say that,' Lauren scolded. 'I know who you are. I'm probably the only person in the world who knows this phone number, so who else would be calling you? And, in any case, most people just say "Hello."'

'Hello,' Meg said, biting her lip in amusement.

'You tried to phone me earlier?' Lauren asked.

'Yes, but I didn't leave you a message, so how did you know to call me back?'

'Because my phone told me that I had a missed call.'

'Oh, I didn't know it could do that.'

'Never mind. What did you want?'

Meg told her that Ana had been charged with stealing Alan's wallet.

'I guess that's why the agency has booked me for a shift tomorrow.'

'You're working here?' Meg asked.

'Yes. I told my manager ages ago that if any shifts ever came up at Britford Lodge, I wanted them. Of course, I told her it was easier for me with Britford being on the bus route in from Downton. I didn't mention you. And finally!'

'I appreciate your excitement, Lauren. But, unfortunately, a very nice young woman is being unjustly detained to give you this opportunity.'

Lauren sobered up as Meg explained that Ana was being held in custody on suspicion of murder. 'That's not fair,' she protested.

'I know, but I think Dan's hands were tied. His superintendent seems very keen to wrap this case up quickly . . .'

'And the easiest thing is to pin the murder on the thief. That's just dumb.'

'I agree, but there's nothing we can do today. I am sure Ana will be exonerated when the DNA results come back.'

'But she is guilty of stealing the wallet?'

'Yes, she confessed to that. And I'm afraid she'll probably lose her job because of it.'

'That sucks.'

Meg agreed with her and then said goodbye, saying she looked forward to seeing her tomorrow.

❁

Her phone call over, Jeannie wanted to know what was happening, having overheard Meg's side of the conversation. Meg succinctly filled her in, begging her to keep Ana's arrest a secret.

'I won't say a word,' Jeannie promised, 'but won't it be rather strange for you to have your friend working here?'

'No, why should it?' asked Meg. 'She was one of my carers at The Cedars.'

They continued to work on their jigsaw, but Meg's mind was on other matters.

Dan had said that the DNA results could take days, and she wasn't sure how long the police could detain Ana for. She really didn't like the idea of that poor girl being held in a police cell. If only she could do something to help prove Ana's innocence. The trouble was, she honestly had no idea who the murderer was. She decided that she needed to focus on who the accomplice might have been, because she was sure it wasn't Ana. That meant she needed to carry on questioning the staff who had been on duty the day before Alan was murdered.

As soon as the outside edge was complete, she excused herself and went to the office. She needed to talk to Sarah. She tapped on the door, but it wasn't Sarah's voice that answered.

'Come in,' summoned Petra.

Meg thought quickly as she pushed open the door. 'I'm sorry to bother you, but I've got this muzzy kind of a headache and it just won't go away,' she lied. 'It's making it difficult to concentrate on my jigsaw puzzle.'

'I'm sorry to hear that. Come and sit down, Meg.' The senior care assistant indicated a chair next to the desk and Meg sat. Petra studied her, eyes full of concern. 'You do look a little pale,' she remarked, taking Meg's wrist and checking her pulse. Then she felt Meg's forehead with the back of her hand. 'I don't think you've got a temperature, but I would like to check your blood pressure. I'll get you some paracetamol too. Just stay here, I'll be right back.'

As soon as Petra had left the office, Meg leapt to her feet and studied the staff notice board. Of course, Petra was in charge on the late shift. She checked her watch. It was later than she'd realised; Sarah must've gone home. There was nothing of interest on the board, so she had a quick look around the office to see if there was anything else worth looking at. There was a folder on the desk marked with Alan's name. She cautiously raised the cover – one eye on the door – and snuck a look. The top sheet of paper was the report into the missing wallet. Meg noted that Ed's surname was Smith and that the address he'd given was in Old Sarum. She wrinkled her brow. That was odd; she was sure he'd mentioned living in Wilton. Hearing footsteps outside the door, she hastily closed the folder and sat back in her seat. Just in the nick of time, as Petra came through the door.

Unsurprisingly, Meg's blood pressure was slightly raised, although that probably had more to do with almost being caught snooping than any medical reason. Meg took her paracetamol and agreed to have a rest on her bed before dinner.

'I'll make sure someone checks your blood pressure again later,' Petra promised.

It was only when she got to her room that Meg realised that Petra was also on the list of suspects. She kicked herself for not questioning her when she had the chance.

❂

As luck would have it, it was Petra who came to check Meg's blood pressure just before dinner.

'Are you feeling any better?' she asked Meg solicitously.

'Oh yes, much better, thank you. And how are you?'

'Very well, thank you.'

'I thought you might still be quite shaken up after discovering Alan's body last week?'

'Not really. At the time, I thought he died in his sleep, and that is something I am used to dealing with, in this job. After, when Dr Baker said he thought it might be suspicious, I was worried that I had missed something. When they said it was murder, yes, I was sad for Alan. But that is all.'

'Did you notice anything odd about his room?' Meg asked. 'Either when you found him or perhaps earlier in the night?'

'I did not see Alan before he went to sleep. After that, every time I looked in, the room was dark so I didn't see anything odd. Only when I saw his hand hanging over the side of the bed. That was odd.'

'That was when you found him?'

'Yes. But his room looked the same as normal. Why do you ask?'

'Well, if someone murdered Alan, I wonder how they got into his room without being seen. You don't have any ideas, do you?'

'No.' Petra seemed completely relaxed, and Meg thought she was unlikely to have been the accomplice.

'It is not a nice thought ... that someone came into this home and murdered a resident like that. I hope the police find out who did it very soon,' Petra said, as she fastened the cuff around Meg's arm. Meg agreed.

'There, all done. Your blood pressure is back to normal now,' announced Petra. 'I don't think there is anything to worry about.'

Apart from the little question of who on earth murdered Alan, Meg thought, as she made her way down to the dining room.

Chapter Twenty-three

Tuesday 17th January 2023

The weather on Tuesday was, if anything, more tempestuous than the day before, but even that couldn't put a damper on Lauren's spirits as she turned up at ten to seven for the early shift. She was shown the staffroom lockers by a pretty dark-haired woman called Lyn. The thirty-four-year-old made Lauren feel very welcome. After handover from the night staff, Lauren was paired to work with Lyn and she set off cheerfully, working in the downstairs corridor to help the residents there to get washed and dressed. When she saw the crime scene tape across the fourth door along, she knew that must have been Alan's room.

'Is that where . . .?' she asked, a little breathlessly.

'Yes, that was Alan's room, the man who was murdered in his bed,' Lyn replied in hushed tones. 'We're forbidden to enter that room. Not that I want to, thank you.' She gave a theatrical shiver.

'Do you know how he was killed?' Lauren asked. Of course, she already knew the answer, but it didn't hurt to play dumb and pretend she didn't.

'He was smothered with a pillow.'

'How horrible! And have the police caught the murderer yet?'

'I don't think so. Come on, we'll get into trouble for gossiping in the corridors. We need to get Jeannie up next.'

Lauren was looking forward to seeing Meg's friend, who she'd met on several occasions when visiting.

Sarah was once again dispensing the morning medications when, to her surprise, Maureen Wilkinson arrived.

'Maureen, I thought you were having a few days away?'

'I was,' the care manager said grimly, 'but there are things that need to be sorted out following Alan's murder. It's lucky we'd only gone to my in-laws in Portsmouth, so it wasn't too far to come back. And, thankfully, my mother-in-law's seventieth birthday was yesterday, which was the main reason for going down.'

'What a shame you've had to come back early. Is there anything I can do?'

'Carry on with what you're doing. I've got some phone calls to make first. Then I can brief you about what's happening.'

Maureen hung her coat on the back of the office door, not bothering to change into her uniform as she had no intention of staying any longer than she needed to. She picked up the card left by the detective inspector and dialled his number, requiring an update.

✿

Meg was very pleased to see Lauren at breakfast time when she wheeled Bill, another of the ground-floor residents, into the dining room. She was accompanied by Jeannie with her walking frame.

'Morning, Meg,' Lauren beamed, having positioned Bill at a nearby table with Donald, Frank and Ray, a hollow shell of a man with dementia who rarely spoke. Jeannie manoeuvred into the seat next to Meg as Lauren sped off to her next resident.

'It's so nice to have your friend working here, my dear,' Jeannie gushed. 'She's given my legs a wonderful massage this morning. It really helped to get the circulation flowing.'

'What's that?' called out Donald. 'Do I understand you already know our new carer?'

Meg explained that Lauren was a friend from her previous care home. 'Is she the one that helped you to solve the murders there?' asked Frank, with curiosity.

'And what do you know about that?' Meg demanded.

'Ah, ''scuse me, old gal, but that might be my fault,'

confessed Albert, arriving to join Meg and Jeannie at their table.

'Albert,' Meg hissed at him, 'what have you been saying about me?'

'Just singing your praises, m'dear. Nothing bad at all.'

'Albert was telling us yesterday how the two of you and one of the carers helped to solve the murders at The Cedars. It all sounded very exciting,' said Frank.

'Oh, he was, was he?' said Meg, glowering at Albert, who had the grace to look abashed.

'Aye, that he did,' chipped in Donald. 'I was asking him if you were going to put your brain to our murder here. And he said you're already working on it. Isn't that right, Albert?'

'Umm, er, yes, I might have said something like that.' Albert tried to avoid Meg's withering look.

'Needn't waste yer time findin' out who done away with that ol' bugger,' grumbled Bill, in a broad West Country accent. 'Ain't no one gonna miss 'im, that's fer sure.'

'Hang on a minute, old chap,' Albert spluttered indignantly. 'Not the done thing to speak ill of the dead, don't y'know?'

'Ye didn't know 'im afore his stroke.' Bill shook his head sorrowfully.

'And you did?' Meg asked.

'Aye, me 'n' Donald, we both knew what 'e were like, din't we?'

'Aye,' Donald sighed. 'I'm afraid he could be quite touchy at times, you know.'

'Oh, in what way?'

'Well, he didn't like anyone knowing his business, for a start. I remember picking up a letter he'd dropped once, and he snatched it out of my hand and damn near bit my head off, he was that sharp; accusing me of reading his private correspondence.' Donald paused. 'Another time, he accused me of listening in to his conversation with that mate of his that visited him regular, like.'

'Ed?'

'Yes, that's the one. They were a peculiar pair, they were. I mean, Alan was all surly and barely had two nice words to say to anyone, whereas Ed was a much nicer fellow, very polite. And erudite too. I remember seeing him do *The Times* crossword as quick as if it were the small one on the back of the *Sun*. There must have been a good few years between them in age n'all. I always wondered how those two had ever become friends in the first place.'

'A good question,' Meg said thoughtfully. That was definitely something to follow up on.

When Lauren was told she could take a ten-minute coffee break, she sought out Meg in the day room. She was on her own doing the jigsaw puzzle this morning, Jeannie having been picked up by ambulance car for a hospital appointment.

'How's it going?' enquired Meg.

'Quite well, actually. Busier than The Cedars, of course, but not as bad as some of the other homes I've worked in since being with the agency. The staff are very friendly here, and there's a nice mix of residents. Plus, the building isn't too old, so the rooms have all mod cons.'

'Are you thinking you might like to work here?' Meg chuckled.

'If I get the chance. Ooh, here comes DI Dan and my sexy sergeant.'

Meg turned to follow Lauren's gaze out of the window in time to see Viv helping Ana out of the back seat. 'Now that's odd, why would they bring her back here?' she mused. 'Will you excuse me?' she begged Lauren, and made her way swiftly to the hall, arriving just as the trio entered.

'Ana, my dear,' she said sympathetically.

'Mrs Thornton, I so sorry.' The poor girl looked at the floor, close to tears.

'I understand, my dear. It wasn't right, but you did what you did to help your father.'

'Yes, I help Papa. But now I have trouble with police. I never have trouble with police before.'

'Meg, you'll need to excuse us,' Dan interrupted gently.

118

'Mrs Wilkinson is expecting Ana. I should take her into the office right away.' Dan moved Ana towards the office door and knocked, entering almost immediately to a tense 'Come.'

Viv waited until the office door was shut. 'We had our orders,' he explained. 'The care manager phoned first thing this morning, demanding that as soon as Ana was released from police custody, we should bring her straight here.'

'Does that mean that you're no longer holding Ana on suspicion of murder?' Meg asked hopefully.

'It does. Ana's DNA is not a match for anything we got from the crime scene. Not that you thought it would be, of course.'

'Of course. Did you get a match with anyone else?'

'Not yet. The lab was asked to rush through the comparison with Ana's DNA because we could only hold her for twenty-four hours. Now we have to wait while they compare it to all the other samples taken from staff and residents. And they'll run it through the national database too.'

'May I ask if you've taken a DNA sample from Alan's friend, Ed?'

'It's funny you should ask that. I went to interview him on Saturday, only to discover the address he gave us doesn't exist. I mean, it sounded very plausible. But he said he lived at 152 Partridge Way, and the house numbers don't go up that high! That number would put him slap-bang in the middle of Salisbury City's football pitch, I reckon.' Viv shook his head. 'Dan's not at all happy.'

'I'm guessing the name might have been false too?' suggested Meg.

'Well, there are two Edward Smiths in the Salisbury area, but as one's in his forties and married and the other's hardly more than a teenager, neither of them are the man we're looking for. We're at a bit of a dead end, to be honest.'

At that moment, Lauren arrived. Viv looked at her uniform with confusion.

'Morning, Sergeant. I hope you're not going to arrest Meg for anything?' she asked, tongue-in-cheek, her eyes shining brightly.

'Er, no. But what are you doing here dressed like that?' he asked.

'Umm, I'm a carer. You know, I work in care homes,' Lauren replied sarcastically.

'But not this one!'

'There's a first time for everything,' she said cheekily. She was about to say something else but the office door opened, so she hurried off down the corridor with a spring in her step, not wanting to be caught gossiping.

Dan came out with a pale-looking Ana and a stern-looking Maureen, who all headed off in the same direction as Lauren.

'I think she's being escorted to her locker to collect her things,' Viv commented.

'Poor girl,' said Meg.

'She did steal a wallet,' pointed out Viv.

'Yes, and it was wrong. But who knows what you or I might have done in her situation?'

Viv considered that. 'That's true,' he conceded.

'What do you think will happen to her?'

'She appeared before the magistrate this morning and was given unconditional bail on surrender of her passport. She's pleading guilty, so that will go in her favour. And she's said that she's willing to return to Romania voluntarily. All in all, I expect she'll get let off with an official caution, along with the revocation of her work visa.'

'At least she'll be happy to be reunited with her family,' Meg sighed.

Chapter Twenty-four

Dan and Maureen returned about five minutes later with Ana between them, hugging a coat and a supermarket carrier bag with a few bits and pieces in it.

'Put that on, girl,' Maureen instructed. 'It's pouring down out there.'

Ana shrugged on her coat whilst the care manager held her bag, then Viv led her outside to the car. Just as Dan was saying his goodbyes, his phone rang and, glancing at the screen, he apologised. 'I need to take this. May I use your office?'

Maureen nodded curtly before turning to Meg. 'I understand you were instrumental in bringing Ana to the attention of the police?'

'I just passed on what little information I had,' Meg replied modestly.

'Thank you. It's not nice to have something like this hanging over the other staff. I just wish Ana would've felt able to come to me about this problem. Maybe I could've helped. I gather she wasn't the only carer confiding their problems in you?'

'I find that young girls sometimes need a listening ear. And I have all the time in the world to listen,' Meg said modestly.

'Again, thank you. I suspected there was something wrong with both Mandy and Kayla. Their work's been off, but I haven't had a chance to get to the bottom of it. I'll make sure they get all the support I can give them. Tell me, is there anything else you think I should know about?'

Meg hesitated. It wasn't really her place. But it wouldn't hurt, would it?

'I expect you recognised the agency carer who's in today, Lauren? She's a regular visitor of mine.'

'I didn't,' confessed Maureen. 'I thought her face was vaguely familiar, but ...'

'I'm sure you've had too much else on your mind,' soothed Meg.

'That's true enough, and now I've got to start trying to recruit a replacement for Ana.'

'That's what I wanted to say to you. I happen to know that Lauren is keen to find a permanent position rather than working for the agency. And I would be happy to give her a personal reference, if that's permissible.'

'Thank you, I'll bear that in mind.'

Just then, Dan came storming out of the office.

'Sorry, Maureen, Meg, I've got to dash.'

'A breakthrough in the case?' asked Meg hopefully.

'Keep this to yourselves, but there's been another murder!' Dan said darkly, before rushing out to the car.

Meg waited on tenterhooks all day, but she heard nothing further from Dan. Of course, he would be very busy; she realised that. But it was frustrating. Was this new murder linked to Alan's or completely unrelated?

Unfortunately, there was no one she could discuss it with. Lauren was occupied with work for the rest of her shift, and she didn't trust Albert enough to share the news with him. Meg did the only thing she could do; she returned to her jigsaw puzzle to think things through.

⚙

Lauren worked her socks off during her shift, determined to make a good impression. So she was a little concerned when the care manager summoned her to the office after the handover to the late staff was finished.

'Come in and close the door,' Maureen instructed. 'Please, sit down.'

Lauren sat in a chair facing the desk, butterflies in her stomach.

'I've spoken to your agency manager, Sharon, and arranged for you to continue working here for the rest of this week. Unfortunately, we've had to dismiss one of our carers, Ana-Maria Matei, but I gather you probably know about that?'

Lauren nodded, not daring to speak as a bubble of excitement was building inside her.

'Well, you'll take over her shifts. The duty roster is posted on the notice board, here. You'll see that she was scheduled to work an early shift tomorrow before two days off, and then a late followed by an early over the weekend. Can you commit to covering all of those shifts?'

'Yes, that won't be a problem.'

'I also understand that you might be interested in applying for a full-time position here?'

Lauren swallowed, trying to keep her excitement in check. Meg must've said something! 'Yes, that's right.'

'Is that just because Meg is a resident here?' Maureen demanded. 'We don't object to friendships between staff and residents, provided they don't get in the way of you doing your work to the high standard I expect. But I need to know that, if anything were to happen to Meg, you would still be just as committed to working here.'

Maureen leant back in her chair and studied Lauren intensely. Lauren knew that it was crucial for her to get her reply right. Crikey, this was a job interview with no time for preparation! She took a deep breath whilst composing her thoughts.

'Meg being here is a factor, of course,' she admitted, 'but I am genuinely looking for a full-time permanent position. I made the decision to become a carer after I left school, and I am still convinced that I've chosen the right career for me. Unfortunately, my job at The Cedars was cut short due to the, er, unusual circumstances there. I've been working through the agency since then, but agency work is unpredictable, and it's not easy going into so many different work environments. I would like to feel that I belong somewhere, get to know the routines properly, and hopefully make friends. I am also aware of the need for ongoing professional development if I am ever to advance up the career ladder, and that simply isn't available through agency work. I know this is my first shift here, but I like the work environment here. There's a nice mixture of residents, the staff I've met so far are friendly, and it is efficiently managed. On a personal level, Britford Lodge is ideally situated for me as I live in Downton. It's easy to get buses to and from Britford without having to cross town or worry about changing buses.'

Lauren ran out of things to say. Was it enough? She couldn't read the care manager's face as to whether she was sufficiently impressed or not. Maureen didn't speak for what seemed like an eternity but was in reality only a few seconds.

'Very well.' She nodded at Lauren and her features softened slightly. 'I've already discussed this with my manager, Mr Percival. Legally, we are obliged to advertise the vacancy properly. But I can assure you that good-quality candidates are hard to come by. I'll give you an application form to fill out immediately, and we'll need references and for the usual checks to be done. You don't know of any reason for those to be a problem, do you?'

'No, there shouldn't be any problems.'

'Good. All being well, we should be able to get everything in place for you to start a three-month probationary period on Monday next week.'

'Th-th-thank you,' Lauren stammered, scarcely believing her luck.

'I should point out that if your enhanced DBS check, references, or the standard of your work is in any way inadequate, the home has the right to terminate your employment at any time during the probationary period. Do you understand that?'

'Yes, Mrs Wilkinson, I understand. And I promise that I will try my very best.'

'I shall expect nothing less.' The care manager's face creased into a smile and she held out a hand. 'Welcome to Britford Lodge, Lauren.'

⚙

Meg was just slotting the last puzzle piece into place as Jeannie watched, when Lauren came into the day room. 'Now that's a huge grin. Have you won the lottery or something?'

'Or something,' Lauren said, bending to plant a kiss on Meg's cheek. 'I don't know what you said, but thank you.' She sank into a seat at their table, her eyes shining brightly.

'For what?'

'Whatever you said to Mrs Wilkinson. She's offered me a chance to work here permanently.'

'That's excellent news!' Meg beamed and Jeannie joined in the congratulations.

When Lauren had shared her news in full, and pointed out that it was okay for her to sit down and chat with them now as it was after three-thirty and she was officially off shift, Meg told her about the second murder.

'Another murder?' Lauren gasped. 'But who? Is it linked to Alan's murder? What does this mean for the investigation?'

'All good questions, my dear. But we don't look like getting any answers anytime soon, I'm afraid.'

Chapter Twenty-five

'Let's see if there's anything online.' Lauren whipped out her smartphone and started tapping furiously with her thumbs. Meg marvelled at the speed with which the girl could type.

'Right, there's a brief mention on the *Salisbury Journal* website . . .

'Man found dead in Wilton. Police are investigating a suspicious death at a home in Wilton but have refused to name the victim until next of kin can be notified. It is believed that the alarm was raised by a delivery girl who spotted something wrong when she delivered a newspaper to the bungalow this morning.'

'Is that it?'

'It mentions that DI Bywater, Dan, is on the scene and that the pathologist, Dr Hamnet, was also seen. Both refused to make any comment.'

'I bet they did,' Meg said wryly. 'Wilton . . . I wonder?'

'What?'

'Well, I'm sure that's where Alan's friend, Ed, said he lived.' She told Lauren about Ed having given a false address in Old Sarum and, it would seem, a false surname.

'Ooh, that's very suspicious,' Lauren commented.

'Yes, indeed, but we mustn't jump to any conclusions. We'll just have to wait for Dan to tell us what's going on.'

'Or we could see what Viv's got to say on the subject!' Lauren pointed out of the window at the sergeant, who was just parking his car.

The young Jamaican strode purposefully in through the front doors and came straight to the day room, clearly looking for Meg.

'Mrs Thornton,' he began.

'Please, call me Meg. Dan does.'

'Meg,' he smiled, showing ivory white teeth against his polished ebony skin. Meg couldn't help thinking how handsome he was. 'May I sit down?'

Jeannie struggled to her feet. 'Here you are, young man. Have my seat. I need to excuse myself.' She trotted off with her walking frame and Viv took her place.

'I hope I didn't offend her?' he asked doubtfully.

'No, she's just being considerate of our need for privacy,' Meg replied.

'You're still here, then?' Viv remarked to Lauren.

'Yep, and I'm off duty now, so here's where I'm staying until you've told us both all about this new murder,' she retorted.

'Well, Dan asked me to talk to Meg. He didn't say anything about taking you into our confidence as well.'

'I'm not going anywhere!' Lauren folded her arms and threw him a challenging look.

'It's okay, Lauren,' Meg intervened, spotting a twitch of a smile on Viv's face. 'I think the sergeant is winding you up.'

Viv chuckled and Lauren blushed. 'You rotter,' she mumbled.

'Right, well. Down to business. Is it okay to talk here?' Viv asked, looking around.

'We can go into the conservatory if you prefer,' Meg offered.

By consent, the three of them decamped into the conservatory and settled in.

'Well, come on then,' urged Lauren impatiently.

'Okay, then.' He leant forward and spoke quietly, Meg and Lauren hanging on his every word.

'Please note: everything I'm about to tell you is strictly confidential.' The pair nodded solemnly. 'And I'm only telling you both because Dan has approved this.'

Lauren wished he would get to the point.

'This morning, we were called to another murder. PC Daly, I think you'll remember him, Meg?' She nodded. 'He got a call out at about seven-thirty to do a welfare check. When he got there, the next-door neighbour was waiting for

127

him. Apparently, a newspaper girl had looked in through the neighbour's living-room window on her way to the front door. She's been doing the round for some time and the house is normally immaculate, so she was alarmed to see that everything was turned upside down. She then noticed that Monday's paper was still in the letterbox. She knocked on the front door and, getting no reply, knocked on the neighbour's door. The two of them tried both front and back doors and couldn't get an answer. But the man's car was still in the drive, so the neighbour phoned the police.'

'And PC Daly attended,' jumped in Lauren, 'but what did he find? And who is it that's been murdered?'

'All in good time,' cautioned Meg.

'If I may continue?' Viv looked at Lauren, an amused expression on his face. 'PC Daly couldn't get any response, either, and he ended up breaking in through the back door. And there, in the kitchen, he found the body.' He paused. 'It wasn't pretty, and that's all I'm going to tell you.'

'We're not wimps, you know,' protested Lauren.

'No, but some things you can't unsee,' said Viv with feeling. 'In this case, the poor man appears to have been tortured; there's no other word for it.'

'You can skip ahead,' encouraged Meg, not wanting all the grisly details.

'PC Daly withdrew immediately and called in the murder team, CSIs, etc. All he could tell us was that the neighbour said that the man was called Ed.'

Meg gasped and Lauren exclaimed, 'Oh my God!'

'The newspaper girl had continued on her rounds but she was tracked down and asked for a statement later, and she only knew the occupant as Mr Smith.'

'Ed Smith, Alan's friend?' asked Meg incredulously.

'Well, therein lies the problem. This man was known just as Ed by all his neighbours and as Mr Smith to a couple of local businesses. But that probably wasn't his real name. We searched the house for paperwork to confirm who he is, but the whole house has been turned over. The murderer had evidently been looking for something. We eventually managed to identify that the house actually belongs to an

Edward Crouch. We ran that name and address through our database . . . and something rather staggering turned up.'

'What?' squeaked Lauren.

'Edward Crouch is, or perhaps was, a convicted murderer out on licence.'

'What?' exploded Meg and Lauren simultaneously.

'Shh!' Viv warned. 'You understand that just because the house belongs to Edward Crouch, it doesn't necessarily mean that he was the murdered man. We need to wait for DNA to confirm that our victim is indeed the same person. But as we have his DNA on file already, that shouldn't take too long. Meanwhile, it's vital that you don't say a word to anyone. Regardless of who he is and what he might have done, we need to contact next of kin before his name gets released. The big question is, assuming the victim *is* Edward Crouch, is he also the man posing as Alan's friend, Ed Smith?'

'And that's where you want my help?' suggested Meg.

'Spot on, as always. You see, we don't know what Ed Smith looks like. You do. That's why Dan sent me here, to show you a photo. If you don't mind looking at it.'

'A photo of a dead man?' Meg asked warily.

'Yes. But we took it after the pathologist and CSIs had finished doing all their stuff, and we'd been given leave to tidy his face up a bit. It's not too bad,' Viv assured her.

'Okay then.'

Viv pulled up a photo on his phone and turned it round to show her. She took a look, pausing in silent sadness for a life lost. Then she nodded. 'Yes, that's Alan's friend, Ed.'

'Wow!' breathed Lauren, grabbing the phone so that she could see the photo. 'How many people did he murder?'

'Directly, none, but he was part of a gang who pulled off a post office heist where the postmistress was shot and killed and another man seriously wounded. All the gang members went down for murder.'

'And did he murder Alan?' asked Lauren.

'It's possible, yes,' replied Viv, 'but we have to gather the evidence to prove that, as we would in any case.'

'But if he murdered Alan, who murdered him?' asked Meg.

129

'Oh yeah. That's a good question,' acknowledged Lauren.

'Exactly,' agreed Viv. 'Now, on the face of it, the two murders had very different MOs, which might indicate two different murderers. But it would be an enormous coincidence for two friends to both be murdered within days of each other.'

'And Dan doesn't believe in coincidences,' Meg commented.

'Nor do I. And, more importantly, Superintendent Wells has accepted that the cases are probably linked, which is why Dan is now heading up both investigations.'

'What else can we do?' Meg asked.

'Absolutely nothing!' Viv insisted. 'My instructions from Dan were very clear; you are not to get involved in this investigation anymore. Ed's murder was brutal and he doesn't want you taking any chances. There's a very dangerous person on the loose out there.'

'Message understood,' Meg conceded, as Lauren looked incredulously at her.

Viv swore the two of them to secrecy before leaving, after which Lauren rounded on Meg. 'You're not really going to sit back and do nothing, are you?'

'Of course not,' Meg smiled. 'I said that the message was understood, not that I agreed to abide by it!'

Before they could say any more, Albert approached, having been waiting for his chance ever since he'd seen the sergeant arrive.

'What-ho? Have there been developments?' he asked, looking at Meg.

'There's been another murder!' burst out Lauren.

'Which we are absolutely sworn to secrecy over,' Meg said sternly to Lauren.

'Oops, sorry. But I thought you trusted Albert?'

'I did until I found out he's been telling all and sundry that I'm investigating Alan's murder.' She looked at him sternly. 'After I told you not to say anything to anyone.'

'Sorry, old gal. It just kind of slipped out, y'know.'

'Well, sit down and stop drawing attention to yourself,' Meg hissed angrily. 'And if I find out you've said a word about this to anyone else ...'

'Won't happen, m'dear. My lips are sealed.' Albert mimed zipping his lips shut, before settling into the chair recently vacated by Viv.

Meg gave him a brief summary of what Viv had told them. She skipped the bit about Edward Crouch being a convicted murderer.

'First poor old Alan, now his friend, Ed. That's a rum do, what?'

Meg was saved from having to give Albert any more information by the arrival of Taska, back on day shifts now, with the tea trolley. She looked at Lauren in surprise. 'You not go home yet?'

Lauren explained that she was just visiting her friend Meg before leaving to catch her bus.

'Perhaps is better if you change uniform before you visit? If you have on uniform, residents think you work.'

'That sounds like sensible advice,' agreed Meg. 'Draw a line between when you're working and when you're here but not on duty.'

'Yeah, I suppose so,' sighed Lauren. She glanced at her watch. 'Crikey, I didn't realise how late it was. Meg, I'm so sorry, I'm going to have to run if I don't want to miss the four-twenty bus.'

Chapter Twenty-six

Meg was delighted to see Taska back on duty as she had a few questions for the young Latvian. 'Do you still have a few more residents to take the tea trolley to, or are we the last?'

'I finish doing teas now,' Taska replied cheerfully. 'Why? You need something?'

'Have you got time to have a chat with us? I wanted to ask you a bit more about when you found Alan.'

'Oh.' Taska's face fell and she looked around as though fearful of something or somebody. 'Policeman say I must not talk with anyone about Alan.'

'I quite understand. But as you already talked to me *before* you spoke to the police, I'm sure it can't do any harm.'

'I not get in trouble?' she asked warily.

'No, I'm sure you won't,' Meg smiled. 'In any case, the policeman in charge of the investigation is my grandson.' She didn't mention that he wasn't actually a blood relative, not wanting to confuse Taska.

'Okay.' Taska sat down on the edge of one of the cane armchairs.

'Could you possibly think back to when you and Petra found Alan? You told me about one of his pillows being on the armchair in his room. Was anything else odd or out of place?'

Taska thought carefully. 'I not think so.'

'Perhaps there was something on the floor that shouldn't have been there?'

Taska shrugged. 'I pick up bit of rubbish, that is all.'

'Rubbish? What ... like a piece of paper or cardboard?' Meg asked eagerly.

'Cardboard,' she replied. 'Like from a box.'

'I say, old gal, that's it, isn't it?' burst out Albert.

'Yes, as you say, that is it. That's what the accomplice jammed the door lock with.'

Taska looked confused. 'This is important?'

'Yes, my dear, potentially very important. What did you do with the piece of cardboard?'

'I put it in rubbish bin.'

'In Alan's room?'

'Yes.'

'And this was at half past four, when you found Alan's body? Before the police came?'

'Yes.'

'This cardboard, what did it look like?'

Taska screwed up her face, trying to remember. 'It was same as boxes in storeroom,' she said, puzzled. 'Blue boxes that have paper towels in.'

Meg looked at Albert and he nodded his understanding. That sealed it. Someone from inside the home had jammed the door open for the murderer. Almost certainly a member of staff. 'That was really helpful, Taska, thank you. Now, I have another question. Think back to the evening before Alan was murdered. When you first went into his room that evening, were the curtains open or closed?'

'Curtains were closed,' Taska answered promptly.

'One of the day staff would have closed them?'

'Yes. Is so.'

'What are you thinking, m'dear?' asked Albert, not comprehending Meg's purpose.

'If the curtains were already closed, the night staff wouldn't have been able to see the cardboard in the door,' Meg explained. 'I think it's quite likely that whoever drew the curtains is probably the same person who put the cardboard there.'

'Ah yes, I get it. They drew the curtains so no one could see what they'd done.'

'Exactly.'

Taska stood up. 'Is that all your questions?'

'One last one. When you and Petra found Alan at half past four in the morning, were the curtains still exactly the same as they had been the evening before?'

133

'No,' gasped Taska. 'Why I not see this? Curtain on window was closed like in evening. Curtain on door was open.'

'Thank you,' beamed Meg.

When Lauren arrived home, her mum was anxiously looking out of the lounge window. 'I thought you'd be home an hour ago?' she scolded, when Lauren came in the front door.

'Sorry, Mum. I missed the earlier bus and had to wait for the four-twenty.'

'But you finished work at three!'

'Yeah, but I had to stay and do a few things. Sorry, I meant to text you. So much has happened today. Let's grab a coffee and I'll tell you all about it.'

Lauren told her mum the good news first whilst they were in the kitchen waiting for the kettle to boil. Her mum was delighted that Lauren had been offered a job at Britford Lodge. 'But what about your references?' she asked. 'You can hardly get one from The Cedars, can you?'

'That'd be kind of impossible,' Lauren agreed, 'but Mrs Wilkinson is happy to accept a reference from Sharon at the agency, plus one from my tutor at college and a personal reference from Meg.'

'That's nice of her.'

'Yeah. If it wasn't for Meg, Mrs Wilkinson would never have offered me the job.'

They took their steaming mugs through to the lounge and sat down, one each end of the sofa. Lauren then told her mum all about her impromptu job interview, how Ana had confessed to stealing the wallet but had officially been cleared of murder, and how Alan's friend Ed had also been found murdered. She didn't mention that Ed was likely a convicted murderer, or anything else about a possible post office heist, for fear of worrying her mum.

'Two murders now. Does that mean there's a serial killer on the loose?' her mum said nervously.

'Well, if there is, he's only killing old men in their

seventies, so I should think I'm quite safe!' Lauren chuckled, but her mum still looked concerned.

'Listen, Mum, it'll be fine. Try not to worry too much.'

'Just promise me you'll be careful.'

'I'll be careful,' Lauren assured her. She could see that her mum was still upset, so she stayed downstairs, chatting and watching TV with her for most of the evening.

By the time she went up to her bedroom and opened her notebook, it was late and she was tired. And she needed to be up early again in the morning. Just a quick search then. She typed the words 'Edward+Crouch+postoffice+murder' into Google. There were no exact matches, but there was a whole raft of close matches. She looked at the first one, wondering if it would be relevant. She found a report into a murder trial at the Old Bailey back in 1988. The trial was that of three defendants, Pete Blackett, Winston Napier and Teddy Crouch, in what was known as the Westbourne Post Office Heist. Teddy? That was a common shortening of Edward, wasn't it? She read on. It sounded very much like the heist Viv had referred to. But, disappointingly, there was no mention of a gang member called Alan. She clicked on a few of the other articles. And that's where she found one that mentioned the missing unnamed 'fourth man'. Her stomach did a little flip of excitement. Could Alan have been the fourth man? Was that the missing link between Alan and Ed?

Just then, her mum tapped on her bedroom door. 'Is your light still on?' she asked, opening the door a little and peering round it. Seeing Lauren with her laptop open, she tutted. 'You're not still doing research into these murders, are you?'

'No, Mum, of course not,' Lauren lied, mainly out of love for her mum. 'I was just replying to an email. And I was just about finished anyway.' She closed her notepad and wished her mum goodnight. After her mum had gone, she found herself yawning and realised that perhaps she ought to settle down to sleep.

Chapter Twenty-seven

Wednesday 18th January 2023

When Lauren arrived the next morning for another early shift, she was bursting to tell Meg what she'd found out online about the Westbourne Post Office Heist. But that would have to wait until her coffee break; she had work to do first and it was essential to impress the senior staff.

This morning, she worked with a different carer, Jess. Jessica Fitzroy was a thirty-four-year-old mother with a three-year-old son, Connor, whom she talked about constantly. It was 'Connor did this' and 'Connor did that'. Only an inch taller than Lauren, who was five foot two, she was quite overweight with short, very curly brunette hair and an easy-going nature. Despite their age difference, the two carers got on well together, and when they were sent to have their coffee break at the same time, Lauren felt that it might appear rude if she didn't sit with Jess in the staff-room. But it meant that she didn't get a chance to talk to Meg until her lunch break.

Meg spent the morning chatting to the terrible twins, Ruth and Pauline. She had realised overnight that these two ladies had not only been lifelong friends, they had boasted about being two of the home's first residents when it opened eight years ago. Therefore, they'd been here longer than Alan and would've known him from when he first came to Britford Lodge.

'Do you mind if I join you?' she enquired politely on entering the day room after breakfast. The two ladies looked up from their knitting almost simultaneously. 'Please do,' encouraged Ruth just as Pauline said, 'Not at all.'

Meg lowered herself into a chair and set about making general polite conversation, not wanting to jump straight in with her questions. Ruth, at eighty-nine, was a few months younger than Pauline, who had recently turned ninety. Both ladies wore tweed skirts and cashmere jumpers and sported almost identical blue rinses. Much to Meg's private amusement, they also appeared to be knitting identical baby cardigans. She couldn't help but ask the ladies about this.

'Yes, indeed,' admitted Ruth. 'We're using the same pattern. It saves money, you see.'

'I'm knitting this for my great-granddaughter who was born just last month,' added Pauline. 'Whereas Ruth is knitting for her great-grandchild that's due in a few weeks' time.'

'You two really do do everything together, don't you?' chuckled Meg. 'Even down to the births of your great-grandchildren!'

The ladies took turns explaining how they'd met at nursery school and had been at both primary and secondary school together, even staying in the same classes for every subject. They'd taken the same O-levels and both gone to the same school of nursing before working in the same hospitals. They'd even got married and had their first children within months of each other.

'Are you sure you aren't twins?'

Pauline laughed. 'We get asked that a lot.'

'Well, I think it's fantastic that you two have such a wonderful friendship,' Meg stated, her eyes sparkling with fondness for the pair. 'Now, do you mind me asking a few questions about Alan?'

'Ooh, are you investigating?' asked Ruth.

'Yes, we heard that you're good at solving murders,' exclaimed Pauline.

'Albert and his big mouth,' muttered Meg under her breath. 'Well, yes, I may have helped once before,' she answered modestly.

'Go ahead, ask anything you want,' encouraged Ruth.

'Yes, we're only too happy to help,' assured Pauline.

'Can you tell me what Alan was like, before his stroke?' Meg asked.

'He was a grumpy old sod,' Pauline quickly replied. 'Kept himself to himself and didn't like anyone poking into his business.'

'Do you remember that time he dropped his wallet?' prompted Ruth.

'Yes, that's a good example,' agreed Pauline. 'He walked by us in the dining room one time and dropped his wallet on the floor. It was of those folded wallets and it fell open. Ruth picked it up and noticed a photo just poking out of one of the compartments. Being nosy—'

'No more than you were!' interrupted Ruth indignantly.

'True, I was just as curious. You see, no one knew anything about Alan. Anyway, she pulled the photo out and asked Alan if it was of his family.'

'And was it?' asked Meg.

'We don't know. He snatched it off Ruth and told her to mind her own business.'

'Except he didn't put it quite so politely,' added Ruth darkly.

'How odd,' mused Meg. 'Why carry a photo if you don't want anyone else to see it?'

'That's what we thought!' nodded Pauline.

'Can you tell me what was in the photo?

Ruth shut her eyes, trying to remember. 'It was a typical family photo. A young man with a strikingly beautiful woman and two quite small children. That's why I asked if it was his family.'

'And it was definitely Alan in the photo?' checked Meg.

'Well, I think so. Or, at least, I assumed it was.' Ruth didn't sound very certain.

'Thank you.' Meg would need time to ponder on the significance of that one.

'Now, what about visitors, did anyone else ever visit Alan apart from his friend Ed?'

'No, never,' asserted Pauline.

'That poor man,' sighed Ruth. 'He was so devoted to his friend. He must be devastated now Alan's gone.'

Meg bit her tongue. The news about Ed's murder wasn't public knowledge yet. 'What about other residents? Was he especially close to anyone in the home?'

'No, quite the opposite,' replied Ruth, frowning. 'He was that rude to everyone, I don't think there was a single person he hadn't upset.'

'It was like he didn't want anyone getting close to him,' added Pauline.

Meg thought for a moment. 'What about Donald and Frank? I mean, in the short time I've been here, he was always sitting with them.'

'Donald and Frank both like watching TV all day,' Ruth said with a frown, 'but I think it was more that the carers chose to put Alan near the TV with them. I'm not sure that it was *his* choice to sit with them, as such.'

Meg thanked the ladies and set off to find a quiet corner to think things through. If Alan had been so surly with everyone else, it made his friendship with Ed all the more curious. What tied the two men together? What did a convicted murderer have in common with a car mechanic? And why had they both been murdered?

❖

When Lauren was told to take her lunch break early, she grabbed her lunch box and sought out Meg in the day room. She didn't have long before the residents would be summoned to their lunch, so she wanted to take the chance to share her news. 'Mind if I join you?' she asked breezily, when she finally found Meg in a faraway corner.

'Not at all.' Meg looked up and smiled.

'Penny for them?' Lauren asked, as she sat down and opened her bright pink lunch box, selecting a jam sandwich and munching hungrily on it.

Meg quickly outlined her conversation with Ruth and Pauline. 'You see, if Alan was such an unsociable person, it makes me even more puzzled about his friendship with Ed. Whatever was it that bound the two together so tightly?'

139

'I think I might know the answer to that,' Lauren burst out excitedly. She told Meg about the Westbourne Post Office Heist and the mysterious fourth man.

Meg nodded enthusiastically. 'Yes, that could well explain it. Teddy and Ed are both common versions of Edward, and that sounds very much like the crime that Viv said Ed was convicted of. But how can we prove that Alan was the fourth man, if the police were never able to identify him?'

Lauren's face fell. 'Yeah, I suppose that's gonna be hard now that they're both dead.'

'Perhaps we should find out more about the other two members of this gang?' suggested Meg. 'But we need to be careful. At least one of them was a cold-blooded murderer. What did you say their names were?'

'Winston Napier and Peter Blackett.'

'Have you goggled them, or whatever it is you do?'

'Googled,' corrected an amused Lauren. 'And, no, I haven't. I didn't have time last night, but I'll get right on it as soon as I get home tonight.'

Meg didn't get a chance to reply, as Jess came into the day room to inform Meg that it was lunchtime.

'Whatever are you doing in here?' Jess asked Lauren. 'You shouldn't be eating your lunch in here, you know.'

'Whyever not?' demanded Lauren. 'Meg's my friend and I wanted to talk to her.'

'But you shouldn't be doing that while you're on duty. If one of the seniors catches you, you'll be in trouble.'

'But it's my break time,' Lauren replied, pouting trucu-lently.

'But you are in uniform, my dear,' Meg pointed out as kindly as she could. 'Other residents might think you're on duty.'

'And Mrs Wilkinson doesn't like it if we spend too much time with one resident,' said Jess. 'You've got to be seen to be helping everyone, not playing favourites.'

Lauren reluctantly conceded that they had a point. 'I'll get back to the staffroom straight away,' she said, disappointed but equally anxious not to get herself into trouble. 'I could always pop in to see you tomorrow, Meg? I've got a day off so I won't be in uniform.'

'Why don't we meet at the farm café?' Meg proposed. 'Have elevenses together. How about ten-thirty?'

'It's a deal.' Lauren winked at Meg as Jess turned and left the day room. They could talk a lot more freely at the café, and there'd be no risk of her getting into trouble.

Chapter Twenty-eight

After lunch, Meg emerged from the dining room to hear Dan's voice in the office. She hovered in the hallway, waiting for him. Regretfully, she couldn't make out what he was saying, and she didn't like to be too obvious about trying to listen in as there was a steady trickle of residents and carers leaving the dining room.

'Meg,' a warm voice said behind her as she was looking at one of the pieces of artwork on the hall walls. She turned round, acting surprised.

'Dan, how lovely to see you!'

'And you just happened to be in the hall, I suppose?'

'Pure coincidence,' she agreed, with a wicked twinkle in her eye.

'How are you?' he enquired.

'Oh, I'm very well, thank you. I have a bit of information for you, if you're interested.'

'I bet you do,' Dan sighed. 'I thought Viv had made it clear to you yesterday that you were to leave this alone. There's clearly at least one very dangerous murderer at large.'

'He made it crystal clear,' acknowledged Meg unabashedly, 'but I've been thinking about our two victims. By all accounts, Alan was not a very friendly person before his stroke, which makes his friendship with Ed all the more significant, don't you agree?'

'Ye-es,' said Dan cautiously.

'Lauren did a bit of research on Edward Crouch. Can you confirm that he was convicted for his part in the West-bourne Post Office Heist that occurred in October 1987?'

'What do you know about that?' Dan asked, astonished. 'Hang on,' he looked around to see who else was nearby, 'not here, it's too exposed. Let's go into the conservatory, where it's more private.'

Once safely installed in the deserted conservatory, Meg repeated what Lauren had told her. 'Do you think it's possible that Alan was the missing fourth man?'

'I don't know how you keep getting to things one step ahead of me,' Dan said, shaking his head. 'But yes, it's what I'm also beginning to think now, having just read up on that old case.'

'Is it true the police had no clue at all about the identity of this fourth man?'

'Apparently not. The other gang members all refused to name him. It was odd, because both Winston Napier and Edward Crouch were quick to give up Peter Blackett as the shooter. Apparently, the gang had agreed in advance to use replica weapons for the heist. It was Peter Blackett who substituted his replica for a real gun without telling the other gang members.'

'And Peter Blackett was the one who shot the post-mistress?'

'Yes.'

Meg shivered at the thought of such a horrible crime. 'I trust he's still safely locked up behind bars?'

Dan hesitated.

'He's not, is he?' Meg demanded.

'Peter Blackett was released on licence three months ago, having served his thirty-five-year term.' Dan then spoke urgently. 'And that's why I don't want you involved in this. He's a nasty piece of work.'

Meg nodded her understanding. 'How come Ed was out of prison so much sooner?'

'The judge accepted that the other gang members had not intended to harm anyone. Winston and Ed both served fifteen years for their parts.'

'If Alan and Ed have both been murdered, doesn't that put Winston in danger too?'

'We're one step ahead of you on that one. I looked into Winston's whereabouts, and he died of natural causes five years ago.'

'So, it's looking likely that Peter Blackett is the murderer?'

'It's a good lead but we don't have any evidence to prove that the two murders are definitely linked, let alone anything to prove that Blackett is responsible.'

'But you're going to question him?'

'He's living in a halfway house in Southall, London. It's not our patch. But we have asked The Met to question him as to his whereabouts for both murders and to check out any alibis he gives.'

'What about the evidence from Alan's fingernails?' Meg asked. 'Won't that prove he did it?'

'It might well do. But, contrary to the public's popular perception, DNA matches aren't instant. We've asked the lab to expedite a comparison as a matter of urgency, but that might still take a day or two.'

Meg was disappointed but, as Dan had said, they had no evidence that Peter Blackett was the murderer, even if that did seem like the most obvious explanation.

'What happens next?' she asked.

'So far as you are concerned, nothing,' Dan said firmly. 'You must stop investigating this, Meg. If that man is in Salisbury . . .'

'I get it,' she said with a nod.

'And tell that to Lauren too. I don't want either of you putting yourselves in danger.'

Meg agreed wholeheartedly.

'And, Meg,' Dan added, 'I know it seems likely that Alan was the fourth man, but we still have to prove that too. We could be putting two and two together and leaping to the wrong conclusion.'

Meg acknowledged that and said goodbye to Dan, who needed to hurry off. Then she started thinking of how she might be able to confirm their hypothesis.

❖

What the hell was that nosy old bitch up to?

She'd been crossing the hall when she overheard the snippet of conversation. She distinctly heard Meg mention 'Edward Crouch'. The name had pulled her up short, and then she'd caught the words 'Westbourne Post Office Heist'.

She'd forced herself to keep moving, not wanting to draw attention. But this was terrible news. It must mean that Teddy's body had already been discovered!

But why would that detective be discussing it with Meg of all people?

Surely, they couldn't have connected the two murders? He'd assured her they wouldn't.

But one thing was certain. Meg Thornton had been going around asking a lot of questions ever since Alan's murder. And she seemed very pally with the inspector. That couldn't be good.

I'll text him later, tell him about the old busybody.

🏵

Lauren had just finished her shift and was leaving the office on her way to the staffroom when she noticed a thin man entering the front door. He looked not much older than her and somewhat harassed. 'Can I help you?' she called out to him.

'Yeah, please,' he smiled nervously. 'I'm Alan Watts' grandson. I was told I could collect his personal belongings this afternoon.'

Lauren thought furiously. She hadn't known that Alan had any family. But a grandson meant he had at least one child. And had presumably been married. Why was she only finding out about this just now?

'Of course,' she said brightly. 'Come into the office.' She knocked and preceded him in. 'Alan Watts' grandson,' she explained to the two senior care assistants, Sarah and Petra, who were both there, the one about to go off duty from the early shift and the other in charge of the late.

'Ah yes, come in.' Sarah seemed to be expecting him.

'Can we release his belongings yet?' asked Petra, surprised.

'Yes, I meant to tell you; that detective inspector was here earlier,' Sarah assured her. 'The police are holding some personal documents and other bits and pieces,' she informed Alan's grandson, 'but they've said that you can collect whatever else is left in his room. If there's anything you don't want to take, you can leave it in the room and we'll dispose of it for you.'

'Er, thank you. Sorry, but I don't know which room was his.'

'Not a problem, I'll take you,' offered Petra.

'Or I don't mind going,' chipped in Lauren.

'You're off duty,' snapped Sarah hastily. 'Let the late staff handle this.'

'Okay then.' Lauren shrugged, disappointed. 'Well, it was a shame to meet under these circumstances, but please know that I'm very sorry for your loss,' she said to the young man, who was looking bemused.

'It's okay,' he replied. 'I never actually met my Grandad Charlie.'

Lauren's pulse suddenly raced. Charlie? The young man must have read her thoughts. 'Yeah, I suppose you knew him as Alan, didn't you? I gather he dropped his first name Charles in favour of his middle name. I've no idea why. Like I said, we never met. But my mum was his daughter and she sent me here when the police phoned to say we could collect his stuff. I doubt there's much we'll want, to be honest, but Mum wanted me to see if he had any old family photos.'

Lauren could scarcely believe her luck. Alan was evidently born Charles Alan Watts! No wonder she hadn't been able to find a birth record or any other information about him. She'd been looking for the wrong name!

'Run along, Lauren,' chivvied Petra kindly. 'It's time you got yourself home. You too, Sarah,' she added. 'I can handle this.'

Chapter Twenty-nine

Lauren had no choice but to go to the staffroom with Sarah, but she changed into her civvies as quickly as she could and called a cheerful goodbye whilst Sarah was still only half-dressed. She hurried along the corridor to Alan's room and peeped through the porthole; Alan's grandson appeared to be alone. She knocked quietly and slipped into the room without waiting.

'Oh, hi again,' said the young man, looking up.

'I just wanted to apologise,' Lauren began.

'Apologise? What for?' he replied, looking puzzled.

'I was so rude earlier, introducing you as Alan's grandson when I should have asked your name and introduced you properly. I'm Lauren Peachy, by the way.'

'Hello, Lauren Peachy,' he grinned sheepishly. 'I'm Kieran Knowles.'

'Nice to meet you, Kieran. Listen, this is going to sound odd, but we like to write a kind of obituary for each of our residents when they pass. Something for the other residents to read. But we know so little about Alan.'

'I really can't help you there,' he replied, shaking his head. 'Like I said, I never met him.'

'No, but I wondered if perhaps I could contact your mother?'

'I'm not sure she'll want to help; she lost touch with her father when her parents divorced. But I suppose you could try her, if you really want to.'

'Could you possibly give me her number?'

'Surely you have it on file already, seeing as you contacted her when Grandad died?' he replied, frowning.

Damn, she hadn't thought this through. *Think quickly!*

'Ah! I don't suppose you have an up-to-date mobile number for her, though? I know the office had a difficult time trying to get in touch with her.' She kept her fingers metaphorically crossed.

'Okay. Have you got your phone on you?'

'Of course.' Lauren whipped it out of her pocket and Kieran sent the number to her.

'Thanks, I'm really grateful for that.' Lauren smiled at him.

'That's okay, I'm just about finished anyway; there's really nothing of interest here. I don't know why Mum made such a fuss about me coming here, to be honest.'

'That's mums for you, isn't it?'

She walked to the door with him, parting ways in the car park as he climbed into a sporty little Golf and she headed for the bus stop.

⚙

Lauren could scarcely wait until she got home. As soon as she'd exchanged a quick 'How was your day?' with her mum and made a cup of coffee, she fled to her bedroom, impatient to make the phone call. But, first, she needed to look up Kieran's family history. She found what she was looking for on her mum's genealogy website, one she'd used numerous times in her research.

Bingo! Kieran was the only son of Christopher Knowles and Theresa Watts.

She pressed the call button on the number Kieran had given her.

'Hello,' a female answered warily.

'Mrs Theresa Knowles?' Lauren checked.

'If you're selling something, I'm not interested,' the female said tersely.

'I'm not selling, honest,' Lauren reassured her quickly, hoping she wouldn't end the call. 'Please, just let me explain why I'm calling you.'

'Go on. But, if this is a scam, you'd better know that I will report this call.'

'That's very reasonable. My name's Lauren Peachy and I'm a carer at the Britford Lodge Care Home in Salisbury.'

'I've already been notified about my father's death.'

'I know. I just wanted to pass on my condolences for

148

your loss and ask for a few minutes of your time to help with an obituary I'm writing.'

'An obituary? What... for a local newspaper or something?' She sounded incredulous.

'Nothing so grand, I'm afraid,' Lauren explained. 'It's just something we do when a resident passes, a mark of respect. Something the other residents can read and remember him by.'

'Ha! I doubt anyone will want to read that!'

'Why?'

'My father was a petty criminal. He lied, he stole, he cheated on my mother, and he was a thoroughly unpleasant person, if half of what she told me was true.'

'Begging your pardon, but is that your memory of him too?'

'Well, not exactly. But I was only a child when I last saw him.'

'May I ask what your childhood memories of him were like?'

'Well!' She sounded taken aback. There was a pause. 'What can I say? He was my dad. I idolised him when I was little. What girl doesn't idolise her dad? But he was always promising me things and then letting me down. Like the time he promised me a new bike for my tenth birthday but then didn't even show up for my party, let alone bring a present. Mum said he was working but I didn't believe her. It broke my heart at the time, thinking he didn't care. Years later, I learnt that he'd been nicked for stealing the bike he was going to give to me. Then, one day, when I was thirteen, he suddenly walked out on us and never came back. I asked Mum about it once, but she told me it was better if I didn't know. Told me never to ask again. Over the years, the more I learnt about my dad and what he was really like, the less I wanted to know about him, so I never asked her again.'

'I'm so sorry . . .' Lauren began.

'Water under the bridge,' Mrs Knowles snapped back brusquely.

'Can I ask if your mother is still alive?' Lauren was kicking herself for not looking that up before phoning.

'No, she died of cancer nearly ten years ago. Now, is that everything? Only, I have work to do.'

'Of course, thank you very much for your time. I'm so sorry—'

The call was ended before Lauren could finish. 'How rude!' she said to herself.

She was picking over what Theresa Knowles had said and doing some more research online, now that she knew Alan's full name, when her phone suddenly rang. Snatching it up, she saw that it was Theresa's number. Odd.

'Hello again, Mrs Knowles,' Lauren began.

'Actually, this is Chris Knowles. Her husband. I demand to know whatever it was you said to my wife that has upset her so much.'

Lauren apologised profusely and repeated her cover story of researching for an in-house obituary once again.

'Well, you've really stirred up a hornet's nest, dragging up old memories like that. You obviously don't know much about the family, do you?'

'No, I don't, Mr Knowles, but that was precisely the reason for my call. I'm genuinely sorry if I've caused any distress.'

'Okay, well, listen to me. I knew Charlie Watts a long time before I started dating Tessa. My parents were friends of Tessa's mum, Rita. Charlie was a petty criminal who spent more time with his so-called mates than with his wife and family.'

'I see. I don't suppose you happen to know who any of those mates were, do you?' Lauren asked hopefully. 'It's just that I'd like to interview them for this obituary, you see.'

'Look, you sound like a nice young lady. My best advice is to keep well away from that crowd. I mean, Charlie was only on the fringes of the gang, but some of those blokes were put away for serious crimes – including murder. They're not people you want to mess with.'

'People like Peter Blackett?' Lauren took a chance.

'If you know about Blackett, you know very well what I mean. He was a right bastard.'

'And Charlie was involved with Blackett?'

'No, he was never into anything big, like some of the stuff they got up to. Charlie was strictly a small-time criminal.'

'Blackett's gang wasn't the reason Charlie walked out on his family then?' Lauren pushed, hoping to get at what she suspected.

'Good grief, no! I don't know where you got that idea. Charlie didn't walk out on his family; Rita kicked him out. She caught him cheating on her with one of the slappers that used to hang around with that crowd.'

'Oh, I see.'

'No, you don't. That slapper accused Charlie of getting her pregnant. But, as Rita said, it could've been any one of that crowd. She got so mad about it that she demanded the woman do a paternity test on the baby.'

'And did she?' asked Lauren breathlessly.

'Yeah, and it wasn't Charlie who was the baby's father. It was Blackett!'

Lauren gasped in surprise before apologising again and saying goodbye.

Chapter Thirty

Thursday 19th January 2023

The rain had finally stopped and a weak sun was trying to break through the clouds. Meg arrived at the farm shop café before Lauren this time. She'd had a difficult job persuading Albert not to accompany her when he found out where she was going. It was lucky she hadn't told him anything about the Westbourne Post Office Heist or the possibility that Peter Blackett had been bumping off his old gang members. He might never have allowed her to come on her own if he'd known! But she couldn't tell him; she didn't trust him not to blurt it out to someone else.

Meg ordered a pot of tea and settled into the same corner table they'd sat at a week previously. Lauren arrived before her pot of tea, so she insisted on going back to the counter to ask for an Americano to be added to the order, then settled in her chair next to where Lauren was now sitting. They waited until the drinks had been delivered before sharing their news, not wanting to be overheard.

Lauren allowed Meg to go first, so Meg shared what she had learnt from Dan. Then Lauren revealed her news about Alan's grandson turning up, and the fact that he'd called Alan 'Grandad Charlie'.

'That meant I could do some proper research into Alan,' Lauren said, pulling her notebook from her large bag and opening it on the table.

'Charles Alan Watts was born in Poole in Dorset on 15th March 1946. He married Rita Jennings in 1969 and they had two children, Philip and Theresa, born in 1972 and 1975 respectively.'

'That ties in with the family photo Ruth described,' put in Meg. 'Alan, or Charlie as he was probably known back then, with his wife, Rita, and two young children.'

'Yes. But the marriage didn't last. Charlie and Rita were divorced in 1989.'

'Interesting, that was not long after the Westbourne Heist,' Meg commented dryly.

'Yeah, and I bet you're thinking exactly the same as I was thinking,' Lauren replied, 'but I did some more snooping and you won't believe what I've found out!'

'Go on.' Meg could tell that Lauren had big news to impart.

Lauren told Meg about her conversations with Theresa and Chris Knowles.

'Goodness gracious, you've established that Charlie, aka Alan Watts, actually knew Peter Blackett!' Meg gasped.

'Yes, but according to Chris, Charlie wasn't involved in Blackett's crimes.'

'That's what he says. He might have been lying, or perhaps he didn't know.'

'That's what I thought,' agreed Lauren, 'but what's really interesting is that Blackett fathered a baby!'

'And you didn't find any record of this before?'

'No.' Lauren repeated what Chris Knowles had told her.'According to official records, Peter Blackett never married and never had children. But if there's an illegitimate child of his . . .'

'He or she could be the accomplice!'

They fell silent for a moment.

'We could be leaping to conclusions, here,' Meg said cautiously.

'But it's obvious, isn't it?' protested Lauren.

'Well, it's a reasonable assumption that Blackett killed Ed, otherwise known as Teddy Crouch, who was a former gang member from the Westbourne Heist. But the police still have to find the evidence to prove that. Then we're assuming that Blackett also killed Alan, which we don't know for sure, yet.'

'But when the police get the DNA results back and the drop of blood and skin samples match Peter Blackett, that will clinch it,' said Lauren.

'Yes, that will prove that Blackett killed Alan. It still

doesn't prove that Alan was the missing fourth man.'

'Yes, but that's the only motive for Blackett to murder Alan, surely?'

'The only motive that we know of,' cautioned Meg.

'What other motive could there be?' exclaimed Lauren.

'Well, if Blackett's intended target all along was Edward Crouch, who we know was definitely involved in the Westbourne Heist, that could mean that Alan was killed because of his friendship with Ed. Perhaps to muddy the waters?'

'Hmm.' Lauren wasn't sure she agreed, but she could see Meg's point.

'If only we could find another piece of evidence to link Alan to the Westbourne Heist.'

'There might be a way,' Lauren suggested. 'Sarah told Kieran that he could leave anything he didn't want to take in Alan's room and we'd dispose of it. Supposing there's a clue left behind?'

'It's unlikely, given that the police will have searched Alan's room thoroughly. But I suppose it wouldn't hurt to see if I can sneak into the room to have a quick look, if it's no longer a crime scene.'

'I'll come with you!' Lauren said excitedly.

'No, my dear, you can't. You're on a day off today, and I think it would be better if you didn't come into the home with me. It might raise suspicions.'

'Why?'

'Don't forget, we believe there's an accomplice among the staff who let the murderer into Alan's room. We should be very careful from now on about being seen together in the home.'

'Ah, and you think the accomplice might be reporting back to Blackett?'

'Assuming he's the murderer, yes. It's quite likely, isn't it?'

Lauren had to concede that one. 'Okay, suppose I do some more research into the possible accomplice this afternoon? I could start by working out how old that illegitimate child of Blackett's would be now and compare that against the list of staff?'

'That would be a good start,' agreed Meg. 'Although we also need to consider what else could connect Blackett and his accomplice. It might also be worth looking into other possible connections between Ed and Alan, in case the Westbourne Heist isn't the connection.'

'Well, I did some research into Ed too,' Lauren informed Meg, after taking a long drink of her rapidly cooling coffee.

'Good. What did you find out?'

'Edward Crouch was also born in Poole in Dorset, on 24th June 1956. He never married, or, at least, not that I could find out. He was arrested in December 1987 for his part in the Westbourne Heist and sentenced to life with a minimum recommendation of fifteen years in prison. He was released in 2002, shortly after which he moved to Wilton and got a job working as a car mechanic.'

'So that gives us another two points of connection,' Meg commented. 'Both men were born in Poole and perhaps knew each other there. And they were both mechanics, so they could well have worked together.'

'Yes,' agreed Lauren, 'but I still think the most likely explanation is that Alan was the missing fourth man.'

When Meg and Lauren left the farm shop café, they agreed to walk back separately so that anyone looking out of Britford Lodge wouldn't see them together. Lauren walked off briskly whilst Meg took a stroll round the shop, succumbing to a small packet of chocolate truffles, before making her way back up the footpath.

She made it back comfortably in time for lunch, where she then struggled to fend off a plethora of questions from Albert. He was getting quite indignant at being excluded, but she couldn't seem to make him see the need for discretion, the dining room being far too public a place to discuss these matters. After lunch, she took him through to the conservatory and read him the riot act.

'This isn't a game, Albert. We suspect that a member of staff aided the murderer by wedging Alan's patio door open. Therefore, we cannot, we *must* not, discuss this matter anywhere where we could be overheard. We just don't know who we can trust!'

'Steady on, old gal. I think you're getting a bit paranoid here, what?'

Meg took a deep breath. It was no good; she'd have to tell him about Ed and the post office heist and Blackett. 'What I am about to tell you is absolutely for your ears only. Don't you dare mention one word of this to anyone else!'

'Look here. I said I'm sorry for giving the game away the other day.'

Meg accepted his apology and succinctly told him everything.

'This Blackett sounds like a very dangerous character,' growled Albert. 'I can see why you're so concerned. Rightly so too. But, surely, all we need to do now is wait for the police to get all their DNA results and what have you, and the case will be solved. No need for you to put yourself in any danger.'

'Don't you see, even if the police prove that Blackett is the murderer, they still have to find him. And they have to prove that Alan was indeed the fourth man. Then there's the little matter of finding out who the accomplice is.'

'Just don't want to see anything happen to you, old gal,' Albert said gruffly, looking awkwardly at the floor. 'Perhaps you'd allow me to escort you next time you need to go anywhere?'

'Thank you, Albert. I appreciate that,' she said softly, touched by his evident concern. 'Maybe you can help me this afternoon. I want to get into Alan's room, have a snoop around anything of Alan's that his grandson might have left behind.'

Albert agreed to act as lookout for her.

Involving him seemed to have bucked him up no end, but Meg just hoped that he would remember to keep schtum.

Chapter Thirty-one

Meg waited until the staff had gone into the office for handover before heading to Alan's room. That meant all the late staff were accounted for as well as Maureen, and the office door was closed. Some of the early staff would still be on their lunch break, and the others were busy helping the stragglers from the dining room. Consequently, the downstairs corridor was deserted, just as she'd hoped.

'Right,' she whispered to Albert. 'You know what you've got to do?'

'I'm on lookout duty,' he answered promptly. 'I'll keep watch port and starboard, and as soon as I see anyone approaching, I'll walk towards them and employ distraction techniques, as discussed.'

'Excellent.' Meg nodded then slipped quietly into Alan's room.

She looked around. The bed had been stripped and the curtains taken down; no doubt everything was being thoroughly cleaned. There were two cardboard boxes next to the dressing table with a yellow Post-it note on top of one. When she approached, she could also see three black bin bags tied up and labelled as clothes to go to a charity shop. The Post-it note read 'Books to be given to the residents'.

Ignoring the bags, she pulled the dressing-table stool closer to the boxes, sat on it and pulled out a pair of disposable gloves from her pocket that she'd acquired from the cleaner. With gloves on, she opened one of the boxes and started methodically taking out each book, shaking it to see if anything was inside, then setting it to one side. Nothing. She quickly returned all the books to the box and started on the second box. Two books in and she suddenly froze, hearing Albert's voice in the corridor outside. 'What-ho, Hazel.'

She couldn't hear her reply but then she heard Albert

again. 'Just stretching my legs, y'know. Taking an inside walk. It's too damn cold outside for my liking.'

Meg waited for a couple more minutes but heard nothing else, so she carried on checking the next book. Three books later, she pulled out a large *Colour Atlas of the World*. She shook it and was about to put it to one side when she realised that something had rustled inside the glossy book jacket. When she examined it, she saw that the edges of the jacket had been almost invisibly taped to the hard cover of the book underneath, so that whatever was contained there would not fall out. Carefully, she prised the tape up. A large brown envelope was inside the jacket. It appeared to have originally been taped to the book's hard cover, but that tape had worn loose with old age. She had a quick peek inside and could see a number of newspaper cuttings, yellowing with age. With trembling hands, she set it on the bed to look at later, before checking the remaining books. There was nothing else of interest, so she quickly returned all the books to the box.

She struggled to push herself up off the stool, having sat with her knees bent for too long. She replaced the stool, picked up the brown envelope and was walking towards the door when she heard Albert's voice again. 'What-ho, Jess.'

Quickly, she flattened herself against the wall to the side of the door so that she wouldn't be visible if anyone looked in.

'I say, are you going into Alan's room?' she heard Albert exclaim loudly, and her heart leapt into her throat. 'Isn't it still a crime scene?'

This time, she could hear Jess' reply, right outside the door, although her thumping heart was doing its best to drown out everything. 'The police have said it's okay, Albert. I'm just going to clear out the stuff Alan's grandson left behind in here and then get the room ready for the new resident arriving tomorrow.'

'Look, sorry to bother you when you've got a job to do, but I've got a bit of a problem.'

'I'm sorry to hear that, Albert. Is there anything I can do?'

'Well, it's a bit embarrassing really. You see, I haven't

158

been able to . . . well, y'know? I haven't, umm, been to the toilet. . . for a few days. Feeling rather uncomfortable.'

'Ah, you haven't had your bowels open?' Jess clarified. Meg could just imagine Albert squirming, as he hated discussing anything personal like that. But bless him for his quick thinking.

'Ah yes, that's it.'

'Come along to the treatment room and I'll get you a dose of Dulcolax.'

Meg heard footsteps retreating and as soon as she could no longer hear them, she cautiously opened the door. Seeing the coast was clear, she hurried back towards the hall, not breathing until she was safely in the lift going upstairs. She hid the envelope in her underwear drawer, removed her gloves and quickly went back downstairs again to find Albert anxiously pacing in the hall.

'Am I glad to see you, old gal!' He heaved a sigh of relief.

'Albert, you were simply splendid! Thank you so much for going above and beyond the call of duty.'

'Don't mention it. You know I'd do anything for you, m'dear.'

'Did she give you some of that medicine?'

'Yes,' he replied miserably, 'and she stood over me while I drank it. Made me swallow every last drop of it too.'

'I'm so sorry.' Meg tried hard to keep a straight face but she just couldn't.

'Harrumph,' Albert snorted, but then even he couldn't resist a smile. 'Tell me it was at least worth it?' he asked.

'Oh yes, just wait until you see what I found.' She beckoned him to the lift.

'Where are we going?' he hissed.

'I've hidden it in my room,' she explained.

'I can't go into your room!' he spluttered, eyes open wide at the thought.

'Come on, Albert. Don't be silly.'

'It's not the done thing, old gal,' he objected, shaking his head stubbornly.

'Well, we can't look at it in a public place where anybody might see it!'

Albert considered that for a moment then, reluctantly, followed her into the lift.

When they got to her room, he edged just inside the door and stood there awkwardly.

'You can sit down,' Meg pointed out.

'I'd rather stand.'

'You're not going to see much from over there. Now, sit in the chair, please, before I have to make you.'

Albert perched on the edge of the chair. 'Where are you going to sit?'

'I can sit on the bed. Now, close your eyes, please,' Meg said, pulling on another pair of disposable gloves.

'Why? What are you going to do?' Albert asked suspiciously.

'I'm going to retrieve the envelope I found from my underwear drawer.'

Albert immediately screwed his eyes shut and refused to open them again until she assured him that her unmentionables were no longer on view.

She opened the envelope and pulled out a cluster of a dozen or so newspaper cuttings carefully paperclipped together. She glanced at the dates written in untidy writing at the top of each and realised they were already in date order. She passed a pair of gloves to Albert and instructed him to put them on, to avoid contaminating the cuttings. Starting with the oldest one, she read it in silence then passed it to Albert, who did the same. Only when they'd finished all of them did they speak.

'Oh, my goodness me,' said Albert.

'Exactly,' agreed Meg. 'That is conclusive proof, I would say, that Alan was the fourth man in the Westbourne Post Office Heist.'

'Absolutely! He obviously followed the case very closely.'

'Well, I suppose he would, wouldn't he?'

'He even highlighted the references to the unnamed man, the getaway driver.' Albert shook his head in disbelief.

'Yes, indeed. I'm guessing that's what he wanted to confess,' Meg wondered aloud.

'Bound to be. But why now? After all these years?'

'I would surmise that he knew that Blackett had been released from prison. Perhaps he was afraid of Blackett coming to get his revenge? After all, Alan, or rather Charlie, got off scot-free,' Meg suggested. Albert nodded thoughtfully.

'I must say,' Albert sounded deadly serious, 'I'm rather bothered by the idea of the missing gun. Who do you suppose had that?'

'Good question.' Meg was silent for a while. 'Viv said that Ed's place had been turned over. I have a horrible feeling that Blackett was looking for something.'

'I wonder if he found it.' Albert pondered. A chill descended over the room at the thought.

Chapter Thirty-two

Albert escaped at the earliest opportunity, terrified at the thought of one of the staff finding him in Meg's room. That was fine with Meg, who had phone calls to make.

First, she phoned Dan. After a predictable lecture about the risk she had taken in searching Alan's room, he thanked her.

'I can't believe the CSIs missed that one,' he said bitterly. 'If it hadn't been for you, we would've lost an important piece of evidence.'

'It's quite possible that the envelope only came loose when the CSI checked the book, and it took me checking it again to be able to hear it move,' she suggested, worried that someone was going to get into trouble.

'I suppose that's possible,' he said begrudgingly. 'I'll send a PC over to pick it up and take it to the lab. I'm guessing you both handled everything?'

'No, we used disposable gloves,' Meg said smugly. 'A DCI's widow knows better than to handle potential evidence.'

'That's great.' Dan sounded impressed. 'If the lab finds only Alan's fingerprints on the envelope and cuttings, that will seal it. He must be the fourth man.'

Meg then phoned Lauren from her mobile.

'I'm sorry,' Lauren began guiltily. 'I haven't done any more digging into the accomplice yet. I kind of, well, I came home and fell asleep.'

'That's okay,' Meg replied with a smile. 'I often have an afternoon nap. But I wasn't phoning about the accomplice.' She told Lauren what she'd found in Alan's room. Lauren was suitably impressed. 'Is it okay if I tell Viv this evening?' she asked.

'You're going on another date already?' Meg asked.

'We're going to the cinema to see the second *Avatar* film. Neither of us have had a chance yet.'

'Who or what is *Avatar*?' Meg asked. Lauren explained, but Meg wasn't sure she was any the wiser.

'Well, I hope you have fun. And, yes, I've already told Dan, so there's no harm in you mentioning it to Viv; he probably already knows. I hope you're not going to pump him about the case, though. He might think you're just using him to get information.'

'Don't worry, I'll make sure he doesn't get the wrong impression,' Lauren said enigmatically. Meg left it at that.

Having finished her phone calls, Meg reviewed her list of the fifteen staff members on duty before Alan was murdered. She may as well finish talking to everyone in case Lauren's theory about the accomplice didn't pan out. After all, they might never be able to identify who Blackett's illegitimate child was. She hadn't mentioned it to Dan, for fear it might sound too fanciful.

Kai was in the day room doing the afternoon tea round when she walked in, and he was on her list. She watched for a moment to assess what direction he was moving in then positioned herself so that he came to her last.

'Hello, Meg. Tea with milk, no sugar?' checked Kai, already pouring tea into a mug. She nodded and he added the milk, stirring it before passing her the mug.

'If you don't mind me asking, is your family originally from China?' she asked.

'My mum is,' he replied.

'Ah, I thought there was something slightly oriental about your looks. Not that you sound at all Chinese.'

Kai laughed. 'My mum came to this country when she went to university, which is where she met my dad. He's a blond-haired, blue-eyed Londoner; they couldn't be more different if they tried! My sisters and I were all born in Southampton, and we've all inherited mum's hair colour and eyes. We get a lot of curious looks when we speak; no one expects a Hampshire accent from someone who looks Chinese.'

'How many sisters do you have?'

'Three,' he replied. 'And, before you ask, yes, they kept trying for a boy until I came along. My mum was just grateful she wasn't forced to stop after one child, the way her friend was back in China.'

'Yes, that must've been very hard if you wanted more than one child.'

'Particularly if the first child was a girl,' Kai remarked sourly.

'Yes, I'm sure.' Meg paused. 'Tell me, Kai, were you on duty Tuesday last week, the day before Alan died? I'm only asking because—'

'You're investigating his murder.' Kai interrupted what she had been going to say. At Meg's surprised look, he said, 'The staff are all talking about why you ask so many questions. Then one of the residents told Stef how you've already helped to solve one murder and now you're investigating this one.'

'Do all the staff know that?' Meg asked, worried.

'I should think so. We do tend to gossip in the staffroom.'

Meg fell silent. That probably meant that the accomplice already knew. She'd have to be very careful from now on.

'It's okay,' Kai wrongly interpreted her hesitation, 'you can ask me anything you want. I have nothing to hide, and the sooner this is cleared up, the better, so far as I'm concerned.'

'Thank you. I've been trying to find out who would've closed the curtains in Alan's room the evening before he was murdered. I don't suppose you've any idea? Or does someone go round closing all the curtains at the same time?'

'No, the residents sometimes close their curtains themselves and sometimes the staff close them, depending on who first goes into a room after dusk has fallen. Of course, Alan couldn't have closed his curtains himself.' He thought for a moment then shook his head. 'I was on night duty that night, with Petra, Taska and Jess. I went into all the downstairs rooms after handover, checking if anyone needed anything. But by then the curtains were all closed. And probably had been for some time; it gets dark so early still. Sorry, that's probably not a lot of help.'

'No, that's fine,' Meg smiled at him.

'If you think of any other questions, feel free to ask. Good luck to you if you can solve this before the police!'

As Kai walked away, Meg metaphorically ticked another name off her list.

Lauren had tried at least a dozen different tops on when getting ready for her date with Viv. She couldn't believe that she was so nervous. She *never* got nervous before a date! As a result, when the doorbell rang, she had barely finished dressing and was yet to comb her hair. She glanced in her mirror, gave it a ruffle with her hands and decided it would do. That was the beauty of having short hair! She raced downstairs, but her mum had beaten her to the door and was chatting to Viv in the hall.

'Lauren, you never told me that Viv was Jamaican!' her mum exclaimed.

'Because it wasn't relevant,' Lauren retorted, wondering why on earth her mum was making such a big deal out of it. 'In any case, he's British, Mum. Same as you and me. His parents were Jamaican, but so what?' She looked at Viv, afraid that he might have been offended but was surprised to see him laughing at her.

'There's no need to get so worked up. Your mum asked if I was of Jamaican heritage, that's all.'

'But why?' Lauren demanded.

'Because your dad and I spent our honeymoon in Jamaica,' her mum replied. 'It was such a beautiful place and the people were so friendly. I was asking Viv where he used to live there, but he tells me he's never actually been to Jamaica.'

'Oh.' Lauren was taken aback. She hadn't known that her parents had ever been to the Caribbean, much less Jamaica.

'One day, when you two have some time, I'll dig out the photo album and I can show it to you both.'

'Thank you, Mrs Peachy. That would be lovely,' Viv said.

'Oh, please, call me Bekka,' her mum insisted.

'Thank you, Bekka. Now, if your daughter is ready, we really need to be going.'

Lauren grabbed her coat and handbag. 'Don't wait up, Mum,' she whispered, as she passed her on the way to the door.

Once Viv had pulled out of Lauren's estate onto the A338 to Salisbury, he asked her how her day had been. She told him about Kieran, her conversations with the Knowleses and her meeting with Meg in the farm shop café. Viv was astounded to learn that Blackett apparently had an illegitimate child. 'We'll look into that straight away,' he assured her. Then she told him about her phone call from Meg and what she had found in Alan's room.

'Yes, Dan told me about that. She really is quite remarkable, isn't she?'

'Oh yes. I'm not sure whether I wish I'd been taught by her, 'cos I'm sure she was a brilliant teacher, or whether it would have been terrifying. She doesn't miss a thing!'

Viv laughed. 'Well, it's great that we can now identify Alan as the missing getaway driver. That ties him to Edward Crouch and makes it very likely that Peter Blackett murdered them both. All we need to do now is get a match with the DNA from Alan's room, and we can ask The Met to arrest him.'

'You won't go to London to arrest him yourself?' Lauren asked, surprised.

'No, we leave that to the local guys. But they'll bring him down here so we can question and charge him.'

'What about Ed's murder? Have you got any news on that?'

'The preliminary post-mortem report says that he'd been dead for between thirty and thirty-six hours when he was first examined on Tuesday morning. That puts time of death sometime late Sunday evening or early Monday morning. He had multiple injuries, but provisional cause of death was exsanguination from a severed carotid artery.'

'His throat was cut?'

'Yes. Like I said, the crime scene was something I won't forget in a hurry.'

'You said he looked like he'd been tortured?'

'Yes, the pathologist thought so too.'

Lauren told him that Meg had a theory that Blackett had been looking for the missing gun from the heist. 'Do you think he could've tortured Ed to get him to tell him where the gun was hidden?'

'Meg is thinking along exactly the same lines as we are,' he replied with a chuckle. 'But, if he did, then Ed obviously didn't tell him.'

'Do you think he found it?'

'Dunno. But, if he did, you and Meg need to take great care.'

'We will!'

By this time, Viv was just pulling into the multi-storey car park so he said, 'Right, no more shoptalk now. I shouldn't have told you anything, really, but I trust you not to tell anyone, other than Meg. I'm sure I can't stop you from telling her! But from now on, this evening is all about the two of us. And *Avatar*.'

'I'm not gonna argue with that,' grinned Lauren, unbuckling her seat belt.

Chapter Thirty-three

On a train from Waterloo to Salisbury

Peter Blackett sat hunched in a corner seat of the carriage. What could be seen of his lacklustre lank hair was plastered to his pallid forehead and trailing untidily over his well-worn coat collar. Most of it was hidden by a beanie pulled down as low as he could get it, and a thick scarf was wrapped around his lower face. It wasn't that he was cold; if anything, it was uncomfortably warm inside the train carriage. But he was trying to stay incognito. Travelling this late in the evening helped; there weren't too many travellers. And some of those who were travelling appeared to be the worse for wear, probably on their way home from a night out clubbing. He stared out of the window, seeing only his reflection as it was dark outside and the moon was hidden by clouds. That was good.

Things hadn't gone according to plan and that rankled. First, Charlie had woken up and fought back more strongly than he'd been led to believe possible. He'd been well covered but somehow Charlie had found a patch of flesh between his sleeve and his glove and had managed to scratch him. Anger had made him press down harder, and he'd heard Charlie's nose crunch. So much for making it look like he'd died from natural causes! And he knew there was a chance that he'd left DNA behind. All that careful planning gone to pot! If that wasn't bad enough, no one was supposed to have worked out how he'd got into the building. But some nosy old bitch had not only worked it out, she'd also been blabbing about how he must've had an inside accomplice. His stomach churned at the thought. That should never have happened.

Then there was Teddy. The bugger had laughed at him

when he'd asked about the dosh. That was long gone, spent on Charlie's care home fees. He ground his teeth in anger at the thought. Then Teddy had refused to tell him where his beloved Walther PPK was, despite some persuasion. But he'd found it, eventually.

Worst of all, that same busybody had connected both Teddy and Charlie with the Westbourne job. *How the hell?*

That left him with a cast-iron alibi for Teddy, despite the rozzers quickly making the association between him and Teddy as predicted, but a very weak alibi for Charlie, whose death should never have been traced back to him.

The Old Bill had already been sniffing around, wanting to question him. But he'd got out of his dingy halfway house just in the nick of time. He knew he should probably be heading out of the country before the net closed in. He hadn't intended to return to Salisbury, but he couldn't leave his daughter in the lurch now, could he? Not after everything she'd done for him.

Resentment snaked around his stomach, bringing the taste of bile to his mouth. He'd suffered on the inside, deprived of liberty and family, discredited and forgotten by those on the outside. Shacked up in a cramped and dilapidated cell with a succession of pathetic scrotes; some whingey, others too cocky for their own good, some obsequious to his status as a lifer, others insolent or downright disrespectful. He'd both given and received his share of split lips and black eyes. His face was grim with determination not to go back inside.

In the end, it had been the education officer who'd thrown him a lifeline with a transfer from A wing – where the gangs ran rampant – to E wing, the reserve of those attending education classes. Not that he'd cared a toss whether he'd passed or failed his GCSEs, fat lot of good they would do him on the inside, but it had earned him access to a computer. Technology! Who'd have thought that you could find out just about anything you needed to know about the outside by simply tapping questions into a machine? Oh yes, he'd learnt all about the internet, emails and mobile phones – even though he wasn't legally supposed to have had one – alongside a whole raft of other things that hadn't existed back in the '80s.

He'd found out that both Winston and Teddy had served their minimum fifteen years and been released on life licence back in '02. That stung, the fact they'd been let off so much more lightly than him. They'd played the dumb innocence card and persuaded the judge that they were unwilling pawns to his desperado. What was it Winston had called him? Buffalo Bill! He remembered it like it was yesterday. The heart-thumping adrenaline of the heist. The slow-motion replays of that blasted postmistress wrestling him for the gun. The whipcrack of shots fired and the smell of cordite stinging his nostrils. The metallic scent of blood as it splattered across the counter. The screams and the shouting that seemed to echo around his head on a constant loop. All that hard work and for what? He'd had only a sniff of the dosh before being banged up. He'd spent thirty-five long years plotting his revenge on the two who'd ratted him out and the one that had got off scot-free. His body shuddered with the anger coursing through his veins.

Fate had deprived him of Winston: the hefty Jamaican had snuffed it unexpectedly five years ago, dead at just sixty. A massive myocardial infarction, according to the death certificate, which was the same as a heart attack, he'd discovered online. Too quick and easy a death, in his opinion. He'd wanted to see the fear in Winston's eyes when he realised that retribution had finally caught up. Teddy had been surprisingly easy to track down, but he'd spent long hours scouring the net for Charlie. What a wonderful concurrence that the two should have so conveniently settled within a few miles of each other!

He'd made parole three months ago and exchanged a grungy cell for an even seedier room in a scrubby halfway house in Southall. Under the watchful eye of his parole officer, he'd signed on and filled out endless forms with little expectation of finding a job at sixty-four years of age. Only a few months 'til he could draw his pension, for Christ's sake, so what was the point? But having been seen to make all the right moves, his PO had lost interest beyond the perfunctory once a week check-in, which is exactly how he wanted it.

So, on Monday last week, he'd checked in with his PO as usual before heading to Salisbury to spend a few days with the daughter he'd not known he had for so many years. Born to a slut called Marlene just months after he'd been banged up, his illegitimate offspring had tracked him down the moment she'd turned eighteen. They'd written at first, and then she'd visited him once. She was a real smart girl, educated, not a bit like her parents, but then again she'd been adopted by a well-to-do couple desperate for a baby. Nicely dressed and quite pretty to boot, he'd asked her not to come again, wary of exposing her to the lecherous leers of the other lags. Instead, they'd stayed in touch via a series of burner phones that were regularly smuggled in and traded around. She'd been happy to help him to plot his revenge, manoeuvring herself into a position where she could be useful to him. Getting close to one of his prey so that he'd be able to slip in and out undetected. And then it had all gone wrong. He seethed with frustration.

The train pulled into Salisbury station and he waited until some other passengers had got off before he slipped through the doors and, sticking to the shadows, made his way out of the station. Ignoring the waiting taxis, he set off on foot for the rundown B&B he'd booked into under a false name. He daren't risk staying with his daughter again. He was just here to tie up a few loose ends and then he'd head for Portsmouth and the Channel ferries.

Chapter Thirty-four

Friday 20th January 2023

Meg woke up early on Friday morning to the sound of rain driving against her window. She waited in the gloomy light for her cup of tea in bed. It was a luxury she had never managed to enjoy before moving into her first care home. Years of teaching had conditioned her into rising early and snatching her tea and toast whilst preparing her bag for the day. And, by the time she'd retired, her first husband had long since buggered off with another woman and her second husband had tragically died of liver cancer. Somehow, having to get up to make it yourself rendered it pointless taking it back to bed. It just wasn't the same as someone else bringing you that first cuppa.

It was Kayla who delivered the long-awaited tea, having just started a stint on nights. She looked even more dishevelled than usual, and Meg noticed fresh bruising on the girl's upper arm when she put Meg's bedside light on for her.

'Has he hit you again, Kayla?' she asked softly.

Kayla flushed and tried to pull the tunic sleeve down. 'It's nothing serious,' she mumbled.

'It doesn't matter whether the injury is serious or not, it's still assault. You don't deserve it, and you shouldn't have to put up with it.'

'I know.' Kayla suddenly looked tearful. 'I just don't know how to get away from him.'

'You need to report it to the police,' Meg urged. Seeing the look of mistrust on Kayla's face, she hastily continued. 'I know you don't want to but they are trained in dealing with domestic abuse. They can arrest Mack and find a safe place for you to go to.'

'But he'll find me,' Kayla moaned. 'I just know I'll get even worse if I squeal on him.'

'Please, will you let me talk to my friend Dan?' Meg insisted gently.

'That detective inspector?'

'Yes.'

'But he investigates murders and serious stuff like that. His only interest in me was when he thought I'd pinched that wallet.'

'He was doing his job, questioning everyone,' she reminded Kayla, 'and he arrested the right person, didn't he?'

'Yeah, suppose so. Not that I can believe Ana was the thief. She was always looking down her nose at me.'

'Oh, I'm sure she wasn't,' Meg exclaimed. 'She's such a lovely person.'

'And a thief. How does that work, eh?'

'Even good people do the wrong things for the right reasons sometimes.'

'What d'ya mean?' Kayla looked baffled.

Meg crossed her fingers and hoped that Ana would forgive her for sharing her story.

Kayla was taken aback when she'd heard about Ana's circumstances.

'Listen, Ana is living in a flat and would've been able to pay her rent on a carer's salary if she hadn't sent all her money to Romania. Why don't you go and see her? She'd be glad of a friendly face, I'm sure. And you might be able to arrange to take over the lease of her flat, if such a thing is possible.'

'She's still in Salisbury? Surely, she'll have gone back home by now?'

'She can't, not until her case comes before the magistrate. Then she will have no choice but to go back to Romania. But, until then, she is stuck in that flat without a friend.'

'She won't want to see me.'

'How do you know until you try?'

Kayla grunted and made an excuse to get on with her work. Meg just hoped she'd sown the seeds of a possible way out in Kayla's mind. And, regardless of Kayla's wishes, she intended to talk to someone about her concerns.

After breakfast, Meg decided to discuss Kayla's situation with Maureen Wilkinson before going to the police. After all, the care manager had said she'd do whatever she could to help Kayla and Mandy. She tapped on the office door and entered when summoned.

'Meg, what can I do for you?' Maureen looked up and then set down the letter she'd been reading.

Meg sat. 'I hope you won't mind me coming to you, but I'm concerned about Kayla.' She explained why and Maureen reassured Meg that she'd done the right thing in sharing her concerns.

'With her consent, I've already spoken to social services about Mandy,' Maureen said. 'They're sorting out her benefits and making sure she's got adequate support. I'm sure they could help Kayla too, if she'll let me speak to them. I know domestic abuse victims often don't want to go to the police, but she needs help to get away from this Mack character. He sounds most unpleasant.'

Meg agreed. Then, a little nervously, she repeated her idea about whether it would be possible for Kayla to take over the tenancy of Ana's flat when she returned to Romania. 'I have no idea,' replied Maureen, 'but I was intending to phone Ana to see if she's okay. Perhaps I could suggest it to see what she thinks.'

Meg agreed to leave it in Maureen's capable hands, and she felt a little lighter when she left the office. Until she remembered that there was still an accomplice to identify. And the possibility of a dangerous murderer on the loose. Although, if he had any sense, he'd have gone a long way away by now to escape capture for his crimes. So, she was probably quite safe, really, wasn't she?

She had just settled down to her jigsaw puzzle with Jeannie when her mobile phone pinged in her pocket. Why did it do that? She drew it out and studied the small screen. Apparently, she had a text message from Dan. She was chuffed to find that she remembered how to open a text. It read simply, *Phone me when you're on your own.*

Intrigued, she excused herself and went back to her bedroom, before calling him. 'Why all the intrigue?' she asked, once they'd exchanged greetings.

''Sorry, I didn't want to alarm you. But I also didn't want to speak to you if you were with a group of other residents. This is definitely for your ears only.'

'I'm alone in my room now, so do go on.'

'Right. Well, firstly, the DNA comparisons came back this morning, confirming that it was Blackett's blood on the bedspread and his skin cells under Alan's fingernails.'

'That's excellent news. You've got your murderer!'

'Ah well, there's a snag. The Met hadn't been to question him yet and when they went this morning, he appeared to have done a runner. All his belongings have gone from his room.'

'Maybe he's left the country?' she suggested hopefully.

'Either that or he's gone into hiding ... or he's heading down here.'

'Do you think he'd risk coming back to Salisbury?'

'I don't know but I don't want to take any chances. That's why I want you to promise me you won't go out anywhere alone.'

'I doubt if Albert would let me,' she chuckled, 'but I won't, I promise. What about Lauren, do you think she could be in danger too?'

'From what I can gather, Viv is planning on driving her everywhere so she doesn't have to use public transport. I'm not sure how that's going to impact his work, but I sympathise. He's really smitten by Lauren, you know.'

'I'm glad to hear it, because I think she feels the same way about him.'

'One final thing before I go, we're going to put out a public appeal on TV and in the newspapers for any information as to Blackett's whereabouts. I'm just warning you, as his accomplice will no doubt see it too and he or she might not be too happy.'

'Thank you for the heads-up, I'll be careful.'

'Good. I don't want any harm coming to you again. Not on my watch!'

'What about fingerprints on the envelope and newspaper cuttings I found?' she asked, changing the subject. 'Did they match Alan?'

'You don't want much, do you?' Dan exclaimed. 'The lab is snowed under at the moment and they only got them yesterday afternoon! It'll probably be Monday before we get confirmation that Alan was definitely the fourth man! However, like you, I think it's pretty much a given now that we've proved Blackett murdered him. It's just about dotting the i's and crossing the t's.'

Meg smiled at hearing the familiar phrase. 'And was there any evidence at Ed's crime scene to prove Blackett murdered him too?'

'Not yet, but that's why the lab is so busy. There was just so much blood and DNA evidence from that scene to process.'

Meg winced. Served her right for asking!

Chapter Thirty-five

That afternoon, Jess came on duty, and she was one of the remaining names on Meg's list of suspects. She'd been on the night shift when Alan died. But getting her alone proved to be frustrating. Eventually, Meg managed to corner her in the hallway when their paths crossed. It wasn't ideal, but she had to take the opportunity.

'Jess, do you have a moment?' she smiled reassuringly.

'Sure, Meg, what do you need?' the carer asked cheerfully.

'I just wanted to ask you about the night Alan died . . .'

'Oh.' Jess' face fell and her demeanour changed. 'I'm actually quite busy right now. And I really don't know anything about it anyway. Sorry.'

'I just had one question; did you happen to close the curtains in Alan's room the evening before he died?'

'What?' Jess looked puzzled. 'No, they were already closed when I first went into his room. Why are you asking?'

'I wondered if you might have noticed anything odd about the patio door.'

'I didn't see the patio door; the curtains were closed. Look, I'm sorry, Meg, but knowing that I was on duty when someone was murdered in this very building really spooked me. I'd rather not talk about it.'

Jess hurried away, clearly reluctant to talk anymore. Was she really just spooked? Or did she have a guilty conscience?

✿

As Meg was about to return to the day room, an ambulance pulled up outside the front door, so Meg lingered a while to watch. The driver eventually got out and strolled into the office casually enough to reassure Meg that they weren't here for an emergency. He reappeared moments later with Hazel and they returned to the vehicle. The senior care assistant hovered impatiently as the ambulance crew brought a frail-looking man out on a trolley before welcoming him warmly. Ah, this was evidently the new resident they were expecting.

Meg waited until the trolley and its entourage had entered the warmth of the hallway before stepping forward and saying hello to its occupant.

'Hello to you too,' warbled a thin reedy voice. 'I'm Jeffrey.'

'Excuse us, please, ma'am,' interrupted the female paramedic, 'but we need to get Mr Hornbeam into his room so we can get back to the hospital.'

Meg murmured her apologies as she watched the trolley disappear down the corridor and into Alan's old room. She couldn't help wondering if anyone had told Jeffrey that his room had so recently been the scene of a murder. She hoped not.

❁

One of the frustrating things about living in a care home was that meal times were decided by someone else. Meg desperately wanted to watch the news that evening to see if Dan's appeal was on TV. But dinner was served at six o'clock on the dot. She kept her fingers crossed that the appeal would be repeated on the local news, if indeed it had even made the national news. She decided to forego her pudding in favour of returning to the day room as quickly as possible.

She made it just in time for the start of *South Today* and sat down breathlessly to watch. The appeal was the main item on the local news that evening.

'Police are asking for help in locating a dangerous murderer,' the presenter began. She recapped the bare bones of the case before going to a reporter at the police briefing that had been given earlier in the afternoon. Dan was sitting in front of the microphone, looking smarter than she had ever seen him, and next to him was a stern-faced woman in a fancy uniform, who was introduced as Super-intendent Monica Wells. Meg watched as photos of Peter Blackett were shown. The first was his mugshot on arrest after the Westbourne Heist, showing a cheeky-looking young man with tousled blond hair. That wasn't exactly helpful, Meg thought, as it was taken thirty-five years ago! But there was also a more up-to-date photo of him holding a GCSE certificate in prison, taken only a couple of years ago. In this photo Blackett had greasy-looking collar-length mousy hair and a rather battered-looking face, partially covered with greying stubble. She studied the face intently as she listened to Dan's appeal. Blackett was described as five foot ten inches tall and of thin build.

'If you see this man, do not approach him. He is danger-ous and could be armed with a weapon. If you see, or think you have seen, this man, call the police immediately on the number on the screen now.'

A telephone number was overlaid across the bottom of the screen. Meg repeated it to herself whilst fumbling to get her mobile phone out of her pocket, but the number disappeared too quickly for her and the next item on the news began. Then she remembered that she had Dan's personal number on speed dial, so it didn't matter.

Peter Blackett was sitting in his B&B room when the appeal came on TV and he cursed. He'd forgotten about that damn photo of his GCSE success. So much for hoping the local fuzz wouldn't know what he looked like!

Fortunately, he'd already taken precautions. He'd gone to a Turkish barber's in a nearby backstreet that morning and had his hair buzz cut and his stubble shaved. He'd then picked up a pair of low-prescription reading glasses in a pharmacy, not because he needed them but because he hoped it would add to the disguise. He just had to hope that the swarthy lad in the barber's either wouldn't see the appeal or wouldn't remember him. Could he take that risk?

Dammit, things were getting more complicated by the minute.

Reluctantly, he pulled on his donkey jacket, beanie and scarf, slunk out of the B&B and made his way back to the barber's. He walked past it first, head down, just glancing out of the corner of his eye to check that it was still open. It was. Good. Then he bought a takeaway at a little kebab shop on a corner, thus killing two birds with one stone as he hadn't eaten yet. He wandered slowly back, pausing every so often. Not that there were many people about, but if anyone did happen to see him, all they would see was a man wrapped up against the cold, eating his takeaway. He casually leant against the wall next to the barber's window and, seeing no one on the street nearby, risked a glance in. The same swarthy lad was there, brushing up the floor. And he appeared to be alone.

Pete stayed there until he'd finished his kebab, taking a glance through the window every so often, confident that he wouldn't be seen from inside. He noted the small TV high up on a wall opposite a few chairs for customers waiting to be served. It was on BBC1, so the lad might have seen the appeal. Flippin' 'ell!

He strolled down the street to a litter bin to deposit his rubbish. No point in leaving it on the street outside the barber's for the CSIs to find! He looked around as he took a pair of black leather gloves from his pocket and put them on. The street was still deserted. He pulled a decep-tively small but deadly flick knife from his pocket and returned to the barber's. He'd make it look like a robbery gone wrong.

Lauren was enjoying a quiet evening in with her mum and had also seen the appeal on *South Today*. Like Meg, she'd studied the face on the screen, trying to memorise its features. Just in case. Then she forgot all about it as they switched over to Netflix to find a film to watch. Every so often, she studied her phone as a text came in from Viv and, with a slightly warm fuzzy feeling inside, she would dash off a reply.

It came as a considerable shock when a text arrived from Viv at about half past eight saying that he'd been called out to a possible murder scene. She felt goosebumps rise on her arms and a tingle run down her spine.

'What's wrong, love?' Bekka asked, seeing her daughter's face suddenly go pale.

Wordlessly, Lauren showed her mum the text.

'It can't be related, surely?' Bekka said, sounding worried.

Lauren certainly hoped not! She texted Viv back, asking him where it was.

Don't worry, I doubt it's related! came the reply, and Lauren heaved a sigh of relief.

They finished watching their film and decided to make some popcorn before watching another, as Lauren wasn't on duty until one o'clock the following day.

❁

Blackett got back to his room to find two missed calls and a text from his daughter. He had deliberately left his phone in his room, even though it was a burner, because he'd learnt inside how the filth could track mobile phone locations. No point risking them somehow getting hold of his phone and finding out that it was at the barber's shop that evening!

The text was to tell him about the TV appeal. He texted back that he'd seen it.

U should get out of country ASAP, came the reply.

No. Gotta sort things out here first

Don't want u back inside!

Don't worry. I won't get caught

Call me

Fuck that! He was tired. He switched his phone off and settled down to sleep like a log right through the night, untroubled by any kind of a conscience.

Chapter Thirty-six

Saturday 21st January 2023

Meg woke to find a text from Lauren on her phone, sent late the night before. It just said, *Call me as soon as you get this*. She waited until Florin had been in with her tea, so that she could make the call without being disturbed. A sleepy-sounding Lauren eventually answered her phone but soon woke up when she heard Meg's voice. She told Meg that Viv had been called out to another murder yesterday evening and that he and Dan were likely to be busy all weekend, what with the two murders they already had and now this one too, as they were the team on call that weekend. She reassured Meg that it looked unlikely that this new murder was related but suggested they meet at the farm shop café at ten-thirty to discuss things – 'And, for goodness' sake, bring Albert with you! Don't walk down alone!'

'But aren't you working today?' Meg asked.

'Yeah, but not until one o'clock. We can have a meeting over coffee and then I'll have some lunch at the café before I come on duty.'

'But how will you get here?'

'Don't worry, I've already asked a friend to give me a lift this morning. It was the only way I could stop Viv from worrying! He kept apologising that he probably wouldn't be able to get away to give me a lift into work today, and saying how he didn't want me to get the bus on my own.'

'Good.' Meg echoed Viv's sentiments and was happy to note how concerned he was with Lauren's welfare.

Albert and Meg arrived at the café just in time to see Lauren being dropped off by a young man about the same age as her in a rather racy-looking Mazda.

'Who was that?' Meg enquired, after he'd revved the engine and sped away.

'Just an old school friend, Jed,' Lauren replied airily.

'That's a very fancy car for someone of his age,' remarked Albert suspiciously.

'Oh, he's a vlogger,' Lauren replied, leaving them none the wiser.

'A video blogger,' she explained, seeing their baffled faces. 'He makes videos and posts them on YouTube.'

'Videos of what?' asked Meg, amazed that such a thing appeared to bring in a considerable income, judging by the car.

'Oh, his gym workouts, spin classes, training sessions; all sorts of things really.'

Meg shook her head and decided to change the subject. 'Shall we go in?'

Once their drinks had been delivered by the waitress, who recognised them and welcomed them back, Lauren updated them on the latest murder.

'Viv says that a young Turkish man was stabbed in a barber's shop in what looks like a robbery. The till was emptied and several things stolen. He doesn't think it's got anything to do with our murders.'

'I'm very relieved to hear it,' said Meg, and Albert nodded his agreement.

'He's really frustrated as this is adding to their already hectic workload.'

'What about finding the accomplice?'

'That's why I've called this meeting,' Lauren explained. 'The super is insisting they only work on this latest murder over the weekend. They can pass it over to another team on Monday, if it isn't solved by then. *She* says that with forces nationwide looking out for him, Blackett will soon be arrested, and then he'll tell them who the accomplice is.'

'If he talks,' remarked Meg darkly.

'Exactly! The super says that finding the accomplice can

wait, as Blackett's already murdered what was left of his gang so he's unlikely to strike again. Viv is absolutely fuming about it.'

'I bet Dan is too,' Meg commented.

'Harrumph! Down to us to find the accomplice, then?' put in Albert.

'Well, I've been doing some more thinking about that,' Lauren announced. '*If* the accomplice was Blackett's illegitimate child, then he or she would have to have been conceived before his arrest in late 1987, because he was remanded in custody until the trial and then sent to prison. Theresa Knowles said that her father walked out when she was thirteen years old, supposedly because he got this ... umm... woman pregnant. Her date of birth was 15th March 1975. That means she was thirteen between March 1988 and March 1989, so that ties in with a baby born in the first half of 1988. Give or take a bit.'

'So that child would be ... what? Thirty-four or thirty-five now?' Albert suggested.

'I think we need to factor in a margin of error,' said Meg. 'The baby could have been born before Blackett's arrest, for all we know. And Theresa's memory might not be all that accurate. But it certainly can't have been born more than nine months *after* Blackett's arrest, if he was definitely the father.'

'Yes, I reckon no younger than thirty-four,' Lauren confirmed, 'and probably not older than thirty-five.'

'Exactly what I said,' snorted Albert.

'And if we cross-check that against our list of fifteen suspects?' Meg asked.

'It leaves us with five suspects,' Lauren said smugly. 'Sarah, Ana-Maria and Jess are all thirty-four. Mandy and Lyn are both thirty-five.'

'Excellent job,' gloated Albert. 'That's a better number of suspects to work with.'

'Assuming that the accomplice *is* Blackett's illegitimate child,' cautioned Meg, 'but I don't think we should count on that to the exclusion of all other possibilities.'

'You don't make life easy for yourself, do you?' sighed Albert, exasperated.

'Meg, how about you tell us where you've got to with questioning your fifteen suspects?' suggested Lauren tactfully.

Meg found her notebook in her handbag, flipped it to her list of suspects and summarised who she'd spoken to and what her conclusions were. 'So that just leaves Sarah and Lyn for me to question,' she finished.

'And only Jess strikes you as at all suspicious, so far?' checked Lauren.

'Yes.'

'So that whittles our five prime suspects down to three, if you've already eliminated Ana and Mandy,' Lauren summed up contentedly.

'Don't want to put a spanner in the works, old gal,' Albert interjected awkwardly, 'but, when you questioned Ana, Kayla and Mandy, wasn't that just about Alan's stolen wallet? Or have you questioned them again since?'

'Botheration!' exploded Meg. 'You're absolutely right!'

'And what about kitchen staff and cleaners who were working that day?' he suggested.

Meg's eyes opened wide with horror at her oversight. 'Dash it! Yes, I've only got the carers on my list.'

'But would they have been able to access Alan's room without being seen?' demanded Lauren.

'I don't know,' replied Meg, 'but we shouldn't discount them, just in case.'

'Let me have a quick look at my spreadsheet.' Lauren typed frantically on her notepad. 'No, it's okay.' She let out a sigh of relief. 'None of them are the right age.'

'Once again, that's assuming that the accomplice is Blackett's child,' said Meg. 'I think we ought to include them in our wider list.'

'Yeah, you're right. Perhaps I'd better do a bit of snooping this afternoon, see if I can find out what other staff were working the day before Alan was murdered,' Lauren conceded.

'Good idea. Meanwhile, I'll continue questioning the rest of my suspects,' said Meg.

'What about me?' said Albert, pouting.

186

Meg thought for a while. 'If I need you to stand lookout again, I'll let you know,' she promised. Seeing him about to object at being sidelined, she added, 'And if Lauren can find out which kitchen staff were on duty over dinner that Tuesday, maybe you could question them next time you see them serving in the dining room?'

'Splendid idea,' Albert beamed, 'but why only dinner? What about breakfast and lunch?'

'Because if anyone had closed the curtains earlier in the day, we would've seen that when we went in to search for Alan's missing wallet in the afternoon.'

'Oh yes.' Albert looked slightly put out for not remembering that himself.

They talked strategy for a while longer, then Meg and Albert set off to walk back to the home in time for their lunch, leaving Lauren to order herself a toasted sandwich.

Chapter Thirty-seven

Lauren spent handover in the office surreptitiously trying, without success, to spot a rota for the kitchen and cleaning staff somewhere on the various notice boards. As she left the office, wondering how she might find some time alone to search again later, she was caught by Florin, who was wheeling their new resident out of the dining room. 'Can you help me put Mr Hornbeam onto his bed for a rest?' he asked cheerfully.

'You can call me Jeffery.' The painfully thin man smiled as she and Florin helped him out of the wheelchair and onto his bed, arranging his pillows and making sure his catheter tubing wasn't kinked. She'd learnt at handover that the poor man was terminally ill with prostate cancer. He had been transferred to them temporarily as the hospice he should have gone to was full, and the hospital had been desperate to unblock as many beds as they could with the current increase in COVID admissions. Poor man, it was almost as though no one wanted him.

'Thank you, Jeffery,' she said warmly. 'I hope you're going to be very comfortable here at Britford Lodge.'

'Oh, I'm sure I will be,' he replied. 'Everyone has been so warm and welcoming. And this room is so much nicer than the hospital ward I just left. Not that I'll hear a word said against any of the nurses; they were all doing the best they could. But they were stretched so thinly and run completely off their feet at times.'

Lauren sympathised. Her mother had said much the same thing on many occasions.

'Tell me,' continued Jeffery with a glint in his eye, 'is it true what I've been hearing over lunch, that the poor fellow in this room before me was murdered in this very bed?'

Florin looked at Lauren and shook his head. Lauren ignored his silent plea to say nothing, guessing, quite rightly, that Jeffery was more intrigued than concerned.

'I say!' he exclaimed breathlessly when she'd told him the bare facts of the case. 'How exciting.'

'It isn't always that exciting here,' warned Florin.

'Spoilsport,' chuckled Jeffery.

✿

When she and Florin had finished making Jeffery comfortable, leaving him to doze in peace, Lauren returned to the office. She was hoping to find it empty but she was out of luck.

'Oh good. You can help me with the weekend cleaning,' said Taska, who was folding a couple of stray laundry items. Lauren was familiar with the concept of weekend cleaning, a rather dreary list of jobs that included tidying cupboards, restocking shelves and doing things that the cleaning staff apparently either couldn't or wouldn't. But how did that apply to the office?

Taska explained that the cleaners weren't allowed to clean the office because of the risk of them seeing sensitive information about the residents. Thus, once a week, one or more of the carers were asked to remove any out-of-date information from the notice boards, file any documents in the out-tray, tidy things away and clean all the surfaces. The evening cleaner would come in later and run a hoover over the floor.

Taska showed Lauren how the filing cabinet was ordered and left her to handle the out-tray, whilst she did the notice boards. Then Taska tidied as Lauren cleaned. As soon as Taska set off to return a blood pressure monitor to the treatment room, Lauren took her chance. She looked through the in-tray, the day book and the top drawer before finding what she wanted in the second drawer down. She studied the 'Rota of Ancillary Staff'. It seemed they worked a fortnightly shift pattern that repeated, which made her task a bit easier. Quickly, she whipped out her phone and took a photo. But just as her phone clicked and flashed, the door opened and Lauren was caught red-handed.

'What on earth are you doing, snooping around?' demanded Sarah, coming in to check on their progress.

Lauren thought quickly. 'I just had a text message,' she explained, 'from my mum. She wanted to know what I was doing. I told her I was cleaning and she said she didn't believe that, because I never do any cleaning at home.' That was a lie, but Sarah wasn't to know that. 'So, I took a photo of the cleaning spray on the desk.'

'You shouldn't be reading or sending texts while you're on duty,' the senior care assistant scolded, 'and you certainly shouldn't be taking any photos at work! In fact, your phone should be left in your staff locker at all times while you're on duty. I suggest you go and deposit it there immediately. And don't let me catch you doing this again or I will feel obliged to report it.'

Lauren apologised and scuttled off to the staffroom. Not that she had any intention of complying, not least because she'd seen other carers with their phones. But she wanted Sarah to think she was doing as she was told.

Meg was disappointed to find that of the carers she still wanted to question, only Sarah appeared to be on duty today. She waited for a chance to get her alone, which finally came as Sarah was putting on her coat and about to head out of the front door to go home.

'Sarah,' she called.

'I'm just going off duty, Meg,' Sarah smiled. 'Can you ask one of the other carers?'

'Oh, it was you I actually wanted to speak to.'

'It's my turn to face the infamous Meg interrogation, is it?' Sarah seemed amused. 'Well, go on then. What do you need to know?'

Meg asked her about the curtains.

'I was on the late shift that day, but I'm afraid I don't remember closing any curtains.'

'Didn't you and Kayla go and search Alan's room for his missing wallet?'

190

'Yes, that's right, we did. His curtains were certainly open at that time, because I remember looking on the windowsill in case his wallet had been left there.'

'What about later?' Meg persisted.

'I'm sorry, I don't think I went into Alan's room again that evening.'

'Did you notice anything odd about his patio door?'

'His patio door?' Sarah looked puzzled. 'Why? Should I have?'

'I just wondered, that's all,' Meg said.

'Sorry, Meg. I keep racking my brains to see if I noticed anything at all suspicious that evening, and I'm afraid, the truth is, I didn't.'

'Not to worry,' Meg reassured her, and watched as Sarah went out to a bright pink Ford Ka parked on the far side of the car park. Another one ticked off her list, although Meg had a sense that Sarah had been humouring her. Was she hiding something?

❁

Towards the end of her shift, Lauren got a text from Jed to say he'd been invited to a party at the last minute and wouldn't be able to pick her up that evening as promised. She swore under her breath then debated whether to text Viv or not. The trouble was, they'd only been out on two dates and she knew how busy he'd been today. She didn't want to come across as needy, so she decided not to text.

When she left Britford Lodge, she hurried up to the bus stop, keeping her phone and her hands in her pockets and staying alert to what was going on around her. Not that she saw a living soul until she got to the bus stop on the main road. She looked at the person waiting at her stop and relaxed when she saw that he had short hair and wore glasses. She didn't give the man in a donkey jacket and scarf a second glance. He politely gestured for her to get on the bus first, and when she made her way to the back seat as usual, he took a seat about halfway down the bus. He was still reading his newspaper when she got off at The Bull, and she didn't give him another thought.

Had she been a little more observant, she would have seen him get off at the next stop and walk back towards her, keeping to the shadows. He followed her at a distance, to see which house she went to. Having satisfied himself that he could find the house again, should the need arise, he retraced his steps and caught the next bus back to Salisbury.

When Lauren got home, she sent Viv a text, as promised, to let him know she was home safely. She didn't mention that she'd caught the bus.

*Glad u r safe, c*ame back his reply.

Have u finished work yet? she sent back.

About an hour ago. Just eaten. Knackered! he replied. *Get to bed nice n early*

U coming with me? LOL

Cheeky!!!

Lauren was feeling a very strange sensation in her stomach by the time their exchange was finished. Sure, they'd kissed a few times, but they hadn't gone any further. Clearly, Viv was interested, and that set her heart rate racing. She hoped it wouldn't be too long before she could see him again.

Chapter Thirty-eight

Sunday 22nd January 2023

Meg was pleased to see that it was Kayla who brought in her early-morning cup of tea. 'How are you?' she enquired.

'A bit sore,' admitted Kayla, 'but nothing I won't get over.'

'Kayla, don't be mad at me, but I talked to Maureen Wilkinson . . .'

'Yeah, I know.'

'You do?'

'She sent me an email. She wants to talk to a social worker about me, but I'm not sure that's a good idea. Mack'll be fuming if he finds out.'

'I can't force you to agree, Kayla, but they might be able to help you to find a way to leave Mack safely.'

'If you say so.' Kayla still sounded doubtful. 'She also sent me Ana's phone number and address. She said she'd talked to Ana, who would be happy for me to visit her, if I want.'

'That's good, isn't it? Will you visit her?'

'I dunno.' Kayla still seemed dubious, so Meg decided not to push it. Hopefully, a drip . . . drip . . . drip approach would work best.

'Kayla, the day before Alan was murdered, you searched his room with Sarah, didn't you?'

'Yeah, but you already know I didn't steal Alan's wallet.' Kayla looked truculent.

'Yes, dear, I know that. But I wondered if you could tell me if you noticed anything unusual about his room that afternoon?'

'What sort of unusual?'

'Perhaps the curtains were closed earlier than normal, or

there was something odd about the patio door?'

'The curtains were open, I remember that,' Kayla said, 'but, nope, don't remember nothing odd.'

'That's okay. Did you see anyone near Alan's room who shouldn't have been there?'

'Nope. You ask a lot of questions, don't ya?'

'I'm just curious,' Meg said, smiling reassuringly.

'Well, if you're done being nosy, I've got a tea round to finish.'

Kayla moved towards the door. Then she hesitated, before turning around. 'There was one odd thing.'

'Yes?' Meg asked, trying not to sound too eager.

'I was the one to take Alan to his bedroom that evening. And the curtains were already closed when I got there. I didn't think nothing of it at the time but, I dunno, it is a bit odd. I mean, usually when I take a resident to their room, the curtains are still open 'cos no one's been in there to close 'em. But someone must've been in his room 'cos they were closed.'

'That's an excellent observation, Kayla, thank you. What time was that?'

'I dunno, maybe eight, half eight, something like that.'

'Before the night staff came on shift?'

'Yeah, definitely.'

'Thank you.'

Kayla hesitated again. 'Do you really think I should go and visit Ana?' she asked.

'My dear, what have you got to lose? Mack surely can't be mad if you visit a friend, and Ana isn't the authorities. And I think you could both do with someone to talk to.'

'Yeah, maybe. I'll think about it.'

Kayla left Meg to drink her tea.

✸

After breakfast, Meg joined Jeannie at their jigsaw puzzle table and relished the opportunity to think whilst they worked together in silence. She was fairly certain now that she could eliminate the night staff from her suspect list –

presuming her theory that whoever wedged the latch on the patio door had then closed the curtains to cover up what they'd done was correct. But what if her theory was wrong? She groaned – that would put them right back to square one! Anyone could have done it, any time before or after the curtains were closed.

'Are you all right?' asked Jeannie anxiously.

'Sorry?' Meg was puzzled.

'You groaned. I thought perhaps you were in pain, or something?'

'Only mental pain,' said Meg, 'from trying to work out who the accomplice was.'

'Accomplice?' asked Jeannie.

Meg remembered that she'd been trying to keep her friend out of it. 'Don't worry about it, my dear.'

'You think someone helped the murderer get into the building, don't you?'

'Well, yes. But it's not for you to worry about, honestly, Jeannie.'

'Perhaps I can help?'

'I'm not sure you can.' Meg shook her head. She really didn't want to get her friend involved.

'A problem shared is a problem halved,' Jeannie said quietly.

Meg gave in and told Jeannie about how the patio door had probably been wedged open from the inside. She also apologised for tearing a piece off the box under Jeannie's bed. Jeannie laughed.

'I wondered how that had got torn. Don't worry, Meg, it's only got books in it. But, listen, you're trying to work out when the door could have been wedged open, right?'

'Yes.'

'Well, don't you think that it can only have been done either by the person who drew the curtains or someone who came in *after* that? If someone had done it earlier, whoever drew the curtains would probably have noticed.'

'You're right,' Meg groaned. 'So that doesn't eliminate the night staff at all.'

'No, but it does eliminate the *early* staff.'

'Why do you say that?'

Well, I went to my room that afternoon to get a clean handkerchief because my nose had been running with the cold weather and the one I had was soggy. That was just after four o'clock. I didn't need to turn the light on because there was still just enough daylight coming in, and I didn't close my curtains on that visit because it wasn't necessary. When I walked past Alan's room, the door was open and there was still daylight in his room too. I'm sure of it.'

'Four o'clock?' exclaimed Meg.

'Yes, dear.'

Meg kicked herself for not talking to her friend sooner. 'By four o'clock, all the early staff would've gone home. They finish at three-thirty, don't they?'

Jeannie nodded.

'You are so right; that eliminates all the early staff!' Meg couldn't believe that she hadn't realised that sooner.

❁

Just to be on the safe side, no longer trusting her own judgement, she went upstairs a little while later and found her diary. Sure enough, sunset on January the tenth had been at four-thirteen. With dusk about half an hour after sunset, it would have looked very odd for anyone to have closed the curtains much before half past four. She got out her suspect list; luckily, she'd marked who had been on which shift. She carefully crossed out the six carers who had been on the early shift. That still left the two she was suspicious about: Sarah, who had been on a late that day, and Jess, who'd been on that night. And she hadn't eliminated some of the others yet.

There was a tap on her door and she hastily shoved her notebook in a drawer, but it was only Lauren, whose head appeared around the door. 'Are you all right, Meg?'

'Yes, of course, come in.'

'I saw you leave the day room and I wanted a chance to talk to you, so I followed.' Meg nodded for her to continue.

196

'I did some research yesterday, but I've drawn a complete blank trying to find any living relatives for Peter Blackett. His parents are both dead. His only brother emigrated to Australia years ago and is also dead. He never married and, officially, he had no children. His only living relative is his illegitimate child, and there's no one we can question about that.'

Meg sympathised with Lauren's frustration and then told her of the conversation she'd had with Jeannie. Lauren agreed; it was unlikely that any of the early staff had wedged the patio door. 'Nor could it have been any of the cleaners,' she announced. She showed Meg the photo of the rota she'd found. 'Look, during the week, the cleaners are in between nine and three. They only do evenings at the weekend.'

'That's helpful,' Meg agreed, 'and it only leaves the one chef in the kitchen after 4pm. Do you know whether the week Alan was murdered was a week A or a week B on your rota? How do we know which chef was on?'

'I've checked, it was a week A,' answered Lauren smugly.

Meg looked at the rota. 'Right then, I'll get Albert to watch out for this guy, Sanjeev Kumar.'

'I've already given him a heads-up,' Lauren replied. 'Sanjeev's on today, so Albert will talk to him at lunchtime.'

'Good work, Lauren.'

❖

Blackett finally got round to phoning his daughter that morning. She wasn't at all happy that he was still in Salisbury but tough! He was only doing this to protect her.

He'd come back to Salisbury precisely to deal with that meddlesome old bitch, Meg Thornton. Taking her out would take the heat off his daughter.

But he was worried about the relationship between Meg and the young care assistant, Lauren. His daughter had reported seeing them together on several occasions and seemed to think they were colluding. That couldn't be good!

He might have to make some additional plans. At least he knew where she lived now. But, first, he had another idea in mind.

Chapter Thirty-nine

At lunchtime, Meg watched as Albert went up to the young chef serving behind the buffet. Sanjeev was a slight Indian man who was probably the politest chef Meg had ever come across. He also appeared to be somewhat in awe of Albert. Meg watched as he swallowed nervously and bobbed his head up and down and shook it side to side, eager to impress upon Albert the veracity of his replies. By the time Albert returned to their table, she had already worked out that he had done nothing and seen nothing on the evening before Alan was murdered.

After lunch, Meg observed Lyn as she went around the day room doing various tasks. She was one of the final suspects she needed to question. When Lyn left the room, Meg followed her at a distance and saw her enter the office. She knocked on the door. 'Come in,' called Lyn.

Meg entered cautiously, fingers crossed that no one else was there. But Sarah was seated at the desk, whilst Lyn was standing by the notice board.

'Meg.' Sarah's mouth wrinkled with amusement. 'Is it Lyn's turn to be grilled?'

'What's this about?' asked Lyn, looking surprised.

'Don't you know? Meg here seems to think she's Miss Marple. She's been asking all sorts of questions about the day before Alan's murder.' Sarah stood up. 'Don't worry, I'll leave you two to it.' She paused as she passed Meg on the way to the door. 'I don't know what you can hope to achieve. Wouldn't it be better just to leave the investigation to the police?' She flounced off before Meg could reply.

'Come in and sit down.' Lyn smiled nervously as she lowered herself into the chair behind the desk. 'What did you want to ask?'

Meg decided there was no point in beating around the

bush after Sarah's introduction, so she dived straight in. 'You were on duty the evening before Alan was murdered. Tell me, did you notice anything unusual at all in his room that evening?'

'No, I didn't,' Lyn replied. 'To be honest, I don't remember much about that shift. You probably know that I only work part time. My son's been sick for the last few days and I've hardly had any sleep. I'm sorry, but I really don't remember anything useful.'

Meg sympathised and asked after her son. Apparently, he'd brought a tummy bug home from nursery school, but he was fully recovered now. 'You know how ill they are one moment, then the next they're as right as rain.'

Meg thanked her and left. She had talked to just about all her suspects now and gained absolutely nothing definitive. Lauren was right; one of them was probably lying. But how to find out which one?

Lauren finished her early shift at three-thirty and made her way up to the bus stop as usual. She knew that Viv would probably tell her off, and Meg was constantly reminding her not to take any risks. But what they didn't know wouldn't hurt them, would it? It was not like she had a lot of choice. Viv was busy working again and she couldn't keep asking her friends. She'd taken the bus last night and again this morning without any trouble. She was confident that nothing would happen.

The wind that afternoon was turning chilly again, and she kept her head down as she walked. One moment she was alone, and then she wasn't!

All of a sudden, a body hurtled into her from behind and almost knocked her to the ground. Whilst she was struggling to keep her balance, she felt arms grappling with her, trying to slip her bag off her shoulder. She held onto it for dear life and received a blow to the side of her head that momentarily made her see stars.

The next thing, her assailant was running off with her

shoulder bag and she was left gasping for breath, winded by the suddenness of the attack. She looked up, determined to have some kind of a description to give the police. All she could see was a person in trainers, jeans and a dark blue hoodie, the hood pulled up over his – or her – head, running back down the road towards the farm. At this distance, Lauren couldn't even be sure of the gender of the person who had attacked her, and neither had she glimpsed his or her face. She groaned. She was going to be in so much trouble with Viv.

She reached into her pocket to phone for help, but her phone wasn't there. Frantically, she felt all her pockets. Had she put it in her shoulder bag? No, she always put it in her pocket for easy access. The bugger had stolen her phone as well as her bag! Seething with a mixture of rage and frustration, she sank down onto the kerb, oblivious to the cold. What the hell was she going to do now?

❖

A couple of minutes later, Maureen Wilkinson drove by, having also just finished the early shift. She braked on seeing Lauren and lowered her passenger window.

'Are you all right, Lauren?' she shouted across.

Lauren tried to stand up but suddenly came over dizzy, so she sank down again.

Maureen pulled on the handbrake and rushed around the car bonnet. 'Whatever's happened?' she demanded, her voice full of concern.

'I-I-I was j-just mugged,' Lauren stammered. 'Someone s-stole my bag. And my phone.' She fought back hot tears and swallowed a wave of nausea.

'Are you injured?' Maureen crouched beside her, looking her over with a professional eye. 'Did you bang your head?'

'I think he, she, whoever it was, hit me.' Lauren was shivering uncontrollably now.

Maureen looked concerned. 'Come on, let's get you into my car and I'll take you straight up to A&E.'

Lauren tried to protest but Maureen was not taking no for

an answer. She helped Lauren up and checked that there were no other injuries apparent. A few grazes but nothing serious that she could see. But she was concerned by the pallor of Lauren's face and the fact that she appeared to be quite dizzy and disorientated. In just a few minutes they were at the A&E entrance of Salisbury District Hospital which, fortunately, was just round the corner from Britford Lodge. Maureen didn't hesitate; she drove up the ramp and stopped in an ambulance bay, before marching into the ambulance-only entrance, reappearing not long afterwards with a nurse, followed by a porter with a trolley.

❀

Blackett ran all the way back down the hill, past the farm, until he reached the footpath that led across the water meadows towards Southampton Road. He needed to act quickly now, before Lauren could report her phone stolen.

He stopped in the lee of a large rhododendron tree, out of sight of the farm buildings. Quickly, he opened her phone, hoping it wasn't security protected. It was. He knew that if you tried your fingerprint and it wasn't recognised, the phone would ask for your PIN code. He did that and the PIN screen appeared. Now, it was really down to luck. Hopefully, she'd chosen something obvious. Like her birthday. He tried 2501 and he could hardly believe his luck. First attempt!

He scanned through her most recent text messages to get a feel for her style of writing. There were loads between her and someone called Viv, some of them quite sexy. Well, Viv was about to be very disappointed, wasn't he. Or she.

There were only a few between her and Meg. He saw that they'd previously arranged to meet at the farm shop café. Excellent. He grinned wickedly, carefully composed a text message and sent it. Then he examined the handbag, which he'd only grabbed to make it look more like a mugging. He hadn't wanted her to know he was only after her phone, now, had he? He grabbed the cash and ditched the rest into the stream next to the path. Then he took the batteries and SIM card out of the phone and ditched all of that into the stream as well. He didn't want to risk carrying it around. Either his text would work or it wouldn't. But he only had one shot at using the girl's phone before she reported it stolen, so it was of no further use to him.

He pushed his hood down and brought a dark blue peaked cap out of his pocket, pulling it down over his eyes. His hair, previously a miserable faded blond colour, was now dyed dark brown. He put a pair of sunglasses on, despite the fading wintry light. Then he strolled back up the lane past the farm to a hiding place he'd identified earlier, about halfway between the old people's home and the café.

He patted his pocket, just to make sure his Walther PPK was still there.

Chapter Forty

Meg was surprised to get a text from Lauren not long after she'd gone off shift. What on earth could've happened in the short space of time since she'd said goodbye?

She read the text. It said, *Got news. Meet at farm cafe ASAP*

She looked at her watch and frowned. It was nearly four o'clock, and didn't the café close at four on a Sunday? She couldn't be sure. Perhaps it was five, not four.

She went and found Albert dozing in a chair next to Frank, who was snoring, and nudged him.

'What? What?' Albert spluttered, looking up at her.

'Albert, I need your assistance,' Meg whispered.

'Righty-oh, old gal,' Albert hissed back, and pushed himself out of the chair.

Meg didn't speak until they were in the lift and then she explained.

'I say, that sounds a bit rum. Isn't she working again tomorrow?' Albert commented.

'Yes,' Meg replied. 'I wonder what it is that's so urgent it can't wait until then.'

'Why don't you call her on that phone of yours and ask her? It's a bit late in the day to go gallivanting off down to the café. It'll be getting dark soon.'

Meg waited until they reached her room; she looked out of her window and agreed. The sun was already quite low on the horizon. Not only would it soon be dark but the temperature would be dropping as it was forecast to freeze again tonight. She dialled Lauren's number, but all she got was a message saying that the number was unobtainable. Now that definitely was strange.

Meg felt torn in two. She had a gut feeling that something wasn't right about this, and that was telling her not to go.

But this was Lauren, who was young and unpredictable, and it might not have occurred to her that older people would be less keen on going out this late on such a cold day. Young people never seemed to feel the cold, did they? And what if Lauren really did have a breakthrough in the case? It made sense that she wouldn't want to be seen coming back into the home having already gone off duty. But then again, why didn't she just phone?

This was most unlike her, but Meg found herself dithering.

'What's up, m'dear?' Albert asked tenderly. 'Tell me what you're thinking.'

She told him and he suggested that if her gut was telling her that something was off about this, she'd be better off not going. Strangely enough, that suddenly made her all the more determined to go. 'I don't want to let Lauren down,' she insisted, as she found her winter shoes and put them on.

'I'll go and get my outdoor togs on too,' Albert said reluctantly, 'and I'm going to take that walking stick of yours, if you've still got it, just in case. I'm fairly certain I could give someone a pretty hard whack with that!'

Meg thought that might be going a bit over the top, but she didn't want to waste time discussing it. She pulled on her coat, hat and scarf, picked up her gloves and retrieved the walking stick from the back of her wardrobe. Then she waited in the corridor by the lift until Albert emerged from his room, equally well wrapped up against the cold.

In the lift going down, she suddenly thought that whoever was in charge might think it was a bit too late for them to be heading out. Just in case someone tried to stop them, they didn't bother signing out. They just walked casually through the front doors with no one any the wiser.

⚙

Lauren was getting more and more concerned. Here she was, lying on a trolley in a cubicle, curtains closed and no one nearby, without her phone to let anyone know where she was. Her mum would worry like mad when she didn't get off her usual bus. And Viv might text to see if she was home safely, and then he'd wonder why she didn't reply. She didn't want them worrying unnecessarily.

At last, a nurse appeared, a thin folder clasped under one arm and wheeling a small trolley full of heart and blood pressure monitoring equipment with the other hand.

'Have you got a phone I could use, please?' Lauren asked urgently.

'There's a pay phone out by the entrance door, but you're not going anywhere until I've booked you in and done some observations,' the nurse replied firmly.

'But I don't have any money!' Lauren wailed. 'You don't understand. I've been mugged. I don't have my phone or bank cards or any cash. But people will be worrying when I don't get home.'

'Just calm down, please. It's important we check you over first, then I'll be able to make a phone call for you.'

Whilst she was speaking, the nurse had slipped an oximeter over Lauren's finger to measure her pulse and blood oxygen saturation, and was attaching a blood pressure cuff round her other arm. Lauren could feel panic rising in her chest as she felt tied down and restricted. 'Please, I've got to make a phone call,' she pleaded.

The nurse hesitated. Any readings she took now could be affected by her patient's agitated state. But, on the other hand, the patient had been admitted as a possible head injury, and any kind of a bleed on the brain could be causing her agitation.

Lauren sensed her hesitation and an idea suddenly occurred to her. 'Listen, I know this is going to sound crazy, but there's a dangerous murderer on the loose out there. What if he stole my phone? He could be going to use it to get to someone I love. Please, if you won't let me use a phone, will you at least phone the police for me? Phone Salisbury police station and ask to be put through to Detective Sergeant Viv Williams. He's my boyfriend. Please?' She was literally begging the nurse by the time she'd finished.

Fortunately for Lauren, the nurse had seen the TV appeal

so she knew that at least part of what her patient was saying was true, even if she thought she was overreacting. But when she heard that her boyfriend was a policeman, that decided it. She glanced at the monitor and ascertained that the patient's pulse, whilst quite rapid, was within normal limits and that her oxygen saturation was perfectly normal. 'Okay, if you promise me not to move from this trolley, I'll go and phone the police station for you. Viv Williams, you said, is that right?'

'Yes. Thank you,' Lauren whispered, leaning back onto the single pillow provided.

Viv was in Dan's car on their way to interview a possible witness when he received a call patched through from the front desk. He couldn't believe what he was hearing!

'Dan, go straight to A&E, please,' he ordered, his voice thick with concern.

Dan made an illegal U-turn on Harnham Road and headed back the way they'd come as Viv continued listening to the female voice on the phone. He waited impatiently for the call to end, unable to hear more than the occasional word.

When the call was finished, Viv quickly filled him in. 'Lauren's been mugged and her phone stolen! The nurse is concerned because she's got a head injury and is very agitated. Lauren was saying something about a murderer on the loose!'

'Blackett?' cried Dan, now very concerned.

'Shit! What if the point of the mugging was for him to get hold of her phone?' Viv exclaimed, horrified.

'Call Meg, now,' instructed Dan. 'Use my personal phone – her mobile number's on there. We need to warn her to ignore any messages or strange calls coming from Lauren's phone.'

Meg and Albert were almost halfway to the café just as the sun slipped over the horizon, and almost immediately the temperature seemed to drop a degree or two. Suddenly several things happened all together in a flash. Although simultaneous, they appeared to be happening in slow motion to Meg. A dark shadowy figure rose up behind the low hedge to her right and pointed something at her. Albert reacted by lifting the walking stick and bringing it down as hard as he could on the attacker's outstretched arm. The phone in Meg's pocket suddenly rang, making her jump, and she turned slightly away from the hedge to reach into her coat pocket. There was a brief flash and a bang so loud it deafened her to whatever Albert was now shouting. And Meg felt something knock her hat off.

Chapter Forty-one

Meg wasn't answering her phone so Dan made a split-second decision at Harnham Junction, taking the Ringwood Road that would take him to Britford, rather than the Blandford Road that would take him to the hospital.

The phone rang out and Viv cancelled the call. 'Try again,' Dan ordered, stepping on the accelerator, impatient with the car in front of him.

This time, Viv got an answer just before it was about to ring out again. 'Meg? Are you there?' he asked, anxiety making his voice husky.

'I think I've just been shot at,' a very wobbly voice replied.

'Are you hurt?'

'No. I don't think so. Albert hit him with my walking stick.'

'Albert's with you? Where are you?'

'We're in Lower Road, between Britford Lodge and the farm.'

'Was it Blackett?'

'I don't know. He was just a silhouette against the sunset.'

'Is he still there?'

'No, he ran.'

'Hang on, we'll be there with you very shortly.' Viv lowered the phone and rapidly relayed everything to Dan.

Dan nodded grimly. 'Radio it in to uniform,' he growled.

'Meg, we'll be with you in less than a minute,' Viv said into the phone before ending the call and grabbing the radio from the car's console.

Dan swung into Lower Road and sped past the care home. Then he spotted Meg standing on the pavement, her hat in her hands. And Albert with his arm around her shoulders. He squealed to a halt beside them.

'Are you all right?' he shouted, as he ran towards her.

'Just a little shaken,' Albert replied.

'Just look what that blighter did to my hat,' complained Meg, holding it out for him to see. There was a groove scorched through the top of her Russian-style faux fur hat. Dan almost went weak at the knees at the thought of what a near miss she'd had.

'Right,' he said brusquely, 'you've had a nasty shock. Let's get you up to the hospital and get you checked out.'

'I'm perfectly fine,' insisted Meg, not sounding it at all.

'Viv needs to head up to the hospital anyway,' Dan said, diplomatically not mentioning that Lauren had also been attacked. 'Here, Viv, take my car and get Meg checked over while you see how our other little problem is.'

'Yes, guv,' Viv nodded his understanding, 'but what about you?'

'I'll stay here until uniform arrive. You'd better take Albert with you too – he's looking a bit pale as well.'

'No need for that,' Albert protested. 'Nothing wrong with me that a nice cup of hot sweet tea won't fix.'

'No,' insisted Dan. 'Viv, you take them both to the hospital and take everyone's statements when they're able to give them. I'll have a look around the scene here before the last of the light goes. Uniform can give me a lift to the hospital when I've finished here.' He turned to Albert. 'Please, go with Meg and look after her,' he said softly, knowing that would get the old boy onside.

Albert nodded. 'Of course. Don't worry, I'll take good care of her. But you'd better tell someone at the home where we are – we didn't check out and I don't want them starting a manhunt!'

'I'll tell them,' Dan reassured him, 'but, before you go, did you see which way the attacker ran?'

'He scurried off down the field towards the farm, like the cowardly rat that he is,' growled Albert. 'I would've chased after him if I was a good few years younger.'

'I know, thank you.' Dan steered him towards the car then helped Meg into the front passenger seat. As soon as everyone had seat belts on, Viv set off at a nice sedate

210

pace, conscious that he was carrying two elderly people who'd just had a very nasty shock.

⚙

The light was fading fast so Dan decided the home could wait five minutes. He examined the ground around where Meg and Albert had been standing. Nothing. He looked up. The sky was lightest to the west, which was behind the hedge and slightly behind him. Turning the other way, it was inky blue. Meg had said that the shooter had been silhouetted against the sunset. So, he'd probably been standing behind the hedge, no doubt having found a hiding spot from which to ambush Meg. It was Blackett; he felt sure it was. But, like everything else, they needed proof.

He crossed the road, all the time keeping his eyes glued to the ground. Still nothing. He returned and walked along the hedge until he could find a gap to push through. He was very careful not to touch the bushes any more than he had to. Then he stealthily avoided the hint of a path in the grass and walked on the undisturbed grass beside it until he was back to the thickest part of the hedge where Meg had been standing. He studied the ground and, to his amazement, he saw a small pistol, dropped at the foot of the hedge. It looked suspiciously like a Walther PPK, but he had no intention of touching it. That was for the forensic team.

He tried to recreate the attack in his mind's eye. Blackett had probably been crouching out of sight. The man was only an inch taller than he was, and Dan could see that it would've been quite easy to stay hidden from anyone on the path. Then he would've stood up, bringing up his arm, aiming the pistol at Meg. She'd said that Albert had hit him with a walking stick. He imagined the stick coming down onto the arm just as it was about to fire. Deflecting the shot, possibly. The blow causing Blackett to drop the weapon. He wouldn't have expected anyone to be with Meg. Blackett, turning to run, in his panic not stopping to pick up the fallen pistol. Of course, he couldn't have been sure whether he'd hit Meg or not.

Flashing blue lights and sirens signalled the imminent arrival of uniform, so he made his way gingerly back to the road to wave them down. He explained the likely scenario and told the officers to get searching for a bullet before it was completely dark, signalling its likely trajectory. He instructed one PC to call in forensics, telling him about the path, the likely place where the shooter had hidden, and the fallen pistol. 'And for God's sake, don't mess up any of the evidence,' he ordered fiercely, before setting off to the care home on foot.

✦

At the care home, no one had noticed that Meg and Albert were missing yet. Sarah was working in the office with the door open. She was very surprised to look up and see the detective inspector marching across the hallway towards her, looking both thunderous and anxious in equal parts.

'Inspector?' she asked, a sinking feeling in her stomach as she sensed that something was definitely wrong.

'I can reassure you that Meg and Albert are safe and as well as can be expected in the circumstances,' he began.

She looked at him open-mouthed. What was he saying?

Dan suddenly realised that the senior care assistant, in charge of thirty or so residents, had no idea that two of them were not present and correct. About to explode, he took a deep breath, sat down and tried to explain as calmly as he could.

Sarah blanched when she heard what had happened and looked only slightly reassured when Dan explained that no serious harm had been done. 'My sergeant has taken them up to the hospital for a precautionary check-up because, obviously, they've both had a severe shock. He'll take their statements there and bring them back as soon as the hospital is satisfied that they're fit.'

Sarah thanked him for telling her.

'There's something else I need to tell you.' He coughed. 'One of your staff was injured in an earlier incident and she is also at the hospital.'

'Who?' Sarah sounded bewildered.

'Lauren Peachy. We think she was the victim of a mugging, but I'll let you know more as soon as I have any information.'

'That's terrible,' Sarah began. She looked close to tears, and Dan realised what a terrible shock this must have been for her too.

Chapter Forty-two

Dan was standing in the hallway of Britford Lodge, about to radio down to the uniforms to get one of them to take him up to the hospital, when his personal phone rang. It was Viv.

'The triage nurse has had a chat with Meg and Albert and doesn't think there's any need for them to wait four or more hours to see a doctor here. He said they'd be better off coming back to the care home, going to bed with a cup of tea and some TLC, and resting. I'm just about to bring them back and take their statements there, away from the hulla-baloo that A&E is right now.'

'That's excellent news.' Dan heaved a sigh of relief. 'What about Lauren?'

'That's not such good news. Apparently, she caught a blow to the side of her head, and the doctor wants her to be admitted overnight for observation. She's not at all happy about that, I can tell you.'

'No, I bet she isn't,' Dan grimaced, 'but she'll be okay, won't she?'

'They're saying it's just a precaution,' Viv confirmed, not sounding at all relieved, 'but she's dreadfully pale, shivery and dizzy when she tries to stand up. And she says she feels sick.'

'When I catch up with Blackett . . .' Dan muttered darkly.

'. . . is nothing to what I'll do if I catch up with him first,' growled Viv.

'Good job the super can't hear us at the moment,' snorted Dan. There was a pause. 'What can I do to help?' he asked, turning his mind to more practical matters.

'Actually, guv, if you don't mind staying where you are, would you take the statements from Meg and Albert? If you don't mind me borrowing your car for a bit longer, I need to drive down to Downton, pick up some overnight things for

Lauren and bring Bekka in to visit. Lauren's phoned her mum already, but you can imagine what she's like. She won't rest until she's seen for herself that Lauren's all right.'

'That's no problem at all,' Dan replied. 'Just get Meg and Albert back here safely and I can take their statements. And, Viv – when you've done that, you're off duty.'

'But, guv—'

'No buts. You need to spend the evening with Lauren and her mother.'

'Thanks, guv, I appreciate that. But what about your car?'

'We can sort out cars later.'

Meg was relieved to be back in her room in her own bed. Granted, she'd been very shaken by what happened, but she hadn't wanted to go to hospital in the first place. She cupped her hands around the mug of comforting hot tea that Stef had just delivered with a concerned face. Stef had also promised to bring her dinner up on a tray as soon as the detective inspector had finished with his questions, so now Meg was just waiting for Dan to come to her after taking Albert's statement. Thoughtful as ever, he'd wanted to give her more time to get herself settled before intruding.

A tap on the door was followed by Dan's worried face.

'Come in, Dan, and do stop worrying,' she commanded with a chuckle. 'I'm not made of porcelain, and I wasn't injured in the slightest, just a little shaken up.'

Dan grinned as he sank into the chair near her bed. 'I'm glad to see you looking more your normal self than you did at the scene,' he commented.

'Well, I suppose anyone would look a bit peaky after just being shot at.'

'I'm so relieved he missed,' sighed Dan.

'Thanks to Albert and Viv.'

'Why Viv? What did he do?'

'My phone rang a split second before the shot. I was turning slightly to reach into my pocket, just as Albert crashed my walking stick down onto the assailant's arm. I think, between the two things, his shot didn't go where it was intended.'

'Thank goodness for that!' Dan exhaled loudly. 'Right, start from the beginning. Tell me why you went off down Lower Lane at such a late hour, and every detail of what you can remember.'

Meg told him as accurately as she could, and he was pleased to note that her statement both corroborated everything that Albert had told him and added to it, Meg being the more observant of the two.

'Thank you,' he said, when she'd finished and he had jotted everything down. 'Now, I'm going to leave you to rest. But I'll be posting a PC on the landing overnight, just in case Blackett comes back and tries again.'

'It was him then?' Meg asked.

'I found a Walther PPK pistol at the scene, which points towards it being Blackett,' Dan grimaced. 'Unless you've got anyone else keen to bump you off?'

'Perish the thought! But I'm sure I don't need protecting in here,' she insisted.

'Blackett got in to murder Alan,' he reminded her.

'With help from an accomplice. He'll need a bit of time to plan something like that again. Who's to say the accomplice is even on duty today?'

'Fair point, but I'm still posting a PC on the landing.'

'Mightn't it be better to let him try?' she suggested. 'If your PC was concealed, and Blackett did come to finish the job, you could catch him in the act.'

'I'm not taking any chances with you,' Dan insisted firmly. 'We already have enough DNA evidence to charge him with Alan's murder, so he's going back inside for the rest of his life. There's no need to take any further risks.'

Meg conceded the point. And she couldn't help feeling relieved that Blackett no longer had his gun!

Blackett was trembling with fury at his own stupidity. So

concerned with staying concealed until the last possible moment, he'd failed to see that the old bitch wasn't alone. So focussed on taking his shot, he'd been taken totally by surprise when that stick had thumped down on his outstretched arm. And in such a hurry to flee the scene, he hadn't realised he'd dropped his beloved Walther PPK until he'd paused for breath back at the rhododendron tree beyond the farm. It had been too late to double back and retrieve it; the place had already been crawling with coppers. How the bloody 'ell had they got there so quickly?

What was worse, his daughter had just texted to say that he'd missed the old bag. He ground his teeth in anger and shame.

He really should head for the ferry port and just concentrate on getting safely away. *But what if that meddlesome Meg Thornton discovered that he had a daughter?*

No – better he took a few precautions and finished the job he'd set out to do. The first thing he'd do was to clear out of the B&B. Eventually, someone there was bound to put two and two together and tell the filth about his changes in appearance. At the moment, they were still working off that old GCSE photo. Best keep it that way.

He'd need to find a safe place to lie low. Then he'd plan how to finish off both the nosy old bitch and her pesky young friend, once and for all.

It took him nearly three quarters of an hour to walk to his B&B, ensuring he took back roads and dark cut-throughs to avoid the brightest street lighting. He pulled his hood up again before entering the dingy terraced house that was laughingly called Elizabeth Court. It sounded a great deal grander than it looked, that was for sure. He snuck up the stairs to his poky room, hastily packed everything into his grubby backpack and tiptoed down again, unseen.

✺

It took him well over an hour to walk to Wilton to where Teddy's bungalow was, still avoiding the main roads. But it was worth it when he discovered the street quiet and dark and no sign of a police presence. It was now a week since he'd done Teddy in, and he'd banked on the scene being unguarded. He made his way stealthily round the back, checking constantly for signs of life from the neighbour. Effortlessly, he prised open the kitchen window. The Old Bill would never think to look for him here! He chuckled as he snuggled down in the dead man's bed. This was a damn sight more comfortable than the lumpy mattress at Elizabeth Court, and it sure as hell beat sleeping rough in this weather!

Chapter Forty-three

Once again, it was Kayla who brought Meg's early-morning cup of tea the next day. Round-eyed and full of curiosity, she asked, 'Is it true you were shot at?'

Meg told her the outline of what had happened.

'I'm so glad he missed. You don't deserve something like that,' the carer observed.

'Thank you, my dear. Now, tell me. Have you thought any more about visiting Ana?'

'I didn't sleep very well yesterday morning, thinking about Mack and everything,' the young woman confessed. 'In the end, I got up about two o'clock to find Mack was snoring his head off in the lounge, totally out of it. I got dressed as quietly as I could and went out for a walk. I must've walked a couple of miles, but before I knew it, I was in the Friary. It was as if my feet took me there of their own accord. So, I took a chance and called on Ana.'

'That's good,' Meg smiled, pleased Kayla had taken her advice. 'And how did it go?'

'She was really timid to begin with, afraid I'd shout at her or something about stealing that wallet and nearly getting me into trouble over it. But then we got chatting. She told me all about her home in Romania and her family. Did you know her dad would've died if she hadn't sent every last penny she had to pay for his operation? It doesn't seem fair, does it?'

Meg agreed that it wasn't fair.

'Well, then I told her all about Mack and me. I've never talked to anyone about some of the things I told her. I can't believe it was so easy to let it all spill out. But she just listened, never once told me what an idiot I was for staying with him.'

'I told you she was a nice young woman, didn't I?' Meg said, feeling relieved.

'Yeah, I guess you were right, 'n' all. Well, you're never gonna guess what she suggested next.' Kayla's eyes were bright and she was more animated than Meg had ever seen her.

'Tell me,' Meg suggested warmly.

'She only asked me to move in with her, straight away, like! I mean, I'll have to sleep on her settee, but that isn't too much of a hardship. I can help by paying the rent. And Mack can sod off for all I care.' Kayla flushed. 'Sorry about the language.'

'Not to worry, my dear. I am very pleased for you. When will you move in? Have you told Mack yet?'

'Nope, and I'm not gonna tell him, neither. I'll catch the bus home after work this morning, pack up my clothes and a few personal bits and pieces, and then I'll take a taxi to Ana's, blow the expense. He'll be down the Job Centre this morning, signing on, and I intend to be long gone before he gets back.'

'And then what?' Meg asked gently.

'Well, Ana said the same as you and Mrs Wilkinson, that I should talk to someone official about it. I ain't going to the police, I just can't do that. But I suppose it wouldn't hurt to talk to someone in social services, would it?'

'I think that's a very sensible move,' encouraged Meg.

'Yeah, well, I'll talk to Mrs Wilkinson when she comes on duty. She can tell me how to go about that. Right, I'd better get on with the tea round before the other residents start complaining,' Kayla said, a little brusquely, turning towards the door. Then she paused. 'Thank you for being so good to me,' she whispered, her back still to Meg.

'You're welcome,' Meg said, as Kayla slipped out of the door.

Lauren was up, washed and dressed nice and early that morning, despite being told that she wasn't going anywhere until a doctor had checked her over and made sure she was fit to be discharged. She'd already been told that someone from Britford Lodge had phoned the ward to pass on a message that she was not expected in to work that day, and that she could phone in later to say if she'd be fit tomorrow or not.

She was feeling a lot better this morning than she had last night, and she was keen to get back to normal. All this waiting around made her feel fidgety.

She was as pleased as punch when Viv arrived shortly after nine o'clock to find her pacing up and down the ward.

'Shouldn't you be working?' she asked, trying to sound cross.

'No, I went in for an early briefing and then Dan insisted I come up here to take you home, once you've been discharged. No more buses for you! And don't even try to pretend you're cross with me. I can see from the light in your eyes and the flush on your cheeks that you're as happy to have me here as I am to be here.'

Lauren blushed even more, remembering that detectives were very good at reading body language. 'Thank you for everything you did last night,' she muttered, as she sat back on the edge of her bed whilst Viv took the chair. 'Going to get my mum and my PJs and stuff. And my notebook. I think I'd have gone mental in here with nothing to do after you both left!'

'You aren't a very patient patient, are you?' he said. They both laughed.

'Now, tell me what happened in the briefing,' Lauren demanded.

'You do know I'm not supposed to discuss anything about the case with you?'

'And you do know that I will keep pestering until you tell me what's happening, don't you? At least tell me whether you've got that bastard Blackett in custody yet?'

'That's what I thought you'd say,' Viv grinned ruefully. 'And, no, there's been no sign of Blackett. However, we did get a caller to the phone number that was put out in last week's appeal. It was the landlady of a B&B in one of the backstreets between the station and Lizzie Gardens,' he said, referring to the Elizabeth Gardens that the B&B in question was apparently named after. 'Turns out Blackett had been staying there since Thursday evening, but he'd already done a runner by the time she bothered to phone us. She says she didn't recognise him straight away, but I think she did. The PC who attended said she was very evasive about when she'd first realised who he was. He says he got the impression that she was possibly looking to blackmail Blackett. Not that that would've ended well! Anyway, it appears she heard someone leaving early yesterday evening and went upstairs to find his door open and the room empty. As he'd buggered off without paying, she was quick enough to phone us then, to complain.'

'So, he's gone?'

'Hopefully, yes. I'd feel happier knowing for certain that he's not still in the area, plotting anything else. We've got all vehicles and patrols on the lookout for him, and we've notified all train stations, ferry ports and airports. He shouldn't be able to get out of the country without being spotted.'

Lauren felt like a trickle of ice had run down her back. She had a horrible feeling that he wouldn't have gone far yet, having failed to get Meg yesterday. From everything Viv had told her last night, her mugging was simply Blackett's way of getting hold of her phone so that he could lure Meg out of the care home. That jolted her memory.

'Dammit!' she exclaimed. 'I don't suppose anyone's found my phone yet?'

'Sorry, no,' Viv replied. 'Do you have an old one at home?'

'Yeah, but it's an old contract phone, so it isn't gonna work anymore.'

'We can stop off on the way home to pick up a pay-as-you-go SIM card, if you like? Just so we can stay in touch, until you can replace your phone.'

'Thanks, that's a good idea.'

'We did learn something useful from the landlady,' added Viv.

'Oh?'

'Yes, she said he's changed his appearance. We've got her coming in this morning to do an e-fit with us. According to her, he's had his hair cut short and dyed dark brown, and he's taken to wearing glasses.'

Lauren suddenly thought of the man at the bus stop on Saturday night. Could that have been Peter Blackett? She shivered.

'Are you all right?' Viv asked anxiously.

'Yeah, course I am,' she replied cheerfully. She kept quiet about her suspicions as she didn't want Viv and her mum worrying any more than they already were. The two chatted quietly until, finally, the doctor arrived. After a fairly cursory examination, she declared Lauren well enough to go home. She couldn't get out of there fast enough.

Chapter Forty-four

Once Meg was comfortably settled into the day room after breakfast, having answered myriad excited and concerned questions in the dining room as politely as she could, she was happy to finally have some time alone with Albert.

'I say, old gal. That was a bit of a close escape last night, what?'

Meg could hear his genuine concern and felt able to say what she hadn't admitted to anyone else, that she had been absolutely terrified. 'If you hadn't insisted on taking my walking stick, I don't know what would've happened,' she said. 'I'm so grateful to you for saving my life.'

'Oh, pish! It's what any gentleman would've done,' Albert said, for once in his life embarrassed. 'I must admit to having the fright of my life when I saw that figure rise up from behind the hedge and realised that he was pointing a gun at you. I don't know what I'd have done if anything had happened to you, m'dear.'

Meg felt herself blush and decided it was time to change the subject. She told Albert about Kayla and Ana. He simply harrumphed and said he hoped she knew what she was doing.

'I'm trying to help, Albert,' she said firmly. 'Those two young women have neither of them had the easiest of lives. If they can help each other now, and if that is in any small part due to me, I am very glad to have been able to help.'

'You're too good-hearted,' grumbled Albert. 'The trouble is, that's one of the things I like about you. You really care about people.'

Meg was saved from having to answer that by the arrival of Mandy with the morning coffee round.

'Tea, milk and no sugar, Meg?' she asked brightly.

'Yes, please. You're looking a bit better today,' Meg said,

pleased to see that the dark circles under the carer's eyes were less defined than before her weekend off.

'Yes, my mum took the kids out yesterday so I could clean through the house. And I was that tired afterwards, I slept right through the night. I don't know if Jack woke up or not, but if he did, he must've settled back to sleep really quickly on his own 'cos I didn't hear a thing.'

'That's very good,' Meg agreed, thinking that possibly Jack had been responding to his mum's improved mood. Young children were very sensitive to their parents' emotions. 'And what about the money side of things?' she asked cautiously.

'I'm seeing a social worker on my day off on Wednesday. She spoke to me briefly on the phone after work on Friday afternoon, just to say she's going to bring some information about claiming housing benefit and reducing my council tax payments, and a few other things. She sounded really nice.' Mandy blushed. 'Thank you so much for listening to me the other day, Meg. I think that kind of made me realise that I needed to get some help.'

'You're welcome.'

Mandy poured Albert's coffee whilst she was speaking and handed it to him.

'Have you put sugar in this?' he demanded suspiciously.

'Two sugars and, yes, I stirred it,' laughed Mandy, before moving off with the trolley. Meg couldn't help but smile.

'I say, m'dear, weren't you going to question Mandy again about the evening before Alan died?' Albert said, after she was out of earshot.

'No need,' said Meg. She explained how she had eliminated all the staff on the early shift the day before Alan's murder, thanks to Jeannie's input.

❁

Lauren spent her unexpected afternoon off alternately racking her brains about the accomplice and dozing off because she could scarcely keep her eyes open. Assuming the accomplice was Blackett's child, and she was convinced it had to be, then they had narrowed the list of suspects down to five, based on age. Of those five, Mandy had been on the early shift, which pretty much eliminated her. And Ana-Maria was Romanian. Surely a baby born in Poole would not have been taken to Romania? Adoptions were more likely the other way round, she thought.

That left Sarah, Lyn and Jess. Meg had thought Jess' answers suspicious when questioned about Alan's death, but Jess had been really nice to her. Sarah was stuck-up and supercilious, but did that make her a murderer's accomplice? And Lyn claimed to have no memory of that evening, with her son having been ill since then, but that seemed like a very lame excuse to her.

No matter how much Lauren thought about the three of them, she simply went round and round in circles until her head began to throb. Eventually, she gave in and settled herself into bed properly for the night. This could wait until tomorrow.

❁

Blackett spoke to his daughter again, but she wasn't being overly helpful. She was in equal parts shocked by the violence of his attacks on Lauren and Meg and upset that he'd failed to take them out. 'All you've done is make things worse,' she insisted. 'At least tell me that you're safely out of the country now?'

She was furious to find out that he was still in Wiltshire.

Eventually, he managed to calm her down. He explained that he wanted to finish off those damned amateur sleuths before making good his escape. He wasn't having anyone getting one up on him!

Reluctantly, she answered his questions as ideas began to form in his head.

With a new plan now formed, he set off as soon as it was dark, once again walking and staying on the back roads. This time, he was dressed all in black and armed with his flick knife. Once in Britford, he took a wide circle around the care home, keeping to the shadows, until he was facing the back of the building. He could see the kitchen door and beside it a bare window with light flooding out. Every so often, a figure would cross the window. That would be the lone chef on duty that evening. According to his daughter, there was a good chance that the back door would be unlocked, as the chef liked to pop outside for frequent illicit smokes. As he watched, sure enough, a bulky figure appeared silhouetted in the doorframe and stood there puffing on a cigarette for a couple of minutes before stubbing it out and returning to the kitchen.

Blackett waited until just gone six o'clock as instructed before stealthily approaching the kitchen door and trying the handle, relieved to find that it wasn't locked.

This part of his plan carried the greatest risk, but he'd always been a believer in the old adage *nothing ventured, nothing gained.*

Chapter Forty-five

Meg spent the evening watching TV with Albert and several others, not liking to do her jigsaw puzzle in artificial light and feeling too worn out to concentrate on her book. Normally, she was one of the last of the residents to go to bed, but tonight she couldn't stop yawning, so she took herself upstairs even before the late-evening drinks had been round. Not that it mattered, as the staff took the trolley round the bedrooms after they'd done the day room. There were always a few of the residents who had retired early of their own volition, plus those who had already been put to bed by the staff. She was tucked up in bed happily doing a crossword puzzle and drinking her hot chocolate when there was a tap at her door.

It was PC Doughty, arriving to spend the night on guard outside on the landing.

'Just checking everything's okay, ma'am,' he said.

'I'm absolutely fine,' Meg replied. 'I do wish Dan wouldn't worry so. I feel sure that Blackett will have run off into hiding, so there's absolutely no need for me to have a guard. And, in any case, we've already proved how difficult it is for anyone to enter the building during the night.'

'Nevertheless, ma'am, I'm here on the inspector's orders. You can sleep safe tonight.'

Meg thanked him and he withdrew back out to the landing.

Quarter of an hour later, she set down her unfinished puzzle and turned the light out. The shock of yesterday's events had evidently taken more out of her than she liked to admit. But it was nothing a good night's sleep wouldn't fix.

Blackett remained hidden until nearly midnight before standing and warily stretching out his cramped limbs. Only when he was sure that there were no pins and needles or cramps to disable him did he silently move from his hiding place and tiptoe stealthily towards the office. A bright light shone out around the edges of the door, which was ajar, and he could hear voices chatting. He listened for a while, trying to judge how many people were in the office. His daughter had told him that there were four carers on at night. Eventually, he was able to distinguish two different female voices and one male voice. That was three out of the four, but where was the fourth? He didn't dare make a move to go upstairs until he could be sure the fourth carer wasn't roaming around up there. He waited motionlessly, listening.

✿

The fourth member of staff on duty that night was Darren Jones, a twenty-five-year-old local lad who'd bumped into PC Doughty earlier during the evening, shortly after he'd come on duty. The two men had immediately recognised each other, having been to St Joseph's Secondary School together. Darren had promised his friend they'd have a catch-up as soon as he was free.

Darren, with his striking bleached blond hair and blue eyes, had gone back upstairs shortly after eleven, the residents all being settled early for once. Having clapped shoulders with his old mate Kev Doughty, the two men had started catching up on each other's news on the landing but were told to keep the noise down. Encouraged by his friend, PC Doughty had abandoned his post and followed Darren downstairs to the day room, where they were having a good chat reminiscing about old times.

✿

Blackett eventually tiptoed past the office door and made it to the hallway. He could hear the low murmur of voices in the day room and wondered who was still up at this

229

time of night. No matter, his business was upstairs. If he played this right, he could be in and out without anyone hearing a thing.

He took the staircase slowly, not wanting to alert anyone downstairs. At the top, he paused to get used to the near-darkness that blanketed the landing. Then he crept cautiously along, counting off the bedrooms until he reached the sixth door along on the left. This should be room twenty-one. It was. He put his hand on the door handle and quietly pressed it down. As the door swung silently open, he could see that the nosy old bitch was sound asleep in her bed.

❂

Albert couldn't fall asleep that night, which was quite unusual for him. He'd been disturbed three times, first when he'd got up to give the two idiots chattering outside his door what for, then by another voice telling them to be quiet, and finally by a carer making his rounds. He'd refused a sleeping tablet, convinced he'd soon nod off and not liking to take unnecessary medication. Sometime later, he found himself still awake and straining his ears to listen to every creak and groan that the building made. Even the slightest noise seemed exaggerated at night, and he could easily imagine someone tiptoeing along the landing past his door. It was probably the copper posted to protect Meg but, in the end, he just had to get up and have a look. To his surprise, the landing was deserted. No sign of anyone, let alone the PC who was supposed to be on guard. He bristled. No man ever dared desert their post back in his day! He used his bathroom and then tried to get back to sleep. But knowing that Meg's room was now unguarded had made him hypervigilant.

There was another flurry of creaking noises on the landing, so he got up again and peeked out through his door. His heart leapt into his throat when he saw a shadowy figure quietly opening Meg's door. He grabbed Meg's walking stick, which was luckily resting just inside his door, waiting to be returned to her. Then he moved as fast as he dared along the landing.

Meg's door was open and Albert could see the shadowy figure bending over her.

'Halt, I say!' Albert bellowed, making the figure spin round and drop the pillow in his hands. It was too dark to make out whether it was Blackett or not, but Albert was sure that none of the staff would be wearing a balaclava. He pointed the walking stick at the figure and waved it threateningly. The figure snarled and reached into a pocket. Albert caught sight of a glimpse of moonlight glinting off steel. A knife!

The figure advanced menacingly, so Albert carefully backed up whilst shouting a warning. 'You won't get away with this, you know.'

The next few seconds were a blur. Footsteps came running up the stairs and along the landing, rough arms snatched Albert and thrust him out of the way, and all of a sudden two men were between him and the assailant.

'Give yourself up,' said PC Doughty firmly, dodging a swipe of the wicked- looking blade.

'Albert, go to the office and get them to call the police,' gasped Darren, whilst trying to flank the man who was directing his anger at the PC.

'Albert?' called Meg, in a tremulous voice, sitting up in bed somewhat dazed.

Albert was torn in two but duty won out, and he descended the staircase faster than in many a year. He burst into the office, crying out, 'Call the police, call the police. Meg's been attacked,' before collapsing into a chair, out of breath and feeling decidedly shaky.

Brandon dashed out of the door and ran up the stairs two at a time.

Sue picked up the phone and dialled 999.

Kayla rushed to Albert, alarmed by his bright red face and ragged breathing.

Albert silently hoped and prayed that Meg would be all right.

Chapter Forty-six

Tuesday 24th January 2023

Meg had fallen asleep almost as soon as she'd turned her light out.

She was dreaming. She was floating on her back in warm water, sunshine on her face, children playing in the background somewhere. Then the delightful sounds of the children had faded and silence had fallen. A large cloud had moved across the sun, darkening the sky, and the water had suddenly become chilly. She wanted to move, to swim away to safer, shallower waters. But suddenly something blocked the sun altogether, pushing her down, down into the water. The water was filling her lungs and she couldn't breathe. She struggled to wake, panicking, to find something soft pushing down into her face. She really couldn't breathe! Then there was a shout and suddenly the pressure lifted and air flooded into her grateful lungs. For a moment, she lay dazed and confused. Where was she?

Then she heard the voice again. 'You won't get away with this, you know.' With tears of relief, she recognised Albert's voice.

This was followed by the sound of running feet and briskly ordered commands. By the time she had struggled to sit up, it was to see a shadowy figure, his back to her, standing in her doorway. Others were outside on the landing and, somewhere in the background, she knew, was Albert. She called out to him but wasn't sure that her voice had actually made any sound.

Exhausted, she sank back onto her pillows, heart pounding in her chest and her breathing deep and uneven. It felt like she'd just run a marathon.

There was a sharp cry of someone in pain, followed by

shouting and scuffling, and the thump of a body hitting the floor.

It was just possible that she had passed out for a few moments because when she attempted to open her eyes again, a light was shining in her face and making her squint. Slowly, two figures came into focus: Brandon on one side of her bed and Kayla on the other, both looking down at her anxiously.

'Meg, thank goodness you're okay,' breathed Kayla.

'Don't try to move yet,' counselled Brandon. 'Just let your breathing and your heart rate come back to normal. You're quite safe now.'

Kayla was holding her hand, stroking it gently, and Brandon continued to talk soothingly. It felt safe.

❁

By the time Dan arrived at nearly one o'clock in the morning, things were calming down again at Britford Lodge. He asked the PC at the front door to brief him, before poking his head around the office door to check if it would be all right to see Meg, then headed swiftly upstairs to her room.

The room was quite crowded, considering the ungodly hour. Meg was sitting up in bed in her dressing gown, cradling a half-empty mug of tea in both hands. She looked surprisingly well for someone who had just been the victim of a second attempted murder in as many days. Albert was sitting stiffly upright in the armchair, his gaze unwavering from Meg's face. Kayla was perched on the bottom of Meg's bed, keeping a wary eye on things. And PC Doughty was standing in the corner, shuffling from foot to foot awkwardly when he spotted Dan.

'Honestly, I can't turn my back on you for one minute,' Dan scolded, before breaking into a smile of relief. 'How are you, Meg?'

'She's fine now, no thanks to this dimwit.' Kayla tossed her head contemptuously in PC Doughty's direction. He looked at the floor, colouring slightly.

'Don't worry, I'll deal with him in due course,' said Dan grimly. 'The important thing is that you're okay, Meg.'

'I'm a little shaken, if I'm being honest, and my chest still feels heavy when I breathe. But I'm told by my excellent carer here that my vital signs have all returned to normal, so I'm doing very well, considering,' said Meg, a little hoarsely.

'I'm very glad to hear it. And, Albert, I gather that once again you came charging to the rescue?'

'Ahem, well, just did what I could, y'know.'

'Do you have any news about Darren?' asked Kayla anxiously.

'Who?' asked Dan, momentarily puzzled, before his brow cleared. 'Ah, you mean the carer who was taken to hospital? Yes, I gather he sustained a fairly deep cut to his upper arm, but luckily there was no serious damage. Although, from the look of the corridor outside, I'd say it must have bled rather a lot.'

'It certainly did,' said Kayla with feeling. 'I thought for one awful moment that someone had been murdered.' Both Meg and Albert shivered at the word.

'I gather that it was thanks to Darren's diversionary heroics that you were able to restrain Blackett, PC Doughty?' Dan asked, his voice frosty.

'Er . . . yes, sir. That and the other carer who came belting up the stairs. He helped to hold the blighter's wrists while I slapped the cuffs on.'

'And might I ask how Blackett managed to slip past you on the landing in the first place?' Dan could barely contain his fury.

'I . . . er . . . I just popped to use the toilet for a moment,' he said, not looking Dan in the eye.

'Poppycock,' exploded Albert. 'He deserted his post, that's what he did.'

PC Doughty cast a despairing look at Albert before studying the floor again.

'You are dismissed from the scene, Kevin,' Dan said sternly. 'I want a full written report on my desk by nine this morning. And believe me when I say I will personally be taking statements from everyone involved, so don't even think about lying.'

They watched in silence as a very subdued PC Doughty left the room.

Dan's voice softened. 'Do you feel up to giving a statement yet, Meg? I could leave it until morning if you need to get some sleep first.'

'No, I don't want to go back to sleep just yet. Please, I'm happy to give you my statement now, although I'm not sure I can tell you very much.' She failed to mention that every time she closed her eyes, she felt like she was suffocating. She was afraid that she'd never be able to sleep again.

'Do you want me to stay, Meg?' asked Kayla.

'I'm sorry,' Dan said softly, 'I'd really rather take her statement independently from yours. Do you think you could accompany Albert to his room and stay with him while I'm here? You're welcome to come back when I go to take his statement. I can take yours later, once Meg is asleep.'

Reluctantly, Kayla and Albert left the room.

✣

Once Dan had taken statements from Meg, Albert and the three remaining members of staff, he headed up to Salisbury District Hospital to speak to Darren Jones. He found the young man garbed in a hospital gown, sitting up on a trolley in one of the cubicles in A&E, his arm heavily bandaged and in a sling.

'You just caught me,' he grimaced as he moved. 'I'm waiting for my girlfriend to bring me a change of clothes and then I'm heading home.'

'I won't detain you for long,' Dan assured him, 'but I really would like to take your statement while it's fresh in your mind.'

He asked Darren to start from the moment he'd come on shift at 9pm and to mention anything that had felt even vaguely out of place or unusual.

'The first thing was me bumping into my old mate Kev.'

'PC Kevin Doughty?' Dan clarified.

'Yeah. We went to school together, you know. I suppose it's my fault, really, isn't it? I mean, we were chatting on the landing upstairs, but first Albert came out of his room and had a go at us to quieten down and then Brandon told us to shut up. We haven't seen each other in ages, and it was a quiet night, so I didn't see any harm in him coming down to the day room with me for a natter.'

'Don't beat yourself up over it,' Dan advised. 'PC Doughty should've known better than to move from that landing. He was the police officer on duty, not you.'

'I suppose he's going to get into a load of trouble over this?'

'That's not your problem,' Dan reiterated. 'Now, please continue.'

'Well, we didn't see or hear anything until Albert shouted out. Luckily, noise carries at night. We shot out of our chairs and ran upstairs. There was Albert, on the landing outside Meg's room, waving a walking stick at this masked intruder who was brandishing a knife. I grabbed Albert and pulled him away just as Kev put himself in between Albert and the intruder. I told Albert to go to the office and call 999, then I tried to help Kev. This guy was just insane, grunting and growling about not going back inside. His eyes were focussed on Kev, who was trying to calm him down. I kind of sidled round to his side, to see if I could take him by surprise. But at the last minute, he spun round to me and lashed out wildly with his knife. He caught me on my arm here,' he indicated with his good hand, 'and I cried out. At the same time, Kev rugby tackled him around the knees and brought him to the ground. I was lying on the floor holding my arm while Kev was wrestling with the guy, trying to hold him still. I thought for one awful moment that he was going to get away, but then Brandon appeared from nowhere and grabbed the guy's arms so that Kev could get the cuffs on his wrists. Kev hauled the bloke to his feet, holding one arm and Brandon took hold of the other 'cos he was wriggling like mad. Then Kev pulled off the guy's balaclava and told him that he was under arrest. He called him Peter something. Black, maybe?'

'Blackett.'

'That's it. Peter Blackett. Anyway, Kev said he was under arrest for murder and read him his rights, like you see on TV. And, all the while, this guy was cursing and swearing. Shortly after that, Sue came upstairs and put pressure on my wound until the paramedics arrived. I wanted them to take Meg to hospital before me, but she refused point-blank. Anyway, two uniformed policemen arrived and they took this Blackett guy away. Kev said he'd stay and make sure that everyone else was okay.'

'Hmph! A bit like shutting the stable door after the horse has bolted, that is,' muttered Dan to himself. What the hell had Kevin been thinking?

Chapter Forty-seven

If Meg thought her arrival at breakfast the previous morning had been greeted with a barrage of questions, this morning's welcome was more like an emotional tsunami. It was amazing how quickly the word had spread. There was clapping and cheering as she walked into the dining room, and almost everyone called out their best wishes as she walked to her usual table. She felt a little like royalty or maybe some famous celebrity but, overall, she decided she didn't really enjoy the attention.

Jeannie had tears in her eyes as Meg sat beside her. 'I am so pleased to see you alive and well, my dear,' she said enthusiastically.

'Not half as happy as I am to be alive,' remarked Meg, rather dryly. She wasn't quite so sure about the 'well' part, seeing as she'd not managed a wink of sleep after Blackett's rude intrusion into her dream. She still couldn't bear to shut her eyes.

It seemed that Albert's role in her survival had also spread like wildfire, because when he entered the dining room some ten minutes after her, the cheers were even louder, and someone started up a chorus of *For He's a Jolly Good Fellow.*

Meg was amused to see that Albert looked even more ill at ease with all the attention than she was.

Lauren's first inkling that anything out of the ordinary had happened was when she was roused from a deep sleep by the insistent ringing of her temporary phone. Who the hell was calling her at this time of the morning? She turned over to reach for her mobile and saw that her clock said it was not even eight-thirty. She decided that whoever it was could wait, and tried to ignore it. But no sooner had the phone rung out than it started up again. Whoever it was, they were certainly being persistent. Begrudgingly, she propped herself up on her elbow and picked up her phone. It was Viv, which made sense as very few people had her new number yet. Shouldn't he be in the middle of a briefing at this time of the morning?

'Yeah?' she muttered sleepily.

'Good morning, gorgeous. Did I wake you?'

'Don't you remember that bit in one of my texts last night when I said I was looking forward to a lie-in?'

'Sorry, but I thought you'd probably want to hear the details from me than get some half-baked story when you walk into work later today.'

'You're not making a lot of sense.'

'Well, I'll tell you the good news first. We've got Blackett in custody.'

That's great.' Lauren sat up, suddenly feeling more awake. 'But what's the bad news?' she asked suspiciously.

'He had another attempt at killing Meg.'

'Flippin' heck, is she all right? Is she hurt? Where is she?' The questions tumbled out of Lauren's mouth incoherently.

'Whoa! Slow down!' Viv explained what had happened during the night.

'You're sure she's really all right?' Lauren asked for the umpteenth time.

'She's not hurt physically, but Dan says she was badly shaken up this time.'

'Yeah, I guess being half smothered would do that to you. Thank goodness Albert was on the ball!'

'Yes, I dread to think what might have happened if he hadn't intervened when he did,' Viv agreed. There was a moment of silence as the reality of what might so easily have happened hit both of them like a freight train.

'But you've got Blackett. Has he told you who his accomplice is yet?'

'Dan and I attempted to interview him last night but, unsurprisingly, he demanded his lawyer and refused to say another word. We are obliged to give his own lawyer

239

reasonable time to attend but, apparently, the middle of the night was not reasonable for Mr Markham. He's coming in at nine, which is why I wanted to phone you before I get stuck in an interview room for goodness only knows how long.'

'Thanks, I appreciate that,' Lauren said, genuinely impressed by his thoughtfulness.

'Am I forgiven for waking you up?' Viv teased.

'On this occasion, yes. But don't ever do it again unless it's for an attempted murder or worse,' Lauren bantered back.

'Fair enough. Listen, I'd better go as Dan wants us to plan our strategy before we start the interview. I'll call you later, if I get a chance, before you leave to go to work. If not, I promise I'll text with any important news and I'll phone you tonight. Or, if you like, I could pick you up from work? You finish at nine-thirty, don't you?'

'It would be great if you can get away to pick me up, but are you sure you won't be too busy, with all that's going on?'

'There'll be a lot to do in the coming days, getting the forensic results in, the evidence all lined up and the paper-work filed. But I'm pretty sure the super will slap a ban on overtime, now that Blackett's in custody.'

'What about that other case?'

'The barber? We passed him off to another team yesterday as it's unrelated.'

'In that case, I'll see you at nine-thirty.' Lauren knew she should be playing it cool, but she couldn't keep the pleasure out of her voice.

'I'll see you later, gorgeous.' Viv blew her a kiss down the phone before ending the call.

⚙

Lauren got to see her sexy sergeant earlier than either of them had anticipated. After Viv's phone call, she was too pumped up to go back to sleep, so she got up and made herself a cup of coffee. By the time she'd washed up last night's dishes and wiped the kitchen worktops down, she'd come to a decision. She needed to see Meg. She hastily popped a piece of bread in the toaster for her breakfast and made some sandwiches for later, then rushed out of the house to catch the ten-fifteen bus.

She was walking down Lower Road when a familiar silver Nissan Juke slowed down as it passed her, tooting its horn, before driving the last hundred metres to the entrance to the care home and turning in. Just as she was cursing it for not offering her a lift in the steady cold rain, Viv's blue Vauxhall Astra pulled to a stop beside her. Her heart fluttered on seeing his beaming face, and she quickly hopped into the passenger seat. 'Thanks—' she began.

'What are you doing here?' interrupted Viv. 'Aren't you just a tad early for your shift?'

'Well, thanks for the welcome!' she retorted, trying to keep the smile out of her voice.

'I could ask you what *you're* doing here. Shouldn't you be questioning a suspect?'

'Ah,' Viv replied ruefully, 'we tried that, and failed.'

'How can you *fail* to interview a suspect?' exclaimed Lauren.

'When he persists in answering "No comment" to every single question.'

'Oh, that must've been frustrating.'

'And some,' the handsome Jamaican said with feeling as he pulled away. He parked next to Dan, who was sitting in his car waiting for them to catch up. They all exited their cars and dashed for the front door.

'I thought Viv said you were working the late shift today?' asked Dan, as he took his coat off and shook it out before folding it over his arm.

'I came in early to visit Meg. Wanted to check she's really okay,' Lauren replied.

'You just can't keep away from this place, can you?' teased Viv gently.

Just then, Maureen emerged from the office. 'Can I help you, Detectives?' she enquired politely, before spotting Lauren. 'What are you doing here so early?' she demanded.

Lauren rolled her eyes and repeated her explanation.

Maureen's tone softened. 'Meg's in the day room, I believe.' She turned to Dan. 'How can I help you, Inspector?'

'We need to identify how Blackett gained access last night, and we're still looking for his accomplice.'

'His accomplice! I don't understand.' Maureen looked most perturbed. 'Are you suggesting that someone inside the home has been helping this murderer?'

'Perhaps we could all go through to the conservatory?' Dan suggested.

Chapter Forty-eight

Once Maureen, Meg, Lauren and the two detectives were settled in the comfortable cane chairs, and enquiries had been made after Meg's health, Dan explained to Maureen why they were certain that Blackett had had an inside accomplice.

'I had no idea the patio doors could be wedged open!' she exclaimed, with a look of horror on her face. 'That is a safety issue we must address immediately.'

'Is that how Blackett got in again last night?' asked Lauren.

'I have no idea,' sighed Dan. 'We're not getting anywhere questioning Blackett. He's sticking to the "No comment" routine.'

'Can't you make him talk?' Lauren demanded.

'Unfortunately, he's entitled to remain silent,' Dan replied, shaking his head. 'For the first time in my life, I've felt like beating a confession out of a suspect.'

'You didn't?' Maureen gasped, disapprovingly.

'Of course not,' Dan reassured her.

'Of course he wouldn't,' Meg insisted, indignantly.

'But you have enough to charge him, don't you?' persisted Lauren.

'We have solid evidence that he murdered Alan, and that he both attempted to murder Meg and assaulted Darren last night. He's been charged with those three offences, for now,' Dan began.

'What about Ed's murder?' asked Meg.

'And what about my mugging?' demanded Lauren. 'Not to mention that bastard shooting at Meg on Sunday?'

'While we're sure that he committed all those offences, we don't have enough concrete evidence to add them to his charge sheet. Yet,' Viv explained.

'Hopefully, the forensics on the pistol and footprints

found at the scene of the shooting will produce some results soon,' Dan said, 'then we can charge him for the first attempt on Meg. But, at the moment, there are too many unanswered questions. In order to make a watertight case for all the charges, we need a lot more solid evidence. And, if we are to charge him with Ed's murder, we need to disprove Blackett's alibi for that night, which The Met are convinced is solid.'

'Or get a full confession,' Viv added grumpily, 'which doesn't look likely to happen anytime soon.'

At that moment, Jess arrived to ask Meg if she wanted a hot drink from the trolley. Maureen insisted that, just this once, they should all have hot drinks. It was that dreary kind of winter's day when the rain and the cold seem to penetrate everywhere. And the subject matter of their discussion was enough to depress anyone, especially Maureen, who took the security of her residents very seriously indeed. Jess obligingly poured teas and coffees to order.

Once they were all warming their hands on identical white mugs, Maureen returned to the question of the accomplice. 'I just can't believe any one of my staff would do something so despicable as to assist a murderer. Are you sure?'

'As certain as we can be,' replied Dan, 'but if you can come up with a viable alternative for how Blackett got into Alan's room, I'd be delighted to hear it.'

After listening to their reasoning again, Maureen conceded that their hypothesis was the most likely explanation, however unpalatable it was to her. 'But what about last night? Don't tell me someone did the exact same thing again?'

'That's a good question,' agreed Meg. 'Perhaps we should look at the staff on duty leading up to both events and see if there's any overlap?'

Dan pulled out his copy of the staff rota whilst Lauren ran up to Meg's room to fetch Meg's notebook and the printed copy of her spreadsheet.

'Now, we've pretty much eliminated the early staff for the

244

day before Alan was murdered, as the curtains couldn't have been closed until after dark without arousing suspicion,' Meg informed them. 'That leaves us with five on the late shift and four on overnight. Let's see if any of those nine were also on duty yesterday.'

Using the same principle, namely concentrating on those staff on the late and night shifts, they came up with four names: Petra, Jess, Kayla and Lyn.

Lauren chipped in, 'Aren't you forgetting that the accomplice is most likely Blackett's illegitimate child?'

'It's one possibility,' agreed Dan. 'Viv told me about your conversations with Alan Watts' daughter and son-in-law, and the team did look into it. But there's only hearsay evidence that Blackett ever fathered a child, and we can't be sure how reliable that is. They couldn't find anything else to corroborate what you were told.'

'Well, I still think we should be looking at the three most likely suspects,' Lauren insisted. 'Sarah, Jess and Lyn are all the right age to be Blackett's daughter, and they were all on duty before Alan was murdered. And Jess and Lyn were also on duty last night. Tell me that doesn't seem suspicious.'

'That's assuming all your suppositions are correct,' cautioned Dan. 'However, there's one very important fact that you're all overlooking. With Alan, we were dealing with a very well-planned murder. Both Blackett and his accomplice had lots of time to prepare for that, so it's impossible to say exactly when it was set up. I know, I know,' he said, waving aside Meg's objections, 'it's always possible that someone might have seen the wedge of cardboard in the door had it been placed there earlier in the day, but that's not to say the murderers didn't take a calculated risk.'

'You make a good point,' conceded Meg. 'Maybe we should consider all fifteen staff on duty in the twenty-four hours before Alan's murder.'

'And that still won't tell us *how* Blackett gained entry last night,' Dan pointed out grimly. 'Last night's attempt on your life, Meg, couldn't have been planned in advance. After all, his first attempt on Sunday might have been successful, so there would have been no need to plan a second attempt.'

There was a momentary silence as his point sunk in. 'In that case, the accomplice might not have been involved last night,' nodded Meg thoughtfully.

'You're suggesting that this Blackett person found *another* way into the building, bypassing all our additional security?' Maureen said, aghast at the idea.

'Well, it seems he did,' said Lauren, pointing out the obvious.

The five of them threw ideas back and forth but came up with nothing.

'We shall just have to question all the staff and residents again,' Dan said finally, 'in the hope that someone saw something useful.'

'You've probably already thought of this,' Meg said carefully, 'but whoever the accomplice might be, do you think he or she might have visited Blackett in prison?'

'We've already checked that Blackett had no visitors in the six months prior to his release, but perhaps we should go back further. Viv, can you ask Moira to get on to the prison authorities and ask them to compare the names of current Britford Lodge staff with Blackett's visitor and mail logs, going right back to the start of his sentence?' Viv nodded. 'As to whether one of the staff could be Blackett's illegitimate child ...' Dan paused then shook his head '... I still think it's too far-fetched, and unfortunately we are now short-staffed, with Kevin on suspension pending his disciplinary meeting ...' He broke off, seeing the look on Lauren's face. 'However, I suppose I could ask Moira to check again to see if any of the staff here were adopted.'

'Perhaps I could do that?' suggested Maureen. 'All of the staff have to provide a copy of their birth certificate when they are hired. I can check our records, if that helps.'

Dan thanked her profusely, before adding, 'Viv, could you ask Moira to check with adoption agencies in the Poole area?' Viv nodded again and moved to one side to phone Moira and brief her.

'I'll start the interviews straight away; in here, if I may?' Dan looked at Maureen, who nodded her consent. 'They

246

have to be our first priority. Someone from forensics should be over later this afternoon, to check all the entry points again. Maybe they'll find something.'

He didn't sound overly hopeful.

Chapter Forty-nine

Emerging from the conservatory, Maureen returned to the office and Lauren went to the staffroom to change into uniform ready for her shift. Meg was amazed to discover that she was late for lunch, so long had they been discussing the case. She hurried into the dining room to find Albert, Jeannie and Betty all very concerned as to what had kept her.

'The detective inspector was just taking my statement,' she told them, casting Albert a warning look not to say anything to the contrary. They cross-examined her as she ate her beef stew and dumplings, but she managed to avoid giving anything away.

Afterwards, Albert collared her and demanded a more detailed briefing.

'Let's take a walk outside,' Meg suggested.

'You and your walks,' Albert grumbled. 'It's been pouring down all morning. The ground will be absolutely sodden, y'know.'

'Yes, and that's why I want to look for clues,' Meg said firmly. 'Don't worry, we'll stick close to the building.'

They gathered their outdoor clothes and slipped out through the front door whilst the late staff were having handover. Mercifully, the rain had slackened to a slight drizzle, and the overhang of the roof protected the path around the building to a certain extent. Once outside, Meg quickly told Albert what had been said in the conservatory. 'We need to find out how Blackett could have got in last night,' she explained. They stopped at every door and window and checked to see if they were secured or showed any signs of being forced, and Meg kept an eye on the damp grass for footprints or anything Blackett could have dropped. When she reached a door at the back of the building, she was thrilled to find a whole host of footprints in the mud beside the tarmac path. *At least three different sets*, she thought. Without thinking, she tried the door and was surprised to find it opened easily.

'Oi, you can't come in here,' yelled a very rotund chef with a bald head. Meg could see the sous-chef, Sanjeev, on one side of the large kitchen prepping vegetables, whilst the chef who had shouted at them was mixing some kind of a cake at an island in the middle.

'I'm sorry to bother you,' Meg smiled apologetically, 'but, I wonder, is this kitchen door always left unlocked?'

'Only when we're on duty,' replied the chef. 'It's locked before we leave for the night.'

'Is there always someone in here, though?' Meg checked.

'What are you nosing about for?' demanded the chef suspiciously.

Sanjeev approached them, paring knife still in one hand. 'You are the lady who was attacked last night, aren't you?' he asked nervously.

'Yes, indeed she is,' Albert said with a nod, 'so, I'm sure you'll want to help us, eh?'

'We didn't have nothing to do with that,' growled the other chef, also approaching the door and not looking best pleased.

'I'm so sorry,' Meg intervened, 'we certainly didn't mean to imply that you did. We know who attacked me, and he's already in police custody. We're just trying to find out how he could have got into the building.'

'Like I said, the door's only unlocked when we're here,' the big chef said dismissively. 'No one could get past us, I'm sure of that.'

'Actually, might there have been an occasion when you were in the dining room?' Sanjeev tentatively suggested.

The big chef paused thoughtfully. 'Huh, you might have a point there,' he grumbled. 'I was serving dinner last night, and it never crossed my mind to check if the door was locked or not before I went through to the dining room.'

'It's possible the kitchen was unlocked and empty for a while?' gasped Meg.

249

'Yeah, it's possible, I suppose. But I'd locked up and gone home by eight o'clock, and you weren't attacked until much later, from what I've heard.'

'That's true,' Meg replied with a nod, 'but he could have come in earlier and maybe hidden somewhere inside?'

'Not in the kitchen, he couldn't,' insisted the chef indignantly. 'I'd have seen him if he was anywhere in here. I was in and out of both the pantry and the cold room, putting things away, and there's nowhere else for someone to hide in this kitchen.'

'Well, thank you very much, Mr . . .?'

'Nokes, but just call me Stuart.' He wiped his plate-like hands on his overalls and offered one to Meg. 'I'm very glad that you didn't come to any harm when you was attacked, ma'am. And, like I said, I doubt anyone could've hidden in here. But I might have left the door unlocked while I was in the dining room, and if that gave some bastard the opportunity to slip in, then I'm right sorry for that.' He looked quite downcast. 'Will you have to tell the police?'

'I think you should tell them yourself,' Meg suggested softly. 'They're interviewing all the staff and residents again this afternoon, and it would sound better coming from you, voluntarily, so to speak.' He nodded morosely.

'I say, do you really think that Blackett fellow came in through the kitchen?' asked Albert, as they continued their inspection of the rest of the building, for the sake of thoroughness.

'Coming in would've been easy enough,' Meg replied with a nod. 'The difficult question is where did he hide until the time when he attacked me?'

'Ah, good point,' Albert agreed.

'Let's say Blackett slipped in through the kitchen somewhere between six and seven pm. He would have to have hidden somewhere for a good five or six hours before attacking me at midnight.'

'Lots of staff and residents moving around during that time, old gal,' remarked Albert. 'Not easy for anyone to stay hidden all that time, what?'

'You're probably right, but let's go in and have a look anyway.'

Albert sighed. He was looking forward to a little nap in front of the television, but that didn't seem to be on Meg's agenda.

Once inside again and divested of their coats, the pair started to consider suitable hiding places. 'If he came in through the kitchen, I doubt he would have risked trying to get past the office and dining room, which were busy with people coming and going from dinner,' Meg theorised. 'Odds are he would have headed down the corridor away from the office.'

On one side were the ten downstairs bedrooms. 'He could have hidden in one of the bedrooms temporarily,' suggested Albert.

'And then somehow got out unseen when that resident came to bed?' Meg asked.

'Hmm, fair point,' he grunted.

They checked the pristine treatment room and then the slightly less salubrious sluice room next to it. 'I think staff would have been into both of these rooms during the course of the evening,' Meg reasoned.

Next was a laundry room with large washing machines, tumble dryers and linen cupboards. 'This looks more likely,' suggested Albert.

'Likely for what?' asked Jess, coming into the room behind them.

'We're looking for hiding places,' said Albert immediately. Meg frowned at him, but there was little point in denying it now he'd said it.

'We're just wondering if my attacker could have sneaked into the building earlier during the day yesterday and then hidden somewhere before coming to attack me,' she explained, as Jess took a clean sheet from the cupboard.

'Well, I don't know if this helps or not, but I came into this room at least twice yesterday evening to fetch clean bed linen,' Jess said, 'and there was no one hiding in here, I'm sure of it.'

251

'What time was that?' demanded Albert.

'The first time was just after dinner – I think perhaps seven o'clock? And then I was back again not long before handover, so just before nine.'

'That's very helpful.' Meg thanked Jess and she hurried off.

The pair continued down the corridor, ruling out the staff-room for obvious reasons. The next door proved to be a large store cupboard. Meg looked inside. It was just possible for someone to squeeze in between the shelves amid the boxes strewn untidily on the floor. She found a light switch and flicked it on.

'Bit cramped for a hiding place,' Albert commented dismissively.

'I'm not so sure.' Meg pointed out a small floor space behind the boxes. 'I reckon a person could sit there, if they were determined enough.' She bent down and examined the area. Was it her imagination or were there a lot of scuff marks on the floor? Like someone's shoes might make if they were fidgeting.

'I say, look at this!' exclaimed Albert, distracted by something on one of the shelves. He showed her a blue box with its lid torn off.

'Well, I'd like to bet that matches the cardboard that was used to wedge Alan's patio door open,' agreed Meg with interest. Sure enough, the box contained paper towels, just as Taska had suggested. 'If the accomplice took the piece of cardboard from here, they could also have suggested it as a hiding place.'

Albert was about to take the box from the shelf when Meg stopped him. 'Leave it, it could have fingerprints on it,' she advised. 'Come on, we need to talk to Dan.'

⚙

Meg had to wait until Dan and Viv were free but then quickly slipped into the conservatory and told them her theories. 'You just can't leave things alone, can you?' Dan scolded her.

'But there's no danger now that Blackett's under lock and key,' she protested.

'Except we still haven't identified his accomplice yet, have we?'

Meg's face fell, so Dan took pity on her. 'But, thanks to you, I can at least save some time and money by getting the CSI to focus on processing the store cupboard, the kitchen and the footprints outside.'

He nodded at Viv, who went to brief the CSI, who had arrived not five minutes ago and was just starting on a similar route to that taken by Meg and Albert not an hour earlier.

'How are the interviews going?' Meg asked hopefully.

'Nothing useful yet,' Dan said morosely, shaking his head. 'And I'm afraid we had some bad news earlier from Moira. Apparently, the prison visitor records were destroyed by a fire during a riot at the prison about three years ago. It's absolutely impossible to trace any visitors Blackett might have had before the records were computerised, after the fire.'

'Coincidence?' asked Meg sceptically.

'Oh, I very much doubt it. Not that we'll ever be able to prove anything.'

'What about adoption records?'

'It's going to take some time, I'm afraid. Moira's working on it, but she's up to her eyes in paperwork at the moment. Now, I really do need to get back to my interviews, if we are ever going to find this accomplice.'

Meg said goodbye and left him to it.

Chapter Fifty

They were no further ahead with the case by the following morning, but at least they had one reason to celebrate: it was Lauren's birthday!

Meg made a special effort to get up and dressed early, which was no great hardship as she'd spent all night tossing and turning and it was a relief to get out of bed. She greeted Lauren as she came through the front door for her early shift, surprising her with a card and a box of chocolates.

'Oh, you shouldn't have!' Lauren exclaimed excitedly, but the look on her face told Meg how much the gesture was appreciated.

Lauren took the card and chocolates to the staff changing room and set them down on a bench so that she could change into her uniform, still smiling broadly.

'You look pleased with yourself,' remarked Jess, already in uniform and shutting her locker. 'Chocolates?' she added, spotting the box. 'From an admirer, perhaps?'

'Whatever makes you think that?' Lauren asked.

'Oh, I've seen you canoodling up to that dishy detective. You two dating, are you?'

'We might be,' Lauren replied, blushing a little.

'No doubt you've got an inside line into the investigation as well,' Jess remarked, winking as she walked past Lauren.

Lauren paused. What on earth did Jess mean by that?

Shortly after Jess left, Sarah entered the changing room. 'Someone's being spoiled?' she asked with a raised eyebrow, on seeing the chocolates.

'It's my birthday,' explained Lauren awkwardly.

'Oh well, then I'd better wish you a happy birthday,

hadn't I? Are you doing anything special tonight? Or perhaps you're too busy investigating with Meg Thornton?'

'Not much left to investigate now Blackett's in custody,' Lauren remarked, not expecting quite the reaction she got.

'What?' exploded Sarah, her face blanching. 'What do you mean, he's been arrested?'

For a second time, Lauren paused. Of course, Sarah had just had two days off, so there was no reason for her to know about either the second attempt on Meg's life or the arrest of Blackett. But then again, she'd said, '*he's* been arrested', not 'who'. Did that mean she knew who Blackett was?

'Peter Blackett made a second attempt on Meg's life on Monday night. But I think you know that, don't you?' Lauren said cautiously.

'Of course I don't! I've no idea what on earth you mean!' Sarah snapped vehemently. She opened her locker and pulled out her uniform tunic as though to start changing. Then she stopped and looked intently at Lauren. 'I was here on Sunday, so I know about the shooting incident. I think I must have heard that detective mention the name Blackett. I was just surprised to hear that he's attacked Meg again. You said a second "attempt", so I assume that he didn't succeed? Is Meg okay?'

'As okay as anyone can be after being nearly murdered two days in a row.'

'Well, I'm pleased to hear that,' Sarah said, with an insincere smile.

Lauren was thinking furiously. Sarah had been on a late shift the day before Alan was murdered. She was also the right age to be Blackett's illegitimate daughter. And she had definitely seemed unduly upset to discover he'd been arrested. But was she jumping to conclusions?

'I wouldn't think too long and hard about it,' Sarah spoke quietly beside her. 'It might not be good for your health.'

Lauren jumped, her pulse racing. She looked quickly around, but they were alone in the changing room. She opened her mouth to scream, but Sarah jammed the tunic top into her open mouth, causing her to gag and fight for breath. She tried to struggle but Sarah was surprisingly strong. She started to feel dizzy and then her vision blurred. She felt her knees buckle and she lost consciousness as she fell to the floor.

⚙

Maureen Wilkinson was sitting at the office desk, tapping her pen impatiently as she waited for the rest of the early shift to arrive so that Brandon could start the handover.

'Has anyone seen either Sarah or Lauren this morning?' she asked tartly, after checking her watch and seeing that it was nearly ten past seven already.

'I saw Lauren in the changing room earlier,' Jess offered.

'Well, that's something, I suppose. I was beginning to wonder if she'd sloped off for the day, given it's her birthday.'

'No, she's definitely in, but that explains the box of chocolates.'

'So where on earth can the girl have got to? Jess, go and check she's not with Meg, will you? I noticed she was already up and about when I came in.'

Jess left the office and almost immediately bumped into Meg. 'Have you seen Lauren?' she demanded, slightly breathlessly.

'When she first arrived, perhaps twenty minutes ago,' replied Meg, 'but I assume she'd be in handover by now?'

'Well, she's not, she was ...' Whatever Jess had been about to say was cut off by the ear-splitting screech of the fire alarm.

Staff rushed out of the office and hurried in different directions, presumably to start evacuating the residents. Jess took Meg's arm and steered her towards the front door. 'Get out immediately!' she yelled in Meg's ear. 'Assemble on the far side of the car park.' She turned and ran back to the office for instructions. Meg walked in a daze in the direction indicated. She was overtired, worried by what Jess had said about Lauren and now doubly concerned by the alarm. What on earth was happening? As she crossed the car park, she was surprised to see a bright pink Ford Ka accelerating towards the exit. She screwed her face up, trying to remember. Wasn't that Sarah's car? Why would a senior care assistant be leaving when there was a fire alarm? Surely, she'd be helping with the evacuation?

All of sudden, the answer flashed into Meg's mind and she turned and hurried back towards the front doors, jostling people who were moving away from the building.

'I say old gal, you're going the wrong way,' reproached Albert, catching hold of her arm. Meg shrugged him off.

'Come on, we've got to find Lauren!' she urged, already moving away from him. He sighed and followed her, not understanding in the slightest but confident that she must have a very good reason for going back inside during a fire drill. At least, he presumed it was a drill. He sniffed the air just before they reached the doors and could smell burning. By Jove, this was serious!

Inside the doors, Meg was being restrained by Maureen Wilkinson. 'You must evacuate, Meg,' she insisted.

'No, you don't understand. I think Sarah's done something to Lauren. We must find her!' Meg gasped, frantically trying to move past the matronly figure.

'What do you mean?' Maureen demanded, just as Albert caught up with them.

'Jess said that Lauren was missing. And I've just seen Sarah driving *away* from here. Don't you see? What if Sarah is the accomplice?' Meg was becoming quite frantic.

'Evacuate, now,' commanded Maureen. 'Go on, I'll look for Lauren.'

Meg nodded and waited until Maureen had turned her back and was heading past the office towards the downstairs bedrooms. Then she followed Maureen, and Albert followed her. A few wisps of smoke were drifting in the corridor as Kayla emerged from the second bedroom along, pushing Bill in a wheelchair in his pyjamas. Maureen responded instinctively, taking the wheelchair from Kayla whilst ordering her to evacuate the remaining residents via their patio doors. 'Don't bring them into the corridor,' she

257

urged. Kayla headed straight into the third bedroom. Seeing Meg and Albert out of the corner of her eye, Maureen rounded on them. 'Albert, take Bill and get outside, now.' He obeyed the direct order without hesitation. 'Meg, go into Jeannie's room and take her out through the patio door. Do you understand? I must help evacuate the other residents.' She didn't wait for an answer, hurrying into Jeffrey's room as soon as she'd finished speaking.

Meg rushed into her friend's room, to find it empty. After checking the bathroom, she hurried back into the corridor, frantically trying to think where Lauren might be. She could see now that the fire door at the far end was wide open. Were the staff evacuating residents that way, or had Sarah escaped by opening the fire door and setting off the alarm? But if that was the case, where was Lauren? She forged onwards, coughing a little as the smoke caught her throat, calling Lauren's name and checking every door to find where the smoke was coming from.

The store cupboard! Smoke was squeezing through all the spaces around the door and then being blown down the corridor she'd just come along by the breeze from the open fire door. She banged on the cupboard door and called Lauren's name. Was that someone groaning? She pulled her sleeve down over her hand, grabbed the handle and threw the door open, turning her head away and covering her mouth and nose with her other hand as smoke surged out and swirled around her. As the rush of smoke subsided, she looked into the cupboard, her eyes desperately search-ing. Flames had flared up in response to the sudden influx of oxygen and, by the eerie dancing light, Meg could see Lauren lying half on the floor, half splayed over a couple of boxes. She sobbed as she bent down, her breath rasping as the smoke clawed at her air passages. She tugged at Lauren's clothing but couldn't move her. Her eyes were smarting as she stumbled backwards, calling for help. Then Maureen was rushing towards her, concern etched all over her face. 'Oh, my goodness!' she exclaimed. Quickly, she grabbed Lauren under her shoulders and dragged her. Meg reached down and caught one of Lauren's arms, and the two of them, coughing and spluttering, managed to pull Lauren towards the open fire door, where the air was clearer. Sirens sounded in the distance, and Meg was vaguely aware of other hands, reaching out and helping them as they tumbled out of the building.

Epilogue

It would have been a birthday party had the circumstances not been overshadowed by recent events. Lauren was propped up in bed, Viv sitting beside her holding her hand, her mother standing with Meg, Albert and Dan; all watching as she attempted to blow out the candles on her birthday cake. Unfortunately, she was still struggling to breathe and had no puff left for candles. 'Can you help?' she whispered, and Viv obliged, blowing all twenty candles out in one breath.

'You'd better make a wish for her too,' Dan advised.

'Hey, it's my birthday!' wheezed Lauren indignantly. They all chuckled.

'I'm so grateful you thought to go back for her,' Bekka said tearfully, for the umpteenth time. 'Imagine if everyone had evacuated . . .'

'It doesn't always pay to imagine,' Dan intervened softly.

'I say, hats off to Meg, though,' said Albert appreciatively. 'She's the one who worked out what was happening.'

'I'm afraid not, Albert. We would've had no idea that Sarah was the accomplice had I not just happened to be in the right place at the right time to see her driving off so suspiciously.' There was a chorus of disagreement, and Meg reluctantly acknowledged their thanks.

'But, tell me,' Bekka asked, once the noise had abated, 'just why did this Sarah do what she did?'

Dan cleared his throat. 'There's still a certain amount of supposition, because Sarah has refused to say a word since she was brought into the station earlier this afternoon. But this is what we know so far. Sarah was adopted as a baby—'

'How did no one find this out sooner?' interrupted Meg.

'For the simple reason that she supplied her short-form

260

birth certificate when she applied for her job at Britford Lodge.'

'I don't understand.'

'There are two forms of birth certificate available, the short form, which shows simply the name, sex, date and place of birth, and the long form, which lists further details, such as the child's parents and their occupations. When a child is adopted, a new birth certificate is issued. The short form shows exactly the same information: name, sex, date and place of birth. It is only the long form that details the date of adoption and the names and occupations of the adoptive parents. Maureen Wilkinson looked through all the birth certificates held in her personnel records yesterday afternoon, after her kind offer to help, but she wouldn't have been able to tell that Sarah was adopted from the short-form certificate that was on Sarah's file.'

'What else do you know about her?' asked Bekka.

'As soon as we knew who we were looking into, Moira, DC Gordon, was able to contact Sarah's parents. Her adoptive parents, that is. They explained that they had adopted Sarah at six weeks old, through an adoption agency in Poole. They had kept the fact a secret from Sarah until she turned eighteen, but then they felt she had a right to know. Apparently, she took the news very badly. She fell out with her adoptive parents and immediately set about tracing her natural parents.

'Moira then contacted the adoption agency, who revealed that Sarah's natural mother was a woman by the name of Marlene Watkins. Moira eventually tracked her down, and she confessed that Peter Blackett was indeed the father of her illegitimate baby. She swears blind that he never knew, and that she never told another living soul. But we think that Sarah must have somehow found out and visited her father in prison. Goodness only knows what stories he spun her, but it seems the two of them kept in touch. We found a burner phone in her handbag with only one number on it. We haven't found Blackett's yet, but I'm convinced he had one too.'

261

'But why would she help him commit murder?' asked Bekka.

'Who knows?' Dan told her about the Westbourne Heist. 'Perhaps he persuaded her that it was some form of justified retribution on his fellow gang members for leaving him to serve the longest prison sentence? Or perhaps she was tempted by the idea that he'd find the missing money?'

'But why Meg? And my Lauren?'

'I think they were simply getting too close to the truth in all their, ahem, amateur sleuthing.' He glanced at Meg. 'Although it's only thanks to Meg that we know how Blackett got into Britford Lodge to murder Alan in the first place. And without that, we might never have known that he had an accomplice.'

'If I hadn't gone around so obviously asking questions, Sarah might never have realised we were thinking along the right lines,' said Meg soberly.

'And if Blackett hadn't returned to Salisbury to come after you, we might never have caught him,' Dan pointed out sternly. 'Like I said, it doesn't pay to imagine what if.'

'You mean, he might have got off scot-free if it hadn't been for Meg,' put in Albert.

'And you and Lauren,' added Meg. 'I couldn't have done it without you both.'

'Well, Blackett and Sarah are both in custody now,' said Dan, 'and more importantly, we're all here to toast Lauren's birthday, albeit somewhat late in the day. Come on, let's get on with the important part of the evening!'

As he popped the cork from a bottle of bubbly and poured it into the waiting plastic cups, Meg glanced at her watch and was amazed to see that it was nearly 9pm. When the cups had been distributed, Dan raised his. 'Happy birthday, Lauren.'

'Happy birthday,' echoed the others.

THE END

I'd be very grateful if you could take the time to

RATE and REVIEW

on Amazon, Goodreads or the site where you purchased this book.

You can also check out my website for details of other books in the series:

https://www.the-salisbury-murders-by-wendy-boynton.com

If you enjoyed reading this book . . . watch out for
my next one!

COMING SOON
The Mystery of the Missing Child

The Salisbury Murders: Book Three

Meg and Lauren are surprised when the sous-chef at Brit-ford Lodge, Sanjeev, approaches them to ask for help. His cousin, Vikram, has been arrested and detained on suspicion of child abduction and murder! Sanjeev is adamant that his cousin is innocent, but DI Barnes of Salisbury Police is convinced that he has his man, despite there being no body and only circumstantial evidence.

Thanks to Lauren passing her driving test, our pair of amateur sleuths are now mobile. After visiting the baby's mother, Mia Jenkins, Meg and Lauren suspect that two-year-old Noah was taken alive, so they set out to find him. Their search takes them into the murky underworld of a racist neo-Nazi group, whose leader is none other than Noah's estranged father, Tyler Ford. Has Tyler organised the kidnap of his own son in order to blame Mia's immigrant boyfriend, Vikram?

Their investigation runs into trouble from the outset, with Lauren's sexy sergeant boyfriend furious that she is interfering in a police matter. Things take a turn for the worse when their chief suspect is himself murdered, but our sleuths continue to unravel the clues in their hunt for the missing child. As the story races towards its thrilling climax, concern for Noah's safety leads Meg and Lauren into a potentially perilous situation; can DI Dan and DS Viv race to the rescue in time?

Glossary of Abbreviations

A&E: Accident and Emergency
BIC: Bournemouth International Centre
CCTV: Closed circuit television
CID: Criminal Investigations Department
CSI: Crime Scene Investigator
CV: Curriculum Vitae
DBS: Disclosure and Barring Service (replaced the Criminal Records Bureau)
DC: Detective Constable
DCI: Detective Chief Inspector
DI: Detective Inspector
DNA: Deoxyribonucleic acid (genetic material)
DS: Detective Sergeant
GCSE: General Certificate of Secondary Education (school exams)
MEM: Marine Engineering Mechanical
NVQ: National Vocational Qualification
O-levels: Ordinary levels (school exams, replaced by GCSEs)
PA: Public Announcement (system)
PC: Police Constable
PO: Parole Officer
SENCO: Special Educational Needs Co-ordinator
TV: Television
WPC: Woman Police Constable (now an obsolete term)

9 781789 635270